ILLUSION

A NOVEL

GINNY L. YTTRUP

SHELTERWOOD
PRESS

To Janet, Susan, and Rebecca, who encouraged me to return to Mendocino.

But the man who is not afraid to admit everything that he sees to be wrong with himself, and yet recognizes that he may be the object of God's love precisely because of his shortcomings, can begin to be sincere. His sincerity is based on confidence, not in his own illusions about himself, but in the endless, unfailing mercy of God.
Thomas Merton

And we all, who with unveiled faces contemplate the Lord's glory, are being transformed into his image with ever-increasing glory, which comes from the Lord, who is the Spirit.
2 Corinthians 3:18

PROLOGUE

Love is our true destiny. We do not find the meaning of life
by ourselves alone - we find it with another.
Thomas Merton

erissa

I LEAN against a side wall of Ellyn's Café, alone. I'm grateful
for a few moments to observe those gathered to celebrate
and to consider the unexpected question this gathering has
scripted in my mind. On my heart. Odd that it hadn't
occurred to me before Miles and Ellyn exchanged their vows
this afternoon.

Will Miles's marriage change the friendship we've shared these
last several years?

Miles is my closest friend in Mendocino Village. My
closest friend anywhere. Perhaps it's a friendship I've taken

1

for granted? No. It's a friendship that's...more dear to me than I realized.

Or is it that Miles is more dear to me than I realized?

I straighten and take a step away from the wall, then refocus my attention. The doors of the café stand open in welcome, and sunlight dapples the wood floors accentuating the old-world Parisian charm Ellyn's created. A coastal breeze drifts through the open windows, ruffling the edges of the white linen cloths covering the tables. The dining room, filled with Miles's and Ellyn's friends and family, is alive with conversations punctuated by laughter. A combo off to one side sets the backdrop with strains of *"La Vie En Rose."*

The romantic lyrics capture Miles and Ellyn's romance, along with the love they committed to "until death do us part." That vow was all the more poignant because it was death that had separated Miles and the first woman he committed his heart and life to nearly thirty years ago, his wife Sarah.

Life is fleeting. As is earthly love sometimes. I twist the thin silver band on my left ring finger. Both are to be treasured.

The servers weaving between the guests offering trays of hors d'oeuvres and flutes of champagne were hired from other local restaurants for the reception. Ellyn's staff, who she considers family, are guests today.

I search out Twila, as I have moment by moment it seems, since I gave birth to her almost twenty-seven years ago. She stands with Miles's son, Will, their hands entwined, near a table where the tiered wedding cake, baked and decorated in the café's kitchen, commands their attention. Heads together, they seem to talk about the cake. The tiny diamond on Twila's engagement ring catches the light and flashes as she points to the white cornflowers, freesias, and lilies atop the cake.

My daughter will soon marry... The thought, that reality, is still so new. Something I've yet to fully process. Not all that long ago, I wasn't certain Twila would survive the eating disorder she had battled. Even just a year ago, the idea that Twila would eat a slice of cake seemed merely wistful. Today, she may do just that. Though her frame is still thin, and will likely remain so, a slight curve exists to her hips now, just visible under her dress. Gone are the layers covering her skeletal figure and warming her. When she turns to look at Will, the flush of her cheeks and her smile reflect health and well-being.

Not only has Twila's emotional and physical health improved, but she offered emotional, physical, and spiritual health to Ellyn as well, or at least an opportunity for growth. *Imago Dei*, the words indelibly inked inside Twila's wrist, serve as a reminder of the truth that we are each created in the image of God. Had Twila not shared that truth with Ellyn, had Ellyn not embraced that truth for herself, would she have dared confess her love for Miles? Not likely. As Twila said, while she and Ellyn may look different on the outside, opposite in fact, the struggles they face with weight share many similarities.

Sabina and her husband, Antwone, both tall and striking, stand together talking to another couple. Sabina's renewed faith in God and her recovery from the depression she'd attempted to run from when she decided to spend a year in the village were also a result of Twila—God through her. I understand healing has taken place in Sabina's marriage as well.

I close my eyes for a moment. The scent of the fresh flowers, not only on the cake but also draping over tall, slender vases on each table, wafts over, the fragrance a sweet reminder of all that is good. *Thank You.*

For this moment. Now. Peace and joy commingle. It is a moment to enjoy, to savor, as Ellyn might say. Because such moments are fleeting. Illusory even, tempting me to believe all is well. And it is, but suffering will come again, as it's prone to do, as we're promised it will in this world.

I open my eyes and then wrap my arms around myself, willing the thought to flee. I won't allow it to rob me of the gifts of this day. This is a day of celebration, not one of suffering.

Miles and Ellyn stand nearby. Miles's dark navy suit sets off his salt-and-pepper hair. The tanned skin around his eyes crinkles as he laughs at something Ellyn's said, and then he reaches for her hand and holds it in his own.

A memory flashes—a look I saw, just once, in Miles's eyes a year or so after Sarah died. At the time, I'd attributed the emotion I discerned to the intimacy that had developed between us as I'd worked with Miles to put together a plant-based diet for Sarah after her cancer diagnosis. An intimacy that had grown during Sarah's battle and remained after her death. But it seemed there was something more in his eyes that day, something I couldn't discern. In the moment, I'd wondered... Did he feel something more? Something for me?

I twist the band around my finger again. I shake my head. He knew of the commitment I'd made, and he respected that commitment.

A feeling sweeps over me, so intense and unexpected that I place my hand over my heart and inhale, air slowly filling my lungs. What is it? Wistfulness? No, it's stronger. Longing? *Oh, Lord...* Maybe it wasn't Miles's feelings I should have wondered about, maybe it was my own I should have examined that day. But no, that's ridiculous, isn't—

"You ever regret it?"

4

Startled from my reverie, I turn. "Rosa…hello. I'm sorry, what did you say?" Though I heard her, I'm not sure what she meant.

She looks down at the ring on my finger. "You ever regret de decision you make?"

I've heard Ellyn speak with some annoyance of her dining room manager's seeming ability to read minds. I consider her question, the one I was just about to ask myself. Do I regret committing the rest of my life to singleness?

I glance down at the ring, then look back to Rosa. I hesitate for just a second before I respond. "No, I don't." I speak the knowledge with certainty. "But how did you—?"

"I know a lot of things."

"So I hear. Why do you ask? You're not thinking of playing matchmaker for me the way you did with Ellyn, are you?"

Her eyes widen. "No." She points to the ring I'm wearing. "Dat serious. I never come between you and your Husband. No, no, no."

I smile as a memorized passage returns to me, "When the soul, then, in any degree possesses the spirit of solitary love, we must not interfere with it…"

"Right. Like I said, I not interfere with dat."

"It's a quote. Saint John of the Cross. What you said reminded me of what he wrote, though so often my own soul, my love, is divided, but thank you for understanding. Most people, at least I assume most people, think I'm a little crazy to wear a wedding band as a reminder of a commitment to Christ."

She shakes her head and her dark curls bounce. "Dat not for me to judge. Anyway, you different than Ellyn."

"How so?"

"She was just scared." She wags her index finger at me.

"Fear can't win. Dat not right." Then she points at me. "You have faith."

"Thank you, Rosa. What about you? You've never remarried."

"True. But I also different than Ellyn. I wasn't scared. I loved my Raul. When he died…" Her brow furrows and she looks out one of the windows, then looks back at me. "I'm content. Like you, I had a daughter to raise. Now, I'm just content. Dat's all."

When Rosa says, *"that's all,"* I suspect she means that's all. Subject closed. "Well, I'm glad Ellyn has you and that you encouraged her to spend time with Miles."

"De doctor is a good man. I tell her that more than once. Now, she knows I'm right."

"Yes, he is a good man." Miles and Ellyn are making their way, it appears, to cut the cake. "I'm happy for him. For both of them."

As Rosa looks in the direction of Miles and Ellyn, Pia and a young man make their way toward the cake. "Your daughter is lovely, Rosa. Does she have a new friend?"

Rosa shifts her focus to where Pia and her date stand. She shakes her head. "He not good for her."

"Really? Pia seems like a wise young woman."

"She only nineteen. Too young to get serious. She has school to focus on, then a career. She has opportunities."

"I'm sorry you're not pleased. She seems so happy."

"I know what's good for her, and he not it. Trust me." She looks back to Miles and Ellyn standing behind the cake table, Ellyn with a cake knife in hand. "I go now before they make a mess of dat cake."

I follow Rosa toward the cake until I reach Twila and Will. I put my arm around Twila's waist and pull her close. "I love you," I whisper.

She leans her head on my shoulder for just a moment,

then I let her go. I look around her and smile at Will. Soon, he and Twila will be the ones standing on the other side of the table, posed to cut their own cake.

Miles and I will also be joined by marriage, the marriage of our children to one another. That sense of longing lingers and disturbs, as it weaves itself in and out of my thoughts.

As Ellyn pushes a too-large bite of what I'm sure is her signature butter cake recipe into Miles's open mouth, those gathered around the table erupt in laughter and applause, their joy at this union undisguised.

But a breeze of disquiet chills me again.

I turn and look out one of the open windows across to the bay where a dark, dense fog hovers. Coastal fog is a given during the summer months, but it typically nestles in during the morning hours, burning off with the heat of the day. The sunlight that shone through the open doors and windows just moments ago is filtered now and casts a gray pall. The warm breeze has turned cold and damp. But the breeze is not the cause of the shiver that trembles through me. *What is it?*

A couple of the servers also notice the change in weather and begin closing the windows against the fog.

"Fear can't win." Rosa is right, of course. And fear won't win. I make that vow now, on this day of vows. Then I turn my attention back to Miles and Ellyn.

This is their day.

Whatever is to come, for each of us, is not mine to control.

With that thought, my shoulders relax and silently I offer my gratitude once again to the One who holds all of us in His hands. *Thank You.*

———

CHAPTER ONE

The more you try to avoid suffering, the more you suffer, because smaller and more insignificant things begin to torture you, in proportion to your fear of being hurt. The one who does most to avoid suffering is, in the end, the one who suffers most.
Thomas Merton

llyn

GIVE UP BUTTER?

That's like asking a monkey to give up bananas, an elephant to give up peanuts, or a platypus to give up... Well, never mind. I'm a chef. Trained in France, Le Cordon Bleu. Butter is a staple. Butter is necessary. Butter is—my mouth waters—nonnegotiable.

Anyway, I tried giving up butter last year. It didn't go well.

I square my shoulders. "When Twila was advising me, she told me butter was a healthy fat. Twila's your daughter and you're both nutritionists, so"—I'm grasping, I know—"I thought you'd share the same nutritional views." I raise my eyebrows in hope as I wait for Nerissa's response.

"Ellyn, butter is a healthy fat. And I didn't say you had to give it up. You asked me to interpret the results of your tests and you're clearly sensitive to dairy, specifically casein and lactose." She glances down at the sheet of results on her desk. "Also egg whites, gluten, and radishes."

"I have no problem giving up radishes."

Nerissa laughs. "Well, that's a start." Then her brow furrows. "I know this is difficult. I'm sorry. Have you tried ghee?"

"Ghee?"

"Yes, it's—"

I hold up one hand. "I know. It's butter without the milk solids, which makes it... Well, it isn't worth talking about." I sigh, then sit up a little straighter, hoping to lift my chins off my chest. "It's fine." I gesture to the test results on her desk. "A lot of people have real issues—this is just a bother." I lean forward. "What I don't understand is why I haven't known this before now. Wouldn't I break out in hives or, I don't know, something?"

"The results aren't indicative of allergies, just intolerances. It's likely your body is reacting in ways you haven't linked to dairy or gluten. It's also possible the sensitivities have developed over time, as you've aged, and your system is just now rebelling. Symptoms could manifest as brain fog, joint pain, GI issues. We can relate a host of symptoms to food intolerances."

"I think I've had all of those. You know, the fibromyalgia diagnosis never seemed like a good fit. Could those symptoms be related to these intolerances?"

"It's possible. You could discuss the specifics with your doctor."

"What about the extra"—I clear my throat—"weight? I can't seem to, well, you know..."

"Sometimes our bodies will hold on to weight as a defense. It's possible that by eliminating gluten and dairy from your diet, you'll drop some weight. Although, you tried a vegan diet for a time, didn't you? Did you see any changes in how you felt or in your weight?"

"Maybe. But gluten was still a staple. It's not like a pat of butter or a croissant will kill me though, right?"

Nerissa leans forward. "Ellyn, why did you go through the testing regimen?"

"Oh. Right. Because I didn't, I don't feel well—aches and pains mostly, low energy, and well, you know. Anyway, medically everything checked out, so Miles suggested... Okay, I get it. But that doesn't mean I like it. Have you ever had a radish just pulled from the garden, washed and patted dry, then spread with a dab of sweet butter and sprinkled with salt? Not your off-the-shelf iodized salt, but a coarse Celtic sea salt, for example?"

"Yes, at your café, actually. I believe the radishes were from your lovely garden behind the café." She picks up the copy of my test results, puts them in a file folder on her desk, then looks back at me. "I'm sorry. I know this is challenging."

For some reason, Nerissa's compassion pokes at me. But for once, the filter between my mouth and brain snaps into place before words fall out. I take a minute to consider what's irritating me as Nerissa continues to offer her condolences for the death of my tolerances. Her thick, dark, chin-length hair, just beginning to show stylish streaks of gray, frames her heart-shaped face. Neither freckles nor wrinkles mar her flawless complexion, reminiscent of pure, heavy cream. And her dark-gray eyes, like the sea on a cloud-covered day, reveal depth, sincerity, and yes, what is likely compassion.

A flock of familiar questions flit through my mind, calling *foul* as they go. Or is it *fowl? Is Miles attracted to Nerissa? She's one of his closest friends. Wouldn't it make sense that he'd find her attractive? How couldn't he?* The final question flaps its wings, battering my heart: *Why did Miles marry me when he could have—?*

"Ellyn?"

"What? Sorry. What were you saying?"

"I asked about the radishes."

"Right. Well, maybe I'll miss them a little bit. So..." I shift in my seat again, ready to talk about something else. "You must miss Twila."

Nerissa eases herself back into the desk chair that seems to swallow her petite frame. Her shoulders rise, then fall with her sigh. "I do, but I'm so grateful for Miles and Sarah's friends in Danville inviting Twila to stay in their guesthouse. It's so generous of them and it's an ideal situation for her. She and Will need time together before the wedding to focus on their relationship. Commuting back and forth on week-ends the last six months has been difficult for both of them. And Twila making that drive alone always concerned me, though she's perfectly capable, I know." She shifts her gaze to the window and stares outside for a moment, then looks back to me. "It's good for Twila to have time on her own, too. She's mature beyond her years in many ways. She always has been. Yet she's so young for her age in other ways. All she went through with the anorexia"—Nerissa shakes her head —"took a toll. It took years from her."

"I'm sure it did. But from the perspective of someone who's learned a lot from Twila, she has great insight. *Imago Dei*, right?"

Nerissa smiles. "Yes, Imago Dei. Twila has certainly embraced that truth. It's reminded her of who she is, and perhaps it's given her purpose, sharing the truth of God's design, His creation of mankind in His own image, with others."

"Well, I'm not going to tattoo that message on this body anytime soon, the way Twila did, but I understand it now in a way I didn't before."

"Thank you. It warms a mother's heart to hear of her child's impact on another." She tilts her head. "Ellyn…"

I wait a moment, but she says nothing more. "What? You're staring at me."

"I'm sorry. I was just thinking. You know it's one thing to believe you're created in the image of God, but it's another to live into that image, isn't it?"

"Live into it? Oh. Sure." One of those fowl starts flapping again. "Right. True. So, so true." I clear my throat. Has a feather lodged there? Then I point to the test results on Nerissa's desk. "So, what comes next? What do you recommend?"

"An elimination plan—beginning with a cleanse, and then slowly adding foods into your diet. If gluten, say, causes issues, you'll know it. I can go over the specifics with you. Beyond that, you might consider your gut health."

"I beg your pardon?"

"Gut health. When the microbe in your gut isn't balanced, the imbalance can lead to inflammation, which could be the cause of some of your symptoms. Actually, eliminating dairy and gluten is a good start toward gut health. But there's more—"

I hold up one hand. "That's more than enough for now."

∿

I STAND outside Nerissa's office across from the headlands surrounding Mendocino Bay, the landscape gray and withered. The wind whips and I push long, unruly curls from my eyes. I reach into my bag for a hair band, gather my hair, then secure it. The cold wind cools my face, which is likely the color of a Ruby Queen beet after the time spent in Nerissa's too-warm office. Or was it the time spent in Nerissa's presence that has me overheated?

I pull the cowl neck of my sweater away from my neck as I turn toward the café. I intended to spend a few hours in the office to wade through a pile of invoices from vendors as the staff preps for dinner this evening, but my stride is slow.

Finally, I stop and turn back the way I've just come. Shops and a few offices tucked into historic buildings line one side of the street and the cliff overlooking Portuguese Beach drops off on the other side. The surf below, agitated by the wind, roars as it crashes against the rocky cliffs.

Maybe it's just the wind that agitates me, too.

Beyond the shops and offices, the street gives way to a few homes—clapboard-sided homes, their white paint weathered. Beyond the bend in the road, the landscape opens to Headlands State Park. Although I can't see it from here, around that bend there's a converted water tower sided with weather-worn shingles standing watch over the open space of the headlands.

A force, almost magnetic, pulls me back down the street. I reach Nerissa's office and continue on. By the time I pass the last building on the street, my breathing is labored. I stop, reach into the pocket of my jacket for a tissue, mop my brow with it, then stuff it back inside. I remove my jacket and drape it over my arm, then continue my trek at a more leisurely pace this time.

Just before Sabina left—has it really been almost seven months?—we'd made this walk together. Did it a few times a week, in fact. And it had become easy. Well, almost easy. Certainly easier than it is today. But the walking habit I'd established went with the move.

Whose move? Mine or Sabina's? Both, I guess.

I stop again, but more from the weight of my soul than the extra weight making my heart pound. Of course, I knew Sabina would leave. I guess I just didn't expect her year here to pass so quickly. Now, she's back living and working, counseling clients again, in the Bay Area. She always said she'd come here to heal and heal she did. I'm happy for her. Really.

But... I gauge how much farther I have to walk to reach the water tower and then start out again. *But what?* I let my mind wander back over the last eighteen months. Back when I didn't even know Sabina. Or Twila. And Miles? He was my doctor, nothing more.

But, like yeast, Sabina, Twila, and Miles were mixed into my life and my heart expanded. In every way.

Then Sabina and Twila left. One right after the other.

"Get over it, Big Girl," I whisper.

"Quoting Earl?" I can almost hear Sabina ask, one perfectly arched eyebrow raised.

Earl, my inner critic. At least that's one person I don't miss. My stint working with a therapist, short as it was, did silence Earl. Well, for the most part. *So, take that, Earl.*

Or...Earleen. My mother, as it turned out. The nearly constant criticisms and prodding, the voice I'd dubbed Earl too many years ago now to count, was linked to my mother's voice. As Shauna, my therapist, helped me understand, it was too painful to attribute the voice to my mother, so I created her alter ego, Earl.

The piece of the equation I'm still working to resolve is how my mother projected her own fears, especially those of

15

men, onto me. She claims she was only protecting me, encouraging me to eat, attempting to stuff me most days, in order to keep me fat. Undesirable. To men. At least most men, I guess. Until Miles...

I guess I'll never truly understand my mother's pain. Especially now. I haven't spoken with her in over a year. She wants nothing to do with me since my "betrayal." My sin? Marriage.

I follow the road around the bend, cross one street, then walk the short distance to the water tower with the small addition jutting out on one side. The rental hasn't been occupied since I moved out of it the week of our wedding, six months ago. Before that, it had been my home for many years.

I stand at the edge of the driveway and take in the appearance of the water tower. The owner decided to do some renovations while the property was vacant. I scan the house but don't detect any noticeable changes. He's certainly taking his time. The place didn't need renovating. It was perfect.

Okay, there were a few issues, like that hole in the Sheetrock under the kitchen sink where I'd finally succumbed to calling Miles to dig a dead rat out of the wall. Miles had covered the hole with plywood, but the Sheetrock could stand fixing. As could that little rodent problem. But that kind of thing can happen anywhere.

I start across the gravel drive for the back porch off the mudroom, eager for a peek at the work being done inside, but I stop short, just a few feet from the porch.

I rest my hand on a new shingle wedged in between the old ones on the addition. Not yet weathered like the others, the bright cedar shingle stands out. Conspicuous. Awkward.

I step back, willing myself to turn away from the water tower and head for the café where I belong.

Where I fit.

But like a cookie burnt to an ungreased baking sheet, I seem stuck here. I swallow the ache in my throat.

What am I doing here?

I crane my neck and look up to the tower and its platform surrounded with a half wall. It was there I first declared my love for Miles. The memory of that night has played over and over like a favorite romantic movie since it occurred just over a year ago.

If I had any expectations that night, our relationship has exceeded them all. Had I dared to let myself hope or dream of marriage, anything I'd have come up with would have fallen far short of the reality.

Miles is a good man. A loving, kind, and thoughtful husband.

I make my way to the back deck and try the handle of the Dutch door between the porch and the mudroom. Locked, of course, and the glass is covered by the curtain I made for it. I move to one of the kitchen windows, cup my hands on the glass, and peer inside. "What...happened?" I stare at the kitchen I'd loved, the space warm, cozy. Okay, it was small-ish, but if it worked for me, then it worked. Period.

I step back from the window and shake my head. "Why would he...?" I return to the window and look in again. The wall that separated the kitchen from the small dining space at the end of the living room is gone. Gutted. An open wound revealing the living room, now visible beyond the kitchen. The countertops have been reconfigured, a sizable island added, and pendant lights dangle overhead. All the old tile is gone, replaced by slabs of marble or granite. New cabinets, still awaiting paint, stand with openings for appliances not yet installed.

The kitchen I knew is gone.

The little house is, or was, filled with memories.

Wasn't it just days ago that Sabina and Twila and I sat at my table together, chatting over warm mugs of coffee or herbal tea? Now that table, along with so many of my things, are in storage, waiting to see if Twila and Will can use it once they move into a place of their own.

"I'm so grateful for Miles and Sarah's friends..."

I swat Nerissa's words away like gnats.

I glance around the kitchen again and then turn away from the window. The grass sways, and beyond the head-lands the surf breaks against rocks offshore. On the horizon today, the sea and sky, the same dull shade of gray, are wed. Just as Miles and Sarah had been wed.

Joined as one.

I swat again.

Then I turn to go.

PACO GIVES the stainless-steel countertop a final wipe down, then tosses the rag in the bin for the laundry service. "Bella, you go. We'll finish here and lock up."

"No, of course not." But as the words leave my mouth, my feet scream in protest and I suspect my sous chef sees me wince.

"Go. You have a drive. We can take care of things."

"I know you can. But I'm fine." I glance at the clock on the wall of the café's kitchen. The thought of navigating the curves of the dark coastal highway between here and the other side of Fort Bragg holds little appeal at almost 11:00 p.m.

"Go."

I silence the debate in my head and the one with Paco. "Okay, I'll go. Thank you. And oh, by the way, I have a couple of interviews scheduled for tomorrow. I am working on getting more kitchen help. You shouldn't have to—"

"Go, Bella. Go."

After grabbing my things from the office, I step outside the café into a thick blanket of fog that's dropped sometime during the evening. I pull on my coat and make my way through the alley to my car parked along the street behind the café. I get inside and start the engine, but the headlights do nothing more than bounce off the fog back in the direction of the car. I dig through my purse for my phone to let Miles know I'm leaving. When I find it, a text from him is waiting for me.

Fog. Sit tight. I'll come get you.

Come get me? No. That's silly. I tap the Call icon, hoping he hasn't already left the house.

"Hi there, I'm just leaving the house."

"Miles, no. Don't. I'm fine. I'll need my car in the morning and anyway, it's not like it's the first time I've driven in fog."

He chuckles. "Well, I'm sure that's true. I know you're capable. But I also know you've had a long day. I'm happy to come get you and drive you back in the morning before I go to the office."

I hesitate. "I appreciate the thought, but I'll take it slow."

He's quiet for a moment. "Okay. See you soon."

"Miles?"

"Yes."

"Thank you. And I'll be fine. Really. I...love you."

"I love you, too."

His words, the smile in his tone, and his thoughtfulness still make my breath catch. And his concern for me, I don't even know what to do with that most of the time.

He knows what it is to lose someone he loves.

So...is his concern genuine? Or is he protecting himself? Or is he thinking about—?

I shake my head, hoping to disturb the thoughts attempting to nest there

Almost forty minutes later, when I finally pull through the front gate of the cliffside property where the house was built, I maneuver the car down the long driveway at a crawl, just as I had to crawl through the fog on the winding highway. My neck and shoulders ache, my hands are stiff from gripping the steering wheel, and my lids are heavy. As I near the house, the landscape lighting creates a gauzy aura in the fog. I pull up to the garage, click the opener, and then wait.

As the door rises, my spirit drops.

I'm just tired. A drive that normally takes twenty minutes, but feels longer on the best of nights, felt endless tonight.

I pull into the garage, park the car, and turn off the engine. But rather than get out, I sit in silence, gaze fixed on the door between the garage and the house. Before I can muster the energy to move, the door opens and Miles looks into the garage, a question on his face as he searches me out. When our eyes meet, I force a smile.

He comes out of the house and heads my direction. As he reaches the car, the image of the water tower as it appeared earlier today flashes in my mind, and with it comes the longing for home my visit elicited.

Miles opens my door and then bends and looks at me. "Tired?"

I nod.

He reaches for my shoulder and rests his hand there, his touch warm. Gentle. "Come on in. How does a hot bath sound? I just turned on the water to fill the tub for you."

Tears threatening, I turn and look at him. "You're too good to me."

"No, I'm not nearly good enough. Come in."

I grab my purse, get out of the car, and follow Miles to the door, which he holds open for me. I hesitate for just a moment, then step over the threshold...

Into the house Miles had built for another woman.

CHAPTER TWO

Indeed, too often the weakest thing about our faith is the
illusion that our faith is strong, when the strength we feel is
only the intensity of emotion or of sentiment, which have
nothing to do with real faith.
Thomas Merton

erissa

THE OCEAN, the same azure as the sky it reflects this afternoon, churns and froths below. Another wave rolls toward
an outcropping of rocks jutting from the ocean floor and
then crashes over the mass, the act untamed, violent. A spray
of mist from the force of the tumbler refracts rays of sunlight
causing a rainbow effect to hang above the rocks for a
moment, then the spectacle begins again as another set of

waves rushes the shore. In the distance, whitecaps dot the unsettled sea.

I step back from the cliff and button my coat against the battering wind, though it does nothing to ward off the chill within. When I slip my hands into the deep pockets of the coat, the letter that drove me here, to the headlands, crinkles. I pull it from the pocket and glance at it again, still trying to make sense of it, though truly, I understand it all too well. I shove it back into my pocket, but I can't hide from the implications it imparted after I had slit the envelope open just an hour ago.

Just an hour ago, when life still seemed ordered, manageable, predictable even. But just when you're certain there are seven waves in every set, the number changes.

I've always known this day would come, haven't I? But it is sooner than expected. I thought I had more time. I thought—

Oh, Lord...

Like sand, I sift the contents of my mind, searching for words to offer, pleas for providence, but find nothing. The watery landscape before me has so often inspired my prayers, informed my prayers even, but now—

There's so much to consider...

Twila's wedding is just the beginning. My stomach churns like the surf below.

"The sea speaks." My father's words, spoken so long ago, echo. We'd stand facing the surf, toes buried in the sand, my hand curled around one ear to amplify the sound.

"Hear it, Sprite?"

I'd strain to hear the words it spoke but could make out nothing but the roar of the swells tumbling one after the other. I'd look up at him and shrug.

His laughter rode the waves as his big hand rested atop my head. *"Someday, you'll understand."*

Will today be that day? "Will you finally release the wisdom you hold?" I whisper. Though my name, chosen by my father from Greek mythology, meaning *sea nymph*, forever links me to its depths, I've yet to hear the sea speak. But I have heard a voice that, as far as I know, my father never listened for or heard. The deaf ear he turned to that voice never fails to rend my heart.

How I long to hear that voice now. But He, like the sea, seems to offer little in this moment.

Another wave, wrought from the depths, crests then slams against the craggy mount of rocks. Even at this distance from the cliff, its spray catches and carries on the wind, its mist chilling as it meets my face. What normally evokes wonder only annoys today. The unending raucousness drowns the peace I'd hoped to find here.

Not only did I come seeking peace, I also seek answers, but I've yet to pin down the questions swirling in my soul. It seems no words exist for the vortex of emotion.

I push myself up from the rock on the bluff where I've sat, brush off the back of my jeans, shove my icy hands back into my pockets, and then turn my back on the ocean. As I walk away from the bluff through the brittle grass of the headlands, a litany of memories plays, each a stone tossed into a pack on my shoulders until the weight feels as though it will press me to the ground. The angst and devastation of the divorce—unwanted yet welcomed with guilt-inducing relief. Twila's tears. So many tears. So many sleepless nights. How I'd tried to make her understand that the father she missed was only an idealized version she'd created. I knew that to be true because I'd once idealized the man myself.

Of course, I couldn't make her understand, and any attempt to do so seemed like sprinkling salt on an open wound. Her heart shattered, and then her mind and body followed with her growing aversion to food and her eventual refusal to eat. My helplessness escalated as I watched her become an empty shell, both emotionally and physically. I knew the nutrition she needed, yet I could not force her to eat. Then came college and her return home, defeated. And finally, the diagnosis and an opening in a treatment program Miles, Twila's doctor at the time, assured me came highly recommended.

It was a decade of single parenting, of attempting to meet needs I couldn't possibly meet, of feeling the pain of one I loved so dearly, all while working to secure a job using a degree I'd earned nearly a quarter of a century before. Working to fill the gap spousal support didn't fill. Working not only to provide financially and emotionally, but to do so in a way that wouldn't drain more of me, what was left of me. The remaining shards of me not given first to a husband who would take all of me, and then some, and to a daughter who has my whole heart but still needed more of me.

However, through it all God was with me. His presence palpable. His provision for me when even those last shards slipped away—His strength through my weakness—was evident. I knew He was there.

I know He is here.

But...

I pull my left hand from my pocket and hold it out in front of me. The silver band is loose around my cold finger. I stare at it a moment, then slide my hand back into the pocket as an unsettling gale whips, nearly flattening me.

Where are You now? I can't feel You. I don't sense You. I know You're with me always. I know. I know that I know. But I need... I'm sorry, but I need Your assurance. Please. I need— I choke back tears I've held at bay. *I need You.* Somehow tears seem to indicate a lack of trust.

I trust You. I do.

Words, something of value it seems, interrupt my plea—

my vow. They land like a dove in my mind and I still, waiting to hear from the One who has so often led me. But the words take flight before I can grasp their message.

Something about tomorrow…

I slow my pace and close my eyes for a moment, willing the words to instruct me. Finally, they land again. *"Don't worry about tomorrow, for tomorrow will worry about itself…"* Words I've taken comfort from so often. But they offer little solace now.

I open my eyes, but my gaze is still focused inward where the landscape is barren and only the utterances of accusation make sense. *I should have worked harder. I should have chosen a more lucrative career. I should have prepared for this day.*

I should have, but I didn't.

Didn't or couldn't?

I don't know.

Somewhere in my confusion is a tightly woven lie, but rather than work to unravel it, I push it aside for later and trudge onward. There is much to do. Although, *what* I'm supposed to do, I'm not sure.

But I must *do* something.

I PULL several checks and the deposit slip from my purse as I wait for the customer ahead of me to finish his business with the teller. Most of my clients pay me digitally, but a few in the village still write checks. I riffle through the slim pile as I wait and stop at Ellyn's check.

When she'd pulled her checkbook from her bag yesterday, I held up my hand. *"Ellyn, we're almost family. No payment necessary."*

She ignored me, filled out the check, then placed it on my

desk and slid it toward me. *"Family or not, we're business owners."*

I couldn't have imagined then, less than twenty-four hours ago, how grateful I'd feel for one more check to add funds to the dwindling balance in my account.

That balance isn't nearly enough to... I close my eyes. *Don't think about it. Don't allow the thought to control your mind, your emotions.* Is refusing to think about my income, or lack thereof, an act of faith? Is it good science? Or is it denial? I pinch the bridge of my nose, hoping to relieve the ache that's settled in my forehead.

"Next."

I open my eyes and step forward.

After making the deposit and verifying the balances of both my business and personal accounts, I leave the bank and, with head down, body steeled against the assaulting wind, I make my way toward my car parked along the street.

"Nerissa."

As I look up, I nearly bump into Miles. "Hello, stranger." Another gust nearly pushes me over and my hair whips, stinging my eyes. Miles, his hand on my shoulder, nudges me back toward the bank. He opens the door and holds it for me and we step into the enclosed foyer where a couple of people stand in front of ATMs.

"Nothing like wind to keep the fog at bay." Miles's eyes, blue as the sky and the sea on this clear day, smile down at me.

I push my hair off my face. "I wish it would keep the fog in my mind at bay."

His expression softens. "Fog in *your* mind?"

I wave away his question, wishing I hadn't alluded to my concerns. "'All shall be well, and all shall be well and all manner of things shall be well.'"

"Julian of Norwich."

"Yes." The familiar words have so often offered comfort, but today, they evoke nothing. Least of all the assurance I hoped they'd afford. I determine to shift my focus, yet again, and smile. "How are you, Miles?"

"I'm well." He glances at his watch. "What brings you to the big city?"

"Fort Bragg? The big city?" I laugh, and the action nudges the fog hovering within aside a bit. "I had a few errands, the bank being one of them."

"Have time for a cup of coffee? It's been a while."

My afternoon holds little—the one client I had scheduled canceled her appointment. Busy time of year, I'd told myself when I listened to her message. Although, typically the beginning of a new year means my calendar is filled with appointments with those who've resolved to either lose weight or get a grasp on a health issue. Or both. But, for some reason, that hasn't been the case this year. There've been a few, like Ellyn, but the usual onslaught didn't occur. "Sure. Dare we brave the walk to the Mercantile?"

"I'll risk it as long as you don't force a Green Giant on me."

"I don't believe I forced it the first time. I suggested it for its health benefits. It's good for you, Doctor."

He chuckles. "Well, that may be, but it didn't taste good."

I reach up and gently tap his forehead. "That's because you didn't think it would taste good. We get what we expect."

"If I expect the Giant to taste like a mocha, I promise you, it's still going to taste green."

I hold up my hands in mock surrender. "Coffee it is."

We dash to the Mercantile, intent on getting out of the weather. Even braced against the wind, my shoulders relax a bit and that weighted pack I've carried all day seems lighter. Once we're settled at a table with our drinks, we sit in companionable silence for a few moments as Miles sips his coffee and I warm my hands on the hot ceramic mug of herbal tea.

"How's your mocha?"

"Bitter." He pats his midsection. "I've put on a few pounds —one of the hazards of marrying a chef. I've traded the mochas for the straight stuff."

"Ah..." I lift my hand and knead a knot at the base of my neck.

Miles's gaze moves from my face to the hand at my neck and then back. "How are you?"

I lower my hand.

"It's nothing. I'm alright. Have you talked with the kids recently?"

He watches me for a moment longer. "Will called last night. He was with Twila—they were cooking dinner together and he wanted to ask Ellyn a question about something they were making. She was at the café, of course." He shrugs. "He sounded good. Preoccupied with what they were doing, but good."

I shake my head. "Twila was cooking... I never imagined how much emotion that image would evoke."

"I'm sure it does, gal. She's doing well." Miles sets his cup down, shifts in his seat, and stretches his long legs in front of him. His demeanor is relaxed. He is a man at ease with himself and with others. More than ease, he exudes peace, which is a gift to his patients, I'm sure. It's a gift I need today, too.

"Ellyn seemed to enjoy her time with you this week."

"Enjoy?"

"Well, she seemed to appreciate your knowledge." He pulls his legs back and leans forward. "How did she seem to you?"

"Seem?" I hesitate, taken aback by the question. "Miles, she's a client, and I don't—"

"No, no, I know. That's not what I'm asking." He runs his hand through his hair. "I mean... Did she, does she seem happy? Content?"

The peace he exuded moments before had evaporated. I consider his question, but he doesn't give me a chance to respond.

"You know, after Sarah died..." He stares at me, but I know he isn't seeing me. "It's just different. This is different."

Is he thinking of Sarah or Ellyn? And then a shadow of knowing passes over me. How many times has Ellyn asked herself that same question since marrying Miles and moving into the home he built for Sarah?

"I know I'm not solely responsible for her happiness or her contentment."

He looks beyond me, lost in his own thoughts, but this time I'm certain he's thinking of Ellyn, and that realization causes a pang somewhere deep within.

"It was different with Sarah." He shakes his head. "I learned that even with all the knowledge I hold, I wasn't in control. I couldn't heal her physically. But with Ellyn? Maybe..." He nods. "Maybe I thought my love for her would be enough, that it would..." He puts his hands on the table, palms flat, resignation creasing his face. "God is reminding me that He's the One who is in control, not me. He's the One who can silence the condemning voice still taunting Ellyn."

"You're right, you know. But there is more to it than that, Miles. God is healing Ellyn, and He's using you in that process. His love for her, through you."

"So, it's both? God is the One in control and He's using me?"

"I think so. It seems He often works that way, doesn't He?"

"He does. You know, after Sarah...I didn't expect a second chance. I didn't think I'd love someone again." His hands relax and he smiles. "Thank you, gal. I want Ellyn to feel supported. She spent so many years alone…" He holds up his hands as though to indicate he's said enough, then leans back in his seat again and chuckles. "Am I making any sense?"

Unsettling emotions, like the tide, have risen as Miles has talked, but I can't consider them now. "Perhaps we're both a little foggy today."

"Maybe so. Marriage can have that effect occasionally, I guess. So that's my excuse, what's yours?"

My grip tightens on the handle of the mug and the silver band on my ring finger presses into my flesh. "My excuse?" I lift the mug and take a sip, then set it back on the table. I know exactly what my excuse is, or I think I do, but… "Just one of those days, I suppose."

I PULL into the driveway just before dusk, turn off the ignition, and then rest my forehead on the steering wheel, eyes closed. Why haven't I told Miles the truth? Was it pride? The money I've put away for Twila's wedding won't even begin to cover the expenses, even though Miles and Ellyn have offered to pay for the reception, and Will and Twila will cover some of the expenses as well. But living month to month means anything extra becomes a burden. And now the small amount I had saved will have to go toward rent, and insurance, and… The list seems endless.

I lift my head and stare into the shadows of late afternoon, then at the empty house. A rip current catches me and threatens to pull me into the depths. It is only when my body shudders with cold that I return my focus to the moment and finally get out of the car.

I set my bag on the bench just inside the front door, then head to the kitchen, flipping on lights as I go. When I reach the kitchen table, I stop. The letter I had received earlier is sitting on the table where I left it after my walk on the headlands. I pull out one of the chairs, drop into it, and reach for the envelope. I open it and pull out the sheaves of paper, unfold them, and read the letter again:

Dear Ms. Boaz,

Attached are copies of documents served on our office by Roland K. Chase, Attorney-at-Law, representing Daniel Boaz. Would you like Cunningham and Bolton to represent you in this matter? Upon receipt of this correspondence, please contact us at your earliest convenience so we can respond to the representing party.

Sincerely,

Kelsey Benning, Paralegal to Michael Cunningham, Attorney-at-Law

I let the letter and its attachments drop on the table. Do I fight? Or do I just... Passivity, my old friend, tempts me once again.

I lean forward and rest my head on my arms. Emotions wash over me as they had threatened to do earlier as I sat across from Miles. This time, I can do nothing to stem the tide. There is no holding back the despair.

What will retaining my attorney cost?

I close my eyes, lids heavy. *"I want her to feel supported, that's all. She spent so many years alone..."* Miles's words play through my mind. His words about Ellyn. Tears crest again and flow now, coming from that deep place where an unknown emotion panged earlier. Miles's words play again and again. Words about Ellyn. Words about his former wife.

I raise my head and stare at the letter that now, through my tears, appears to float on the table. This is nothing God can't handle. I know that. Yet…

What will retaining my attorney cost me? Too much.

What will a fight cost me? Too much.

I have nothing left to give.

I've given it all. Alone. For too long.

Alone?

No, Lord. I know better.

But tonight, all day, in fact, what I know and what I feel have warred against one another. It's a battle, all of it, I no longer possess the energy to wage.

CHAPTER THREE

A man who fails well is greater than one who succeeds badly.
Thomas Merton

ia

I STARE out the windshield of the parked truck, seeing nothing but the crack in the glass. A dividing line. Before Manuel confessed the lie, and now, after I know the truth. The impact totally slammed me, cracked me wide open, and I'm left with a gaping, untreatable wound.

I swipe at something wet and hot on my face. Blood? I pull my hand from my cheek. Only tears? I double over in the passenger seat wanting to hide from this pain, but there's nowhere to go, nothing to do. I literally don't know what to do.

"Pia…" Manuel rests his hand on my back and I jerk back up at his touch.

"I have to go," I mumble as I push open the door of the truck. Mama stands in the doorway of the café, her expression telling me all I need to know, and more.

Manuel leans toward me. "Wait!"

"No. She'll… No." As I reach for my bag, he grabs my hand, lacing his fingers with mine, and holds tight. Hands clasped, the color of our skin, each a variation of rich, California soil, melds as one. But his hand, unlike mine, is callused, hardened from his work in the vineyards, and feels rough against my palm.

Was my mama right? Should the calluses, or rather the cause of the calluses, have warned me? Should I have refused to go out with him when I learned he was a laborer? *Just a laborer*, some would say.

"You only date boys in school. Boys with a future. Boys who belong here, Pia."

It isn't that Manuel is a laborer, that isn't the issue. My mama respects hard work. Demands hard work. It's what the labor represents, the possibility it implies. The color of our skin may be the same. We may have thought we are the same. But we are not. I know that now. And whether we want it to or not, the difference changes everything.

His thick dark hair falls over his dark eyes, and he combs it back with his fingers, a motion I've seen hundreds of times. The pain in his eyes flows like Big River into the sea, clouding what once seemed clear to both of us. As I look into his eyes, I know I look into my own.

"I have to go," I tell him again. When I peel my hand from his, I wonder if I haven't left my skin on his palm. I get out of the truck, the door rattling with my slam, and run up the pathway and then up the two steps leading to the café. I stop only because Mama uses her small frame to block my entrance.

"You okay?"

I don't look at her. I can't look at her. Head down, I nod. How long has she been standing here? What did she see?

"You late."

I keep my face down. "No, I'm not." I start to push past her but stop myself. No reason to disrespect her.

"You want to get promoted to server, you be on time."

I look at my watch—4:00 p.m. exactly. "I am on time."

"You cut it too close, Pia."

She looks past me to where Manuel is still parked, watching us, I assume. "You cutting too much too close right now."

I nod again.

"Look at me."

She doesn't know what she asks. How much she asks.

"Pia." Her tone is firm.

I glance at her again but without letting our eyes meet, then I peer back over my shoulder toward Manuel. He sits in the old ranch truck, pallets filling the bed. He shrugs, as if to ask what she's saying. When I turn back, Mama reaches up and puts her hand on my cheek. I tower over her, as most people do, but we all know she is the bigger person. That, at least, is still clear.

"Tears?" Her tone has softened.

"No. I mean... It's nothing." *Nothing?* I rub my palm, still raw from Manuel's touch, against my pants. Nothing or everything? There is no in-between, no little bit. It is all or nothing.

"If he hurt you—" she says, sharp as a blade.

"It's not like that, Mama!" I strike, defending him, as is my habit with her. Then I take a deep breath and slow down. "He didn't…" *Didn't he?* "I'm fine." *Fine?* Whether I mean to disrespect her or not, my lie does the job.

She looks past me again, then turns and points toward the dining room. "You go."

I slip around her, cross the dining room, and push through the swinging door into the kitchen, where I head straight for the time clock in the back room. I drop my bag on the long, rustic wood table, *the family table*, as Auntie Ellyn's always called it.

"Pia, you are my family. We are we. There is no me, no you. It is only 'we' now."

Hands shaking, I clock in. Mama's right. I cut it too close, and it isn't the first time.

"Bebe, I'm sorry. I am. But I can't change it."

Tears blur my vision. I can't think about it now. Not here. Anyway, it's pointless. He's right. He can't change what he did, the lie he told. And his lie made me a liar. A new thought, dart-like, pins me in place. *Just like Manuel's parents' lie made him a liar?* Lies swarm like flies over a decaying carcass.

I close my eyes and press my palms to my temples. It's too much. I can't. Not now. I open my eyes and pick up my bag. I stare at the table where my bag sat, then rub my hand across the smooth surface where I've spent almost every Sunday afternoon for as long as I can remember. The table where Ellyn hosts her restaurant family.

My family? Or is Manuel right? Is he my family now?

The wood is firm, solid under my hand. I celebrated my sixteenth birthday here—sixteen, when all I wanted to do was grow up. How much easier things were before…

Before Manuel.

Before love.

If I didn't love him, none of this would matter.

A sharp rap on the back door jerks me from my thoughts.

I fumble for a piece of Kleenex in my jacket pocket, pull out a crumpled wad, then rub the damp tissues under my eyes. I stuff the black mascara-streaked mess back into my pocket, then go to open the door just as whoever is on the other side bangs again.

Ellyn, holding a basket, stands on the stoop. "Oh. Sorry, honey. I forgot to grab the key before I went out, and I didn't think anyone in the kitchen would hear me knock." She takes a step to come in, then stops and looks at me, her expression full of questions.

Please don't ask. Please.

She pauses, puts her hand on my arm, and gives it a squeeze. "Here, take this for me." She hands me the basket filled with winter lettuces from the garden.

When it's clear that's all she'll say, I breathe again and then follow her into the kitchen where the clang of utensils on the metal countertops, the sizzle of meat on the grill, and the raised voices of the staff turn the volume up a few notches, which is good. I need the distraction right now.

"Pia, *hola.*" Paco, who is stirring something on one of the ranges, nods in my direction. Others smile or wave without stopping what they're doing.

"Hey, you guys." I don't stop and talk. There's no time for that now and I don't have it in me, anyway. The energy in the kitchen is always high. Maybe I can absorb some of that energy tonight. I'll need it.

I set the basket on a side counter, then go to the lockers where I take off my jacket and hang it with my bag in one of the spaces.

"Pia, have a minute?" Ellyn stands in her office doorway.

"Um, sure. Be right there." Great. Now she'll ask. I check my face in the small mirror hanging on the locker door, wipe under my eyes again, then grab a tube of foundation from my bag. I rub a dab under both eyes. It's all I can do for now.

When I walk into her office, she's already sitting at her desk, so I take the seat next to the desk.

She swivels her chair so she's facing me and then points to a brown paper grocery bag sitting on the floor by the door. "That's for you. I thought you could use it for one of your mosaics."

I rise out of the chair and peer into the bag. "Oh no. What happened?"

"It fell off the shelf—came crashing down. Just one of those things. I thought you could use it."

I glance again at the pieces of the broken platter, the aqua ceramic is familiar. "That was one of your pieces from France."

"It was."

"I'm sorry it broke, but yeah, I'll use it. It'll still be beautiful. Thank you."

"So…" She searches my face. "How are you?"

I shrug. "Okay, I guess." Not a lie. But not the truth either. I sit down again, assuming she wanted more than to give me the pieces of the broken platter.

"Okay?"

I don't say anything else, afraid the words won't get past the ache in my throat.

"Well, I guess I'll have to take 'okay,' but only for now." She waits until I look at her again before she continues. "Listen, you've shadowed Andrea several times, and I think you're ready to serve. What do you think? Can you handle it tonight?"

I nod. "I can handle it, Auntie El— I mean…"

"Honey, I hope you'll always think of me as Auntie Ellyn. You've grown up here in my kitchen. Tonight, instead of the hostess station, I need you in the dining room. Andrea called in sick and that leaves us short. Your mom will seat guests, while managing the rest of us, that is."

"She does that well," I mumble.

Ellyn stares at me a moment. "Very well. Now, go grab yourself an apron."

"Thank you." I get up, pick up the bag, and turn to go.

"Pia?"

I turn back.

"If you ever need to talk about anything, you know where to find me. Auntie first, boss second. Got it?"

I nod, then I look down as tears threaten again.

"Honey, whatever's going on, it'll turn out okay. I promise."

I swallow the lump in my throat and look back up. "How do you know?" I whisper.

"Experience."

As I walk out of Ellyn's office, I bump into my mama coming into the office.

"Oh, Rosa...Pia, hold on a minute," Ellyn calls after me.

I return to the office to stand next to Mama.

"Pia's going to serve in Andrea's place tonight. Andrea called in."

Mama plants her hands on her hips. "She din't call me."

"She's terrified of you."

I read the humor in Ellyn's eyes, but Mama doesn't seem to see it. She straightens to her full height and squares her shoulders. "Dat not—"

"Okay, maybe not terrified, just scared to death." Ellyn winks at me, then looks back at Mama. "I just happened to pick up the phone, okay? Anyway, I wanted to let you know of the change. I'll need you to work the hostess station."

"Of course."

Ellyn looks to me, then back to Mama. "Pia can handle it."

"Yes. She do a good job." Mama turns to me. "I know you do a good job. And I here if you need anything."

My mama has always expected a lot of me—set high standards. I get it. She wants me to appreciate the opportunities I have and make the most of them. Opportunities she didn't have. Opportunities most of the world doesn't have. When she left Mexico, she left a life, she assures me, I will never understand. She wanted more for her only child, and I have more than she ever had growing up.

Her expectations include respect, gratitude, loyalty, hard work. And one other thing. Truthfulness. Always. How many times has she pointed at me to say, *"You always tell de truth, Pia. Always. You understand?"*

Yes, I understood. I understand. But now... It's literally just so complicated.

I get why she's pushed me, why she continues to push me, but I haven't always liked it. She hasn't expected me to accomplish things alone, though. She's always been there to support me. To help me. Even when I haven't wanted her help.

Like when I didn't want her help, or her *interference*, with Manuel. Of course, I got her opinion where he was concerned whether I wanted it or not.

And now I know. Both the truth about Manuel and that, in some respect, she was right.

"What you doing staring off into space like you have nothing to do?" Mama nudges me as she passes me in the kitchen. Then she looks back at me as she pushes through the swinging door. "C'mon. You got work to do. You know what specials on de menu tonight? No? You got work to do."

I put the bag from Ellyn with my things in the locker, pull a black apron from the pile of laundered aprons, tie it around my waist, then go into the dining room where Mama hands me the list of house specials for the evening. I read through the offerings but can't take any of it in—can't make sense of it.

What does make sense, what I do understand now, is why

she kept pushing me and questioning me about Manuel. If I'd listened to her, how would I feel now? Better. That's for sure. Or is it? To never have gotten to know Manuel? To never have loved him?

How could that be better?

And how could it be worse?

She won't support me now, though. How could she? After all the times she warned me? No.

I review the list of specials again, including the ingredients, and work to memorize them before guests arrive, but the memory of Ellyn's words interrupt. *"Honey, whatever's going on, it'll turn out okay."* Is there any way she can be right? I can't see how this can possibly turn out okay. But I want her to be right. I so need her to be right. Then I remember what she'd said when I asked how she knew. *"Experience."* I crumple the list in my hand.

As much as I want to believe her, I guarantee this is one experience she's never had.

CHAPTER FOUR

The spiritual life is first of all a life. It is not merely
something to be known and studied, it is to be lived.
Thomas Merton

erissa

I BOLT UPRIGHT, heart pounding, thoughts tumbling. *What's
wrong?* I untangle myself from the sheets and blankets, then
stare at the blank canvas before me. The numbers on the
digital clock on my nightstand cast a blue hue, otherwise,
darkness envelops me. I glance at the clock: 3:23 a.m.

Unmoving, I listen for the sound that woke me but hear
nothing. I strain to listen, to hear. The hum of the refrigerator? The sigh of the heater? A breath of wind outside? But
there's nothing. Not even the creak or groan of a settling
house.

The silence, the stillness, is deafening in its completeness. I am alone. Utterly alone.

"No. That's not true." I whisper, hoping my own voice will break the spell. But the blanket of oppression only grows heavier.

My already racing heart quickens and fear, like a viper, strikes fast and hard, sinking its fangs into my soul.

I swing my legs over the side of the bed and fumble, hands trembling, with the switch on the bedside lamp. As light floods the room, I'm certain I'll see something, though what, I'm afraid to consider. But nothing is out of place, nor does anything out of the ordinary appear. What was I expecting?

I hold out my hands, willing them to stop shaking but to no avail. I glance back at the clock on my nightstand, then reach for the Bible next to the clock. I set it on my lap and open it. I put on my glasses and begin reading where my gaze lands. I care not what book, chapter, or verse.

"...in order that the world might be saved through Him." I stop to find the beginning of the verse and then read it in its entirety. *"For God did not send his Son into the world to condemn the world, but in order that the world might be saved through him."*

Yes, Lord. The anxiety of yesterday and the fear that holds me— I stop myself midthought and reframe the sentence— the fear that *held* me begins to ebb. *Thank You for saving me...* I pause as the circumstance presented nags again. "Thank you for saving me moment by moment, over and over again, for now and all of eternity."

I inhale, filling my lungs. *You save me.* I slowly exhale. *Thank You.*

I inhale again. *You save me*, and again, I exhale. *Thank You.*

I lie back down, pull the covers over my now-chilled body, and begin to relax under their warmth. I inhale. *You save me.* My heart rate begins to slow. I exhale. *Thank You.*

The trembling subsides, my body stills. *You save me.*

I continue the meditation and intentional breathing, refusing to leave space in my mind for other thoughts. Keeping my mind focused on God's saving grace and offering gratitude quells the fear and whatever evil I sensed surrounding me.

AWARENESS COMES LIKE A KITTEN, gentle and soft. I open my eyes to the pale hues of dawn shrouding the room. I luxuriate in the moment, lingering in the warm cocoon the covers create until reality rudely disrupts. My mind shuffles the memories like a deck of cards, each card a reminder. The letter. Its implications. The angst of the day before. The fear in the early hours. I toss the covers back and climb out of bed with the resolve that rest, and the time spent meditating during the night, afford.

After shrugging into my robe, I stop at the thermostat in the hallway and reach to turn up the temperature, then hesitate. Fifty-eight degrees. I leave the thermostat set as is. I make my way to the kitchen, where I set the teakettle to boil.

I take a mug of steeping tea to the kitchen table, intent on making some decisions. The letter is where I left it last night, along with the documents that came with it. I push the letter aside and pick up and scan the documents the letter references. I glanced at them yesterday, just long enough to determine most of the content is written in legalese I don't understand. But the point is clear: Daniel has filed a motion of intent to stop paying spousal support.

Why now?

Based on the marriage settlement agreement we signed during our divorce proceedings, he was to pay support until retirement age, which is now close to seventy years of age in

California. Daniel, who is several years older than me, won't turn seventy for almost eleven years. I was sure I had at least a dozen years to continue building my business and, eventually, begin putting something away for my own retirement. I set the documents aside and cross my arms on the table. Retirement will never come, will it?

He shouldn't have to pay you anything. Certainly not now, not after all these years. Why haven't you worked harder? Worked smarter?

"Stop," I whisper. I place my palms flat on the table and take a deep breath.

The truth is that under California law, ours was considered a long-term marriage—Twila was almost twelve when we'd separated. And as such, based on the fact that I sacrificed my career to help Daniel get a business started and later to raise Twila, which was no sacrifice at all, upon our divorce Daniel was ordered to pay spousal support.

Our decision to have me stay home freed Daniel to travel throughout the Pacific Northwest that his business, *our* business, necessitated. He was to pay both spousal and child support.

That order was modified when Twila turned eighteen. The child support was discontinued, the spousal support continued. While I could have fought then to have the amount Daniel paid me increased based on the steep incline of his income since our divorce, I chose not to do so. I wanted, I want, more than anything, to provide for myself. I didn't want more from Daniel, then or now.

But so many obstacles have stood between me and a steady income. Haven't they? Twila's illness and recovery come to mind, as they did yesterday. She needed my support, my presence. While Daniel may have sent the checks each month, he'd abandoned Twila in every other way. She needed a father. I tried to make up for what she lacked, which was impossible, but my presence offered stability. And love. Of that, I'm certain.

And I did work. Hard. But opportunities in the village and surrounding areas are limited, and a move would have added more stress to Twila's already-fragile existence. As strong as she is, she is also sensitive in so many ways. I couldn't uproot her. Not then. Not after what she'd lost when Daniel left and then didn't stay in touch with her.

The thought that's plagued me for many years, the one I can never get away from for long, knocks. *There is nothing good about divorce.* Yet divorce is sometimes necessary for the emotional health of those involved, as was ours.

Truth?

I close my eyes, weary of the accusations. I am familiar with the enemy who hurls them, and he is not deserving of my attention. Nor was I deserving of Daniel's verbal assaults, manipulations, and his many lies, among other things. Neither was Twila.

While Twila did need me, especially when she returned home from college, she also needed professional care—life-saving care. *Emotional health?* The divorce came too late to save Twila's health. I stayed too long. I should have... "Truth, Nerissa, what's true?" I whisper.

A small portion of the inpatient treatment program where Twila was a resident was covered by Daniel's insurance. He paid the deductible but refused to cover the remaining amount. Not a surprise, really, his abandonment of Twila was nearly complete. Yet, I'd let it surprise me, and wound me, again.

I agreed to pay the remaining amount. Of course I'd pay it, there wasn't a question. And I trusted God would provide the means. But He's not chosen to do so, yet.

That debt remains, accruing interest—along with other debt I've incurred when my income didn't cover the monthly expenses. Yes, the spousal support helps, but it isn't enough to... My breaths have become shallow and my heart races. I need to think about something else, do something else, put all of this behind me, somehow.

But no. This is reality. Any attempt to escape it will just delay the inevitable. I have to—

The phone rings in the pocket of my robe, startling me. I pull it from my pocket and read Twila's name on the screen. I let it ring again as I force my mind back to the present before I answer. I clear my throat, then breathe deep. "Good morning."

"Hey..."

"Hi, honey, how are you?" Thoughts still sprinting, I continue talking without waiting for Twila's response, but I can't seem to stop the rush of words. "I heard you and Will were cooking dinner together the other night. That sounded like fun. How'd it—?"

"He cooked. I was just... Mom, how are *you*?"

"Me?" What does she know? Or suspect? Much like Rosa, Twila's always had a sense, even stronger than a sense, more a knowledge and understanding of other people's pain or heartache. Divine knowledge, I believe. A gift God's given her that neither of us fully understands. But what occurred yesterday, the news I received, is not something I want Twila to know. Not yet. Not now. It isn't her concern, not for her to—

"Mom?"

"I'm sorry. Fine. I'm fine. I'm glad to hear from you." I glance at the clock on the microwave. "You're awake early for a Saturday. What are you up to today? Do you have—?"

"Mom, wait. So, like, you're totally fine? You're okay, really?"

I close my eyes and work to quiet my mind. "Really." On some level, I know that's true despite what I feel. I open my eyes again and focus on the conversation. "How are you doing? How are the wedding plans coming?"

Twila's silent for a moment. "Um, I'm okay, I guess. I just —I don't know. I thought maybe something was wrong."

I hear her confusion and reconsider my response. "Honey, life comes with stressors, we both know that. I've had a few this week, but I trust God is providing even as we speak."

As I hear my own words spoken to my daughter, I vow to hold on to them, to operate in faith, the belief in what I can't see, as I've done many times before. Why is this circumstance, this time, any different? It isn't. God is the same and that's all I need to know.

"Yeah. Okay."

"Have you and Will finalized the guest list and looked at invitations?" Though I know they're planning a small ceremony and reception, the cost of just the postage to mail the invitations presents itself, followed by the cost of the invitations themselves, at least what I imagine they'll cost. And then there's... I reach for the phone I've cradled between my ear and shoulder, tap the icon to set it to speaker mode, then set it on the table. Do I dare ask Daniel to help with the wedding expenses?

No. Twila wouldn't want that. When Daniel showed up last year, it was clear to Twila he was only there to serve his own purpose, not because he cared about her. Her decision to set a firm boundary in the relationship was for the best. I can't undo what she did. Nor do I want to. It's just...

I knead the knot that's formed in my shoulder. Both shoulders, actually. I work to focus on faith. On the words I've only just spoken. How quickly they fled.

"Not yet. We've had a lot going on with work and stuff. I was thinking about coming home for a couple days, maybe this weekend. Does that work?"

"Of course, you know you don't need to ask. Can Will join you?"

"I…don't know. I'm not sure."

Do I imagine Twila's hesitation? Read too much into it? "Honey, are *you* okay?"

"Sure."

Her response comes too quickly for my comfort. "Well, if you can make it, I'll look forward to seeing you. Keep me posted."

"Yeah, I will."

We chat a bit more, but it's a brief exchange. After we end the call, I sit, hands wrapped around the now lukewarm mug of tea, and consider the conversation and the seed of concern it's planted in my soul. Did I project my own worries onto Twila? Or is there something going on with her? Is she truly okay?

"I'm fine," I had told her.

"Sure," she said when I asked if she was okay.

Were we each protecting the other? If so, what is she protecting me from? That seed sprouts and takes root as old fears rise. Is she eating? Did something trigger Ed, as she came to call her eating disorder. Are things alright between Will and her? Their engagement came so quickly.

Like my engagement to Daniel? I was so young.

No, Twila and Will are not only older, but so much more emotionally mature. And they share a spiritual maturity that neither Daniel nor I possessed when we had met. I came to faith in the early years of our marriage, when the hardships of the relationship had already settled in—when I realized the mistake I'd made.

I look down at the silver band on my finger. My faith is just one way I've seen God work all things for good, especially out of, trying circumstances.

No, Twila and Will are nothing like Daniel and I were.

Still, unease prickles again, though there's nothing I can do about it now. If they're struggling in their relationship, God knows. My prayers for them will continue.

I pick up the paperwork my attorney's office sent and glance at it one more time. Why now? I don't know, nor does it matter. And retirement? I smile. What in the world would I do with myself?

I love what I do—I value the opportunities I have to help others heal or to help them choose habits with enduring benefits. But there will come a day when I'm too old... I shake my head. "Stay present, Nerissa." This isn't a time to look too far ahead.

I fold the paperwork, stuff it back into the envelope it arrived in, then get up and take it to the spare bedroom I use as a home office. I tuck the letter into the top drawer of the desk. I'll call my attorney first thing Monday morning.

The call will cost me, yes. But I won't know what I'm truly up against until I collect some information and look at the facts as they stand now.

It's time to set emotion aside. Emotion isn't bad, but it can't be counted on. And it isn't serving me well at the moment.

The only thing that will serve me well is my faith.

Oh, Lord, I need Your help...

I stand in front of the desk in the silent room, in the silent house, eyes closed, attention fixed on the unseen. Praying. Waiting. Hoping...

He'll break the silence.

But I hear nothing.

Sense nothing.

CHAPTER FIVE

The light of truth burns without a flicker in the depths of a
house that is shaken with storms of passion and fear.
Thomas Merton

llyn

WHEN THE BACK of my neck prickles, I tighten my grip on the
framed photo I'm staring at—a picture likely taken some
time in the last five years, not long before Sarah's death. Will,
Alex, and his wife, Kimberli, stare back at me. Miles and
Sarah look at one another, a look anyone could identify as
love between them. The family stands, arms around one
another, smiling, hair blowing in the breeze off the crys-
talline water behind them. It appears the photo was taken at
one of the area beaches.

Without turning around to confirm what I already know

—Miles has come into the room—I swipe the dust rag across the top of the nightstand in the guest room, then set the photo back in its place.

"If the photo bothers you, we can put it away." His tone is gentle.

I leave the dust rag on the nightstand and reach for the decorative pillows on the guest bed, pillows chosen, I assume, by Sarah. Bedding she chose, in a house she helped design and decorate. "Bother me? Why would it bother me?"

I fluff the pillows before I place them back on the bed. "This is Alex and Kimberli's room when they come to stay. Just because you've remarried, doesn't mean Sarah's memory should vanish. She was their mother. You were a family. I'm sure the photo represents a special memory for all of you. I'm just doing a little light cleaning, freshening up before—"

"Ellyn?"

"Hmm?" I turn back to the nightstand and busy myself straightening the bedside lamp, the framed photo, and the digital clock. The longer Miles is silent, the more I flutter until finally, I make myself turn and face him. I raise my eyebrows in question as I will my face, which I'm sure is watermelon red, to return to its usual fair and freckled combo.

But when our eyes meet, when I see the concern in his expression, my will fails me, as usual, and I'm certain the color of my face deepens another shade or two. I can't hold his gaze so I look down at the floor. Soon, I'm looking at two pairs of feet rather than just one.

Miles places his hands on my arms, his touch tender as always. Then he leans forward. His lips are soft and warm on my forehead. He says nothing as he pulls me into his embrace and holds me there.

I close my eyes, lay my cheek on his shoulder, and wrap my arms around his waist, and then, once again, will my body to do something it won't seem to do on its own: relax. I long to truly rest in Miles's arms, to melt into him, to trust—

Get over it, Ellyn. It isn't like there are photos of Sarah all over the house.

Miles was thoughtful before I'd moved in and boxed up most of the photos that included Sarah and him. He's tried. Of course he has. This is the only family photo on display. Only here, in a room where Sarah and Miles's children stay. It's only natural.

Don't make something out of nothing. You're always making a mountain out of a molehill. What is wrong with you, anyway?

Earl's voice? No. It's Earleen again. How often did my mother tell me I was making something out of nothing?

When Miles pats my back, it's still rigid, as though steeled for...

What?

Then he steps back and looks down at me. What appears to be confusion clouds his eyes. He stares at me a moment longer, then turns and walks out of the room.

"Miles?" I follow after him. "How about some breakfast?"

He glances over his shoulder and smiles. "I had the same thought. What can I make you?"

He's paused and I catch up to him in the hallway and give him a peck on the cheek. "You can make nothing. But you can keep me company in the kitchen, if you have time, that is. I don't want to take—"

"I have time and I'd love to." The confusion I thought I'd seen in his expression is gone. Had I imagined it?

I gather ingredients—eggs, butter, cream, chives—from the refrigerator and place them on the island. Then I grab a couple of croissants I brought home yesterday and go back to the fridge for a jar of rhubarb marmalade from Mendocino Jams & Preserves.

"I forgot to tell you that Will called the other night. He wanted to talk to you." Miles sits on one of the bar stools at the kitchen island, today's *San Francisco Chronicle* next to him.

I open the carton of eggs. "Me?"

"Yes, he and Twila were cooking and he had a question for you."

"What was the question?"

"I don't know. I didn't think to ask him." Miles chuckles.

"Well, that's sweet that he thought to ask me."

"I assume they worked through their culinary issue, whatever it was." He picks up the French press I prepared, pushes the stopper down, and fills his mug as he talks. "Nerissa was pleased to hear Twila was cooking. I think she still worries about her weight and a possible relapse."

I pause, egg suspended above the edge of a small mixing bowl. "Nerissa?"

"Yes, I had coffee with her. I guess I forgot to mention that, too. We've been going in opposite directions this week, haven't we?"

I bring the egg down and crack it on the rim of the bowl. "You had coffee with her?"

"I ran into her at the bank."

"Oh. Good." Good? "That's great." Great?

I reach for another egg, bring it down on the rim of the bowl, but rather than crack, it smashes into smithereens. Tiny shards of shell float atop the cracked eggs in the bowl, too many pieces to fish out.

I glance up to see if Miles has noticed, but he's picked up the newspaper and is reading the front page. I carry the bowl to the sink, empty it, and then return to the island to begin again. "So…how is Nerissa?"

"WHAT...IS...WRONG...WITH ME?" Phone to my ear, I stop walking, turn my back to Mendocino Bay, and lean against the whitewashed split-rail fence that separates the thin strip of the headlands overlooking the bay from the street and the village while I try to catch my breath.

"Girl, you're asking the wrong question."

"Sabina, just...answer— Wait, what do you mean I'm... asking the wrong question?" My heart hammers in my chest. Who thought taking up walking again was a good idea? After my encounter with the photo, and Miles, and *Nerissa*, who wasn't even there, I decided a brisk walk once I got to the village this afternoon would be good for me. Who was I kidding?

"I mean you're wise to look at yourself, but not at what's wrong with you, but rather why you're feeling what you're feeling. Miles is a good man, one who loves you, yet you don't feel loved. You don't trust his love. Why?"

I nudge a pebble out of the dirt with the toe of my walking shoe, then kick it into the street. "So...why do you think that is?"

"I can't answer the question for you. Only you can unearth the reason. Only you can do that work. But, I think you know the reason."

"Oh." I look up from the ground where I've focused as we've talked. I've stopped just across the street from Nerissa's office. "Here's another question for you. Why didn't Miles marry Nerissa?"

"Really?"

"Yes, really."

"First you're worried about his lingering feelings for his first wife. Now you're worrying about Nerissa? Ellyn, this isn't about either Sarah or Nerissa."

"Is it about my mother?"

"What do you think?"

"I think you're doing that therapist thing. Answering a question with a question. And since I'm not one of your clients, as you like to remind me, how about just telling me what I want to know?"

"I'm your friend. One who knows the value of discovering the answer for yourself. Call Shauna. Get back in there and finish the work you started with her. She's a good therapist. It may relieve you."

"I'm not *worried* about Nerissa. I just asked. It seems like a valid question. Miles had coffee with her a few days ago."

"So?"

"So nothing, I guess."

"Exactly. It means nothing. They were friends before you married, and they remain friends. Miles loves *you*, Ellyn. Call Shauna."

"Are you and Antwone coming for the long weekend next month? Hey, you know my water tower? It's still vacant. Maybe you two could rent it—you know, as a second home here."

"Now that's the first reasonable thing you've said. But no, we're heading east—incorporating the holiday weekend into a week of vacation. Going to spend some time with the girls while they're still living back there. Before we know it, they'll both have graduated and moved on to other things, other places."

"Oh, well, that will be nice. But still, think about the water tower."

"We're not in a position to rent a place full time right now, though the water tower is tempting. But I'm still paying for the year I took off work and spent there. You know we're talking about retiring in Mendocino. And we'll come for the summer—I'll commute back and forth a couple days a week to meet with clients, but we can spend at least two full months there, maybe a few weeks more. If the water tower is still vacant, maybe the owner will rent it to us short term."

"You could practice here, you know. People here need therapists, too."

"No kidding?" She laughs. "So, you going to make that call or not?"

After I end the call with Sabina, I stare at Nerissa's office —the golden glow of the light within on this gray afternoon makes me think of melting butter. I close my eyes and can almost smell the nutty scent of butter as it browns, which makes me think of the butternut squash and sage toast I've considered adding to the brunch menu. Well, when and if I ever decide to open the café for brunch. Thick toasted slices of crusty French bread brushed with browned butter, then topped with butternut squash roasted with a dusting of nutmeg, fresh crisped sage, and a dab of creamy mascarpone.

My shoulders droop. Mascarpone is cheese. Made from cream. A dairy product. As is butter, of course, but I refuse to consider that fact. *"Have you tried ghee?"* I shake my head at Nerissa's suggestion. Maybe I'll skip the nutmeg and use a mild herbed goat cheese instead. And gluten free bread? That can't be good, can it?

"Ellyn?"

I open my eyes. Nerissa stands on the sidewalk across the street, as though I've conjured her like an evil spirit. Well, not evil, obviously. *I'm sorry, Lord.* She's a very kind, thoughtful, lovely woman, which is why I don't understand why Miles wouldn't—

"Are you okay?" She shields her eyes with her hand.

Okay? No, I'm definitely not okay. "Of course." I push off the fence, then cross the street. "I was just thinking about cheese. Goat cheese. I can eat that, right?"

"Yes. With your culinary skills, you'll come up with all kinds of wonderful substitutes for dairy and for gluten, if you want to. Have you begun eliminating them from your diet, to see how you feel?"

"Not yet." I shrug. "It's a lot to figure out."

"Well"—she hesitates—"pay attention to any negative impacts you experience. When you're ready, I'm here to help. I'd be happy to walk you through an elimination diet. I've seen wonderful results with clients who've committed to that type of plan."

"Right." Wrong. Diets and I haven't formed a friendship in the past, and I don't see that changing now. "I'll keep that in mind."

"I could put together a package of appointments. To save you some—"

"Whatever you normally do is great."

She nods. Is she flushed? I'm not sure, but something about money seems to make her nervous. "Businesswomen, remember? You charge me whatever you charge everyone else. If you normally sell packages, let me know the cost and I'll give it some thought."

"Businesswomen? I think I still have some things to learn in the business arena."

"If I can help, let me know. It took me a while to get beyond just wanting to cook, to create, to feed people. I had to figure out how to run a business, how to not only earn a living for myself but sustain a model that could support my employees as well." I glance at my watch. "Speaking of business, I need to get back to mine."

"Thank you, Ellyn. I may take you up on your offer, if you're serious?"

Serious? Am I? "Whatever." My tone, I realize too late, was cooler than I intended.

I'M SUCH A DORK. I mean, I did offer to help her, so then I toss out the *"Whatever"* line? Good grief. What I meant was *"Whatever works for you."* As in, I'm here if I can help. But what comes out? *"Whatever."* Now I meter my words? When have I ever done that?

I stump my way back up the street toward the café. *What is wrong with me?* I have got to get a grip. Nerissa is one of Miles's closest friends. I knew that when I married him. Sabina's right, nothing's changed. Plus, now that Twila and Will are engaged, Nerissa will be part of the family.

Maybe even more a part of the family than I am?

That's the thought I carry with me into the café and then the kitchen, where Rosa is passing through with an armload of freshly laundered napkins, her dark curls bouncing with each step.

She stops midstride when she sees me. "What wrong with you?"

"*That* is a very good question. One I'd love to figure out the answer to." I hold up one hand. "Wait. On second thought, I don't need you to answer it for me. I'm fine."

"Fine."

"Fine?"

"You say fine, not me."

"What?"

Rosa shrugs. "You know what your problem is?"

"I told you, I don't—"

"You need a mother. From now on, I be your mama."

I stare at Rosa, then turn away. "What are you talking about? I'm forty-eight years old, and I don't—well, never mind. Anyway, I have a mother," I say over my shoulder.

"Oh, you do? Then where she when you get married? Why she not at the wedding?"

I shrug, hoping that will appease her. But really, who am I kidding? Appeasing Rosa would take an act of God.

"Why? You tell me why."

The last thing I want or need is to think about my mother. To consider her manipulations, the ways she worked to control me, to "protect me" from men. But even as anger rises, so does empathy. She did, in her own wounded way, try to protect me. If only she'd done her own emotional work. I push the thoughts away. Again. As I've grown accustomed to doing this year.

I sigh and turn back to face Rosa. "You know why."

"Exactly. That's why I your mama now."

"You can't be my mama. I'm your boss."

"What dat have to do with anything? You always say we're a family."

"A work family, Rosa."

"Oh, there's a difference? Well, only to you." She heads for the dining room, then pauses and looks back at me. "No matter." She points at me. "I your mama." Then she pushes all five feet of herself through the swinging door into the dining room.

I stare at the door as it swings shut.

"She's a good mama, Bella." Paco chuckles as he wipes his hands on his apron. "Anyway, she's been mothering you since you hired her. She just made it official, that's all."

"I get no respect here. You with the 'Bella' thing and then her—well, she's never respected me. She thinks she owns the place."

Paco's laugh is deep and full this time. When he stops laughing, he grows serious. "We respect you, but"—he puts his hand over his heart—"we also love you, Chef."

"That's more like it." Unexpected tears prick my eyes. I clear my throat, then shake my head as I walk out of the kitchen. "I don't know what to do with any of you." I push through the door into the dining room where Rosa now sits at one of the tables folding napkins.

I sit across from her. "You're not old enough to be my mother." Why I continue to argue with her when I know it's futile is beyond me.

"I older than you think."

"How old—?"

"No!" She holds up one hand. "There's laws against dat kind of question."

Pia walks into the dining room, headed for the hostess station. When she's out of her mother's range of view, she waves at me, then shakes her head as if to tell me what I already know: This is a useless discussion.

I return my attention to Rosa. "Oh, so now you're an HR expert, an employee, and my mother? You can't be all three."

"I certainly can. Now, you tell me what wrong. You come in here with your forehead all creased—something wrong."

I sigh and then lean back in the chair. "I don't know. I'm just…" I raise my hands, palms up. "I don't know."

"You call dat doctor lady?"

"Doctor Norman? Courtney? Why? I'm not sick."

"Not dat doctor, de head doctor. You call and talk to her."

"The head… The psychologist? How do you know about—?"

"I know. You call her. She help you like she did last time."

"Did Sabina call you?"

"Sabina? No. I not talk to her."

"So just because my forehead is 'all creased,' as you put it, you think I need to see a therapist?"

"No. Dat just part of it. I know you." She points her index finger at me. "A mama knows."

"Rosa…"

"Unless you want to tell me about it, you call de doctor. It's for your best, okay? I tell you what best for you." She turns and looks at Pia, who's still standing at the hostess station, her arms now filled with the menus she'll insert the list of the evening's specials into. "Isn't dat right? I tell you what best for you?"

Pia glances from Rosa to me and rolls her eyes. "You might as well just do whatever it is she's telling you to do."

"But—"

"She's usually right." Then Pia looks at Rosa. "But not *always*." It's clear Pia's making a point, although I don't know what exchanges have come between them before this one.

I lean back in my chair, defeated. "Fine."

"Fine?"

"I said fine." With that, I get up and head for my office. Apparently, I have a call to make.

I drop into my desk chair, reach for my phone, and scroll through the list of contacts until I find Shauna's information. I stare at her number for a moment, then click on it to make the call. When the call connects and her line rings, my insides quiver like a molded blancmange. I pull the phone away from my ear and, with fingers trembling, end the call.

Good job, Big Girl. You don't need her.

"Shush, Earl! I thought you were gone," I whisper.

I sit for several moments, phone still in my hand. Once my jellied insides have settled, I scroll through my list of contacts again until I find the name I'm looking for. As I stare at the name and number, I let an idea I've pushed down for several days take form.

"Businesswomen, remember?" The words I spoke to Nerissa earlier come back to me.

When the call goes to voice mail, I leave a message. "Hi, Jim, this is Ellyn DeMoss. It appears the water tower is still vacant, and I'd like to talk to you about it. Give me a call when you have a moment." I leave my number and then end the call.

It's business. That's all.

CHAPTER SIX

It is not we who choose to awaken ourselves, but God Who
chooses to awaken us.
Thomas Merton

ia

THE ALARM on my phone yanks me from sleep. I roll over
and slap at the phone on the nightstand until the beeping
stops. I roll back over and pull the covers up around my chin
to preserve the fuzz of sleep. *Just a few more minutes...*

Voices murmur outside my bedroom door.

What day is it?

I roll to my other side.

Thursday.

And then the memories assault me. Manuel. His texts.
Texts I've mostly ignored since he told me. And then I recall

the truth. Or is it the lie? What difference does it make now?

The alarm did its job. Wide awake, I roll onto my back, open my eyes, and stare at the ceiling. The TV is on in the living room. Mama is up.

When Manuel asked why I wouldn't respond to his texts or calls, I finally did respond.

What good would it do? It won't change anything.

And what did he say?

I'll give you time, Bebe. Take your time. I love you. I get it. I'm living it too, remember?

I do remember. I just wish I could forget. But that it isn't true. Forgetting means letting go of Manuel, and I can't do that. And Manuel's response, his respect, and his understanding just make everything more confusing.

I sit up in bed, push my hair off my face, and look around the room, which is large considering the small size of the bungalow—a two-bedroom guesthouse in Mendocino, so far from the main house and separated by so many redwoods, cypress, and other trees that we rarely see the owners. We've rented the house for as long as I can remember.

Spread out on my art table across from my bed are the pieces of Auntie Ellyn's broken platter, along with a stack of chipped or cracked plates I'd picked up at a thrift shop in Willits last week. The owner of the shop sets the broken pieces aside and gives them to me. *"Won't sell anyway, you might as well take them,"* she told me the first time I asked what she'd charge me for a cracked teacup—an English china pattern.

I climb from the warmth of the bed, go to the table, and

finger a ridged piece of aqua-colored ceramic—one of three raised shells in the center of the platter. I pick up the piece and turn it over and see the stamp: *Gien, France*. When I searched for the piece online, I learned it was circa 1880s. Where the shells are raised, the edges of the platter are covered with a seaweed pattern etched into the ceramic. I can see why Auntie Ellyn chose the piece while in France— how it might have reminded her of home and the Pacific.

I pick up another piece, a fragment from a plate— Portuguese pottery—the intricate design hand-painted. The broken pieces of the varying ceramics are like pieces of a puzzle I'll put together to create a new pattern, a new vision. But there won't be time today to lose myself in the pieces. Work comes first, and today that work is school.

When I come out of my room to use the bathroom, the TV lights up the living room. My mama stands in front of the TV, hands on her hips. She shakes her head and rattles off something in Spanish under her breath.

"What? What's going on?"

She stares at the screen where a newscaster on one of the early shows rambles on about something.

"Politicians arguing about President Obama's amnesty for de illegals." She pulls her gaze from the screen and looks at me, but I sense she barely sees me. "You sleep?" Her question is automatic.

I nod, then make my way into the bathroom where I close the door and then lean against it, chin to chest, hair hanging over my face, stomach clenched. The newscaster's voice, void of emotion, slides under the door. As much as I know I need to pay attention, to hear the reports, I can't. Not now.

I straighten, reach for the faucet, and turn on the water to drown out the sound. Then I stare for a moment at my reflection in the mirror. I did sleep but not enough, as the dark circles under my eyes prove. Auntie Ellyn's always said my eyes are like molten chocolate. What molten has to do with anything, I don't know, but it definitely doesn't apply today. Instead, the eyes staring back at me from the mirror are cold, lifeless.

∼

MAMA'S MUTED the volume on the TV and sits at the kitchen table now, a cup of coffee in front of her. I drop my backpack on one of the kitchen chairs and then grab a yogurt from the fridge.

"You sit for a minute."

"I have to go—I'll eat this on the way." I pull a spoon from the drawer.

"You don't eat while you drive. No, you sit. You have time."

I glance at the clock on the microwave even though I know she's right. "Yeah, okay." I take the seat across from her, as I have hundreds of times before. Just the two of us at this table for so many years.

"Something bothering you."

It's a statement, not a question, and I hesitate a moment too long before I respond. "Bothering me?" I stare down at the cup of yogurt and focus on prying the plastic lid off the cup.

"Since Saturday—since you been with him and he make you cry—you upset. You try to hide, but I know."

I know she cares, but I also know the truth will anger her, and I'm not ready. I can't do this with her. This is why I've hidden. This is the conversation I've wanted to avoid.

"We had…" I search for words that are true but not all of the truth, "a disagreement." Still not looking at her, I set the lid from the yogurt aside and reach for the spoon.

"Truth, Pia." Her tone has tightened.

I set the spoon down, take a deep breath, then meet and hold her gaze. "Mama, that is the truth. It just isn't the whole truth. I'm not ready to talk about it yet. When I'm ready, I will tell you."

She says nothing, just watches me. Finally she nods and pushes back from the table. But before she gets up she points her finger at me. "If he hurt you, he has to deal with me."

The picture of my barely five-foot mama *dealing with* six-foot-three Manuel induces a smile in spite of my angst. "He knows that, Mama. You've made that clear many times."

"Well, you make sure he remember dat."

RAIN PELTS THE WINDSHIELD, and the strong coffee diluted with caramel-flavored creamer in my thermal mug sits cooling in the cup holder. The coffee holds no appeal. My stomach is tight as a fist. Just the sound of the coffee sloshing inside the cup as I maneuver the car around the sharp curves between Fort Bragg and Willits causes acid to rise in my throat. I lift my foot off the accelerator, the movement rote as I approach a sharp turn around another bend. I know every curve, every turnout, every inch of this winding road through the dense, dark forest. I make the drive between home and Mendocino College in Ukiah every Tuesday and Thursday—114.8 miles round trip, which averages just a few cents under eleven dollars each day, twenty-two dollars a week, eighty-eight dollars per month. I calculate a little extra every month to cover the fluctuating cost of gas. When prices drop, I end up with a few dollars extra to apply to tuition and books. I fill the tank in Ukiah, where the price per gallon can be several cents less than in Fort Bragg.

When I come up short, Mama makes up the difference. *"We're a team, Pia. We do this together."* My mama has talked of me attending college, getting a degree for forever. It is her dream for me. It is my dream, too. But now, I also have other dreams.

I have always believed, always been taught, that everything is possible. In America, with God, all things can be mine if I trust and work hard.

Is that still true?

Is everything Manuel and I talked about, everything we dreamed about together, still possible? I don't see how. *"Dat's when you trust, Pia. When you can't see. Dat's faith."* But would my mama say that now? If she knew the truth? No. She would say my relationship with Manuel holds only impossibilities.

How are all things possible and impossible at the same time?

As I approach the campus, sunlight streams through the windshield warming the car's interior. And my wipers screech on the dry windshield. When did the rain stop? And how did I miss Willits? I don't recall driving through the town that marks the halfway point of my commute. Goose bumps rise on my arms as I realize I have no memory at all of driving the last hour or so. I sit up straighter in the driver's seat and grasp the steering wheel so tight my fingers ache. I was so deep in my head. I blink a few times, then intentionally take in my surroundings. The angular lines of the library building, the rolling coastal range set as the campus backdrop, the drought-resistant landscaping.

I maneuver through the parking lot searching for a space. The college is a commuter school, drawing from the coastal region and the rural areas surrounding Ukiah. *"You'll make friends there, maybe even meet a nice young man."* My mama's encouragement was well intended when I started classes, but it was not well founded. It came from her desires for my contentment, I know. The few close friends I had in high school left soon after graduation. There's not much worth staying for—jobs are few in the area, the economy depressed.

I plan on leaving too after I complete my general ed requirements. I plan to transfer to one of the state universities. I am working to pay my way, to save. College is one of my dreams, but the dream is still a little abstract. A degree, yes. In what, I don't know yet.

But making friends hasn't been easy. Between school, homework, and my work at Ellyn's, I've had little time to get involved in anything. Plus, there's my art, and my other interest. My primary interest—the *"nice young man"* Mama hoped I'd meet. She was certain I wouldn't find him in Mendocino or Fort Bragg. Those I knew who've stayed in the area? Mama would kill me if I ever thought of going out with one of them.

"No meth heads, Pia. You hear me? You don't get wrapped up in dat."

I did meet him though, just not at school as she'd hoped. No, I met Manuel in the village, at Auntie Ellyn's café. He was delivering cases of wine from the vintner he works for in Philo, the northwestern end of the Anderson Valley, one of the state's renowned wine regions. Of course, Manuel taught me that. I won't even be old enough to buy wine for another year, but I've learned a lot about the vineyards and winemaking from Manuel who is following his father in the work he's done since coming to the states. It is work Manuel loves—work he is proud of.

When I met Manuel, my dreams began to take on a new shape. His dream of owning his own vineyard became my dream, too. My dream of graduating with a degree became his also. But now? I don't know. How is any of it possible?

Like an overexerted muscle, the thought of our dreams aches. That ache has been constant since Saturday. It's all I've focused on. As frustrated as I can get with my mama, she would never lie to me. I can't even imagine it. And as much as this has hurt me, I can only imagine how it's hurt Manuel. I need to support him. To be there for him, even though... I inhale sharply. Even though it will hurt.

For the first time, I understand what love as a sacrifice means.

It also occurs to me that yes, his parents' lies hurt him, but he's had time to adjust. He's known the truth for several years. I've just discovered the truth. It is new to me. The wound still raw. What does Manuel feel now? Do I even know? No. I was too angry to ask—too focused on how the truth impacted me. Us.

The morning news story comes back to me—the word I've heard but have paid little attention to: amnesty. I know what it means, but what does it mean for the illegal immigrants? Last week it didn't matter to me. Suddenly, it matters more than most things. More than anything. And it's time I pay attention. It's time I learn.

After I park, I reach for my backpack, get out of the car, then click the button on the worn key fob to lock the doors. I stand for a moment, staring at the faded blue 2009 Toyota Camry I saved for all through high school, working first at Harvest Foods in Fort Bragg, stocking shelves and bagging groceries for customers during summers, then later hostessing at Auntie Ellyn's in the evenings and on weekends.

Hard work pays off. It's how things get done.

Does that apply to my relationship with Manuel?

I turn away from the car and head for the campus, the question churning in my mind. If hard work is how things get done, then it's time to get to work with Manuel—to view the issue as a possibility rather than an impossibility.

An issue to work through. There has to be a way...

Something small and warm rises within me.

I can do work.

Like an ember, it rises.

I stop at the restroom as is my habit before going to class, but before going into the stall, I stop at the mirror. I pull my comb from my backpack and run it through my hair, considering my next step as I do. If we're going to work through this issue, then we need to do it together, me and Manuel.

Then I think of my mama, of what she'll say when she learns the truth, and the ember cools. I slip the comb into my backpack and turn away from the mirror.

No.

There has to be a way.

There is a way. I may not know what it is now, but I'll find it.

What smoldered, ignites now, and I turn and look back into the mirror. My dark eyes stare back at me, no longer cold and lifeless. Instead, I see passion, I see fire.

Molten chocolate.

I can do hard work. It's doing nothing that's impossible.

CHAPTER SEVEN

Whose silence are you?
Thomas Merton

erissa

THE DOOR of the old church building turned health food store scrapes closed behind me as I leave following my Thursday shift. I cross the small parking area out front, gravel crunching beneath my feet. When I reach the street, I turn and look back at Corners of the Mouth, the co-op where I've worked since Daniel left. The building, including the steeple, is painted barn-red. The multicolored stained-glass windows shimmer in the afternoon sunlight.

After a couple years spent researching customers' questions about supplements, gluten-free options, dairy-free options, whether soy is beneficial or harmful, the impact of

GMOs, and a host of other inquires, I felt ready to step into the role my degree had prepared me for so many years before: nutritionist. My work at Corners of the Mouth not only helped prepare me, familiarizing me with new research and products, but most of my clients have connected with me through the store, too—either as customers or through the store's website.

Standing there in the milky winter light looking at the store, I recognize, again, all it's afforded me. Not only income, but also satisfying work. And friendships. All so necessary after the divorce. It is, I believe, the work God gave me. The work, perhaps, that He created me for. Yet, the income hasn't met my needs.

I should have done more.

What more could I have done?

The argument in my mind, the one that's replayed almost nonstop since the day before yesterday, goes nowhere. I need to let it go. I can't change what was. And if I need to change what is, then God will make that clear. Or maybe He is making it clear. Maybe the inadequate income is the clarity I seek. It isn't enough, so I need to make a change. But…what would I do?

Lord? Please. I wait, hoping for an idea, a word, inspiration, a sense of some sort. But I'm given nothing. *If You created me to do this work, even if it doesn't provide what I think I need, isn't it still worth doing? Sacrificing for? You've promised to meet my needs, so maybe I need too much, maybe I need to adjust my expectations and—*

"Hey."

I look over my shoulder and stare for a moment. "Twila?!" I go to her, arms open. "I wasn't expecting you until Saturday. You got a couple of days off?" I give her a hug, her frame is thin, but not as thin as it once was. I step back from her, hands still on her shoulders, and wait for her response to my question. When it doesn't come, I search her face. Her complexion looks good, healthy, the dark ink of the small tattoo of a thorny branch on her upper right cheek—her sign of solidarity with those who suffer—always seems to make her already-pale complexion appear lighter, but color blooms in her cheeks, and though there are shadows beneath her eyes, she appears well. "Honey?"

"I just...I thought..." She tucks a long strand of dark hair behind one ear. "I got here about an hour ago and decided to walk over to meet you. You're done for the day?"

"I'm done here. I have a couple of things to finish at the office." Though she didn't answer my question, I let it go and wrap my arm around her shoulders. "I parked over by the office. I had a couple of appointments this morning before my shift."

"Cool." She glances at me as we walk side by side. "So, how are you?"

I pause and step back so I can see her face again. "Are you worried about me?"

She shrugs. "I'm just asking, like, you know, how you're doing."

"I'm okay. Just some stress. Nothing for you to worry about." Her concern warms my heart, but I don't want her worrying about my financial issues. Those are mine to own, not hers. "Thank you for caring."

We walk up the street to one of the walkways that cuts between blocks, many of which are landscaped with mounds of soft verdant ground cover or the colorful perennials or succulents that thrive in the mild coastal weather. We cross the second street and then cut through another block. Twila is quiet as we walk, which isn't unusual. We speak on the phone often, so there isn't much to catch up on. I simply enjoy having her close, the comfort of our relationship. And, if I'm honest, someone other than myself and my own concerns to focus on.

We reach Main Street and turn toward my office. "Would you like to stop in and say hello to Ellyn?"

Her steps slow as we approach the café. "Maybe. Do you mind?"

"No, of course not. I don't know if she's here, but we can check."

We take the walkway around the side of the café to the back where Ellyn's organic garden, sectioned like a quilt in squares of color and texture, sits behind a low, weathered split-rail fence, alongside a small greenhouse, its glass speckled on the inside with condensation.

As we approach the back door, it swings open, and Ellyn steps out, then catches sight of us. "Twila!" She clamors down the steps, crosses the space between us, and wraps Twila in a hug, then she steps back. "I didn't know you were coming. Will didn't let us know."

Twila doesn't respond so I fill in, "Will didn't come this time."

"Oh."

"She's just here for the weekend. A long weekend."

"I bet you two have wedding plans you're working on. Let me know if I can do anything to help. We still need to talk about the menu for the reception."

Twila, hands in the pockets of her jacket, shoulders lifted to her ears to ward off the cold as she's done since she was a child, says nothing. Instead, she takes in the volley of conversation between Ellyn and me but doesn't enter in.

I fill the gap again. "We do have plans to discuss."

"Can you come in for a few minutes? I was heading to the greenhouse, but it can wait."

Twila looks at me, eyebrows raised in question, and again I respond to Ellyn, "If you're sure it's not a bother."

"Bother? Of course not. Come in and we'll have a cup of coffee or that healthy tea you both drink. I'll steep some fresh herbs for you. I can spare a few minutes."

Twila's shoulders relax and she takes her hands out of her pockets. I notice something I hadn't noticed before, and I slow my steps. I trail behind Twila and Ellyn, then I stop. "On second thought…" They both turn back and look at me. "I may go on to the office and finish up. Twila, why don't you join Ellyn, and when you're finished you can meet me at the office."

"Sure. That works."

"Thank you for the invitation, Ellyn. I'd love a cup of your fresh herbal tea another time. I'll let you two catch up."

Ellyn wraps her arm around Twila's shoulders, just as I had earlier, and leads her into the café. As I walk back to the street, then toward the office, I recount the last fifteen or so minutes. Why hadn't Twila let me know she was coming? That isn't like her. Why didn't she respond when I asked her about the time off? Why didn't Will join her here this weekend? Was her silence typical, or did it seem more pronounced?

Her silence wasn't atypical. What wasn't typical, what raised the red flag of concern, now that I have a few minutes to process our conversation, was her evasiveness. Twila is quiet, thoughtful, and when she speaks, she speaks truth. I've not known her to evade, to sidestep a question.

As I approach my office, questions spin in my mind, including the one question that could have multiple logical answers.

Why isn't Twila wearing her engagement ring?

CHAPTER EIGHT

Everyone of us is shadowed by an illusory person: a false self.
We are not very good at recognizing illusions, least of all the
ones we cherish about ourselves.
Thomas Merton

llyn

I FILL the tea infuser with fresh mint, lavender, and lemon
balm cut from the plants in the greenhouse. I fill the pot with
boiling water and then set the lid, plunging the infuser into the
water. "There you go." I slide the pot across the stainless-steel
countertop toward Twila. "Let that steep a few minutes." I grab
two mugs, hand her one, and then go fill mine with coffee.

When I come back, Twila's leaning against the countertop, staring at the teapot, hands in her pockets.

"May I take your jacket?" She's usually cold, or used to be, but I ask anyway.

"That's okay, I'll keep it on."

I wink at her. "I thought you might."

I pick up the teapot. "Let's sit at the table in the back."

Once we've landed at the table, Twila reaches for the teapot and the tattoo inside her wrist peeks out from under the sleeve of her jacket. When she sets the teapot down, I reach out and put my hand on her left arm. "May I?" Something flashes in her eyes, and she pulls her arm away from me.

Did I startle her? "I'm sorry. I just wanted to see your tattoo again."

"Oh, sorry." She pulls back the sleeve of her jacket and holds out her arm, wrist up. I gently turn her wrist so I can read the words inked there, even though I know what they say. I rub my thumb over the tattoo, contemplating again the wonder of the reality the words represent—that I am created in God's image. "Amazing."

She pulls her arm back and stuffs her hands back into her pockets. "Yeah, it is. So how's that going—you know, living that truth for yourself?"

I pick up my mug of coffee and lean back in my seat. "Good. It's so helpful. I haven't weighed myself in months, and I'm content, just as I am. Not fretting anymore about every bite I take and whether or not I love food too much and wondering if God is disappointed in me because I ate a croissant, with butter. And jam. Or a crème brûlée. And no more listening to that negative voice, all those condemnations. Nope. I'm God's creation, and as it says in Genesis, God saw that it was good, and that's good enough for me."

As I take a sip of the hot coffee laden with coconut cream, I realize my mouth was off and running before I really considered Twila's question. But everything I said was true, wasn't it?

"You know it's one thing to believe you're created in the image of God, but it's another to live into that image, isn't it?" It's the first time I've thought of Nerissa's comment since meeting with her last week. *Live into it?* That's what I did with Shauna, right? *Live into it?* A shadow of doubt niggles, but I push it aside to consider later.

"Nice. I'm happy for you."

Twila's smile seems genuine, but there's something in her eyes that I can't read. I take another sip of the rich coffee, then set the mug down. "You know, I'm still using coconut milk, at least in my coffee. You taught me a lot, Twila. I still have a lot to learn about nutrition, but I'll get there. In fact, I met with your mom recently. But that's more than enough about me. I want to hear about you." I lean forward. "How are you? You've made a lot of changes, girly—engagement, a move, a new job. How's it all going?"

"You met with my mom?"

"Yes, but—"

"Are you going to keep meeting with her, like, professionally?"

"Maybe. Why?"

"She's..." Twila pauses, then shakes her head. "I don't know. I just wondered."

"So what about you? How's the new job?"

"It's okay. The customers are different than here, you know? More affluent. And some of them are more assured of themselves."

"More arrogant?"

She smiles. "Maybe. But not all of them. I've learned some new things from a few of the customers, so that's good."

"Hey, speaking of new things, those vegan recipes you helped me create? They've done well. In fact, I ran a report for the last quarter and the polenta with roasted vegetables was one of our most ordered entrées. We'd roast whatever vegetables were in season and available. It's been a hit. The spaghetti squash"—I make air quotes with my fingers—"pasta with the crushed tomatoes, garlic, and oregano has done well, too. Go figure, right? Maybe while you're here, we can come up with a couple more recipes using seasonal ingredients. I'd like to add something new for spring."

"You don't need me to do that."

"Maybe not, but it would be more fun to do it with you."

Twila appears thoughtful, like she has something to say, so I lift my mug to my mouth to keep more words from flowing out.

She leans forward, her gray eyes, so like Nerissa's, shine. "So, like, do you think cooking, owning a restaurant, is God's purpose for you?"

"Oh. Good question. And admittedly, not one I've given much consideration. I guess I'd say that God gave me a talent, and opportunity, and a love for food and people. But 'purpose' is a big word. There's probably more to His purpose for me, for each of us, than what we choose to do as careers, though that probably factors into it for some people. Why do you ask?"

"I've just been thinking about it, like what God wants me to do."

"Long term?"

"Maybe."

"Well, He's certainly gifted you, Twila."

"How? I mean, in what ways do you think?"

"That seems so obvious."

She shrugs. "I used to think I knew, but now...I'm not sure, I guess."

I sit back in my seat and consider her question for a moment. "Okay, so you asked what I think, what I see. First, foremost, is the way you interact with people. Maybe it's that sense of knowing He's given you, the way you can assess what someone is going through and offer what they need in the moment, even before they know they need it. Like you did with me. And with Sabina. Remember? But it's also just who you are. Remember the first time we met at Corners?"

"Sure."

"You put me at ease immediately, and that's not easily done. You speak truth but without judgment. You accept people with all their foibles, and believe me, I have a few, and you help them..."—I search my mind for what it is, exactly, I've seen Twila do in my own life and in the lives of others —"move beyond the beliefs that hold them back. Does that ring true?"

Those thin shoulders she just shrugged, now seem to slump a bit. "Yeah, I guess."

"Were you hoping I'd say something else?"

"Kind of. I mean, I'm not sure what to do with that sense, what's revealed to me about others. The helping them move forward, that's easier. It's what I've watched my mom do my whole life—with me and with others. But knowing stuff about other people and having to act on it... I don't know."

"What does Will think?"

She looks down at her cup of tea. "We sort of see it differently."

"Differently? In what way—?" The back door swings open and Rosa, followed by Pia, blow in with a cold gust. "Hey, you two, look who's here."

"Twila, hello." Rosa stops at the table, Pia behind her. "Good to see you." She moves to take off her jacket and Twila helps her, then Rosa takes her jacket and drapes it over her arm. She glances between Twila and Pia, then back again at Twila. "You remember Pia? You two meet, right?" She looks over her shoulder at Pia again. "Come here." She points to the floor next to her and Pia comes and stands next to her.

"Yeah, we've met. Hey, Pia."

Pia smiles but before she can respond, Rosa jumps in again. "When you here,"—she says to Twila—"you two should get together." She points back and forth between Twila and Pia. "You two could be friends. Pia is older now. You be good friends."

I shake my head. "Here she goes again. Rosa—"

"What? What I do?"

"This is exactly what you did to Sabina and me, and Miles and me, come to think of it."

"Yes. And how those turn out? Hmm?" Rosa doesn't wait for a response. "I know these things." She walks off and leaves Pia standing at the table.

"Sorry," Pia says to Twila, "that's just how she is. How long are you here for?"

"Um...I'm not sure, exactly. But, like, I'm totally up for getting together. We could take a walk sometime or, you know, get coffee or something?"

Rosa may have pushed, but I sense Twila's invitation, her desire to get together with Pia, is genuine. As much as I hate to admit it, Rosa may have made another good match. There's a depth to both Twila and Pia—they're both mature beyond their years. And again, Rosa is right. Pia is older now, an adult, and there comes a time when age is no longer a factor in friendship. There are so few young people in the community, and although Twila no longer lives here, she and Will will always come back. They have family here.

I get up to leave them to their plans. "The kitchen calls."

Pia's eyes widen. "I have to clock in."

"No rush, honey. You were here on time, I know that. A few minutes isn't going to make a difference."

"It will to my mama."

"Well, I'm still boss here, at least I was the last time I checked." Rosa may argue that point. I pick up my mug and then bend down and wrap my arms around Twila and give her a quick hug. "Will I see you again before you leave?"

"Sure. I'll be around."

"Good." As I head for the kitchen, something nags at me as I go. What was it Twila said to Pia? She's not sure how long she'll be here?

Didn't Nerissa say Twila was just here for the weekend?

I LEAVE the house early on Saturday morning to make the drive to the café while Miles heads to his office where he sees patients one Saturday morning each month. I sip a mug of French press as I drive, catching glimpses as I round bends in the road of a thick blanket of dark clouds slung low over the Pacific. I turn the thermostat of the car's heater to high and count the mile markers I've established as I go: Cowlicks Ice Cream on the right in the center, or thereabouts, of Fort Bragg. That marker never fails to trigger a craving for a pint of their black raspberry-chocolate chunk ice cream. Then comes the bridge over Noyo Harbor on the south end of town. Next is a redwood to the left of the highway—a jagged black scar on its trunk marks where it was struck by lightning. The drive seems to take longer each time I make it. I finally catch a glimpse of the old, weathered church steeple in Caspar on the ocean side of the highway, which means my turnoff on Lansing Road is just a few miles ahead.

In between mile markers, my mind wanders to the water tower, as it's done too many times in the last week, and the conversation I had with Jim, my former landlord, when he returned my call. A file of paperwork he sent over is locked in my desk drawer.

I slow, signal right, and make the turn onto Lansing. As I drive toward the village, I pass the house overlooking Agate Cove that Sabina rented, and loneliness tugs at my heart. Having Sabina here—having a friend to share life with, the laughter and the tears—was special. I have Miles, of course, and I'm grateful, but...

But what? "I love Miles," I tell myself as I pass through the Village. And I do. So much so that tears prick my eyes at the thought of it. He's a wonderful friend and husband. But there's something different about that special friendship between women, something I hadn't really known before Sabina.

I pull into my parking spot behind the café, a place where the shoulder of the road is a few feet wider, and put the car into *Park*. I enjoy my phone conversations with Sabina, but it's not the same as having a friend here, someone to really talk to. Not exactly, anyway. I sigh, grab my things, and push the thought from my mind.

I am, if I do say so myself, becoming an expert at not thinking.

Wait, that can't be good, can it?

I shake my head. "Just don't think about it."

THE KITCHEN IS SILENT, absent of the usual clang and clatter, the sizzle and simmer, and voices raised above the commotion. The whir of the computer in the office is my only companion, the monitor on my desk alive as I click the mouse and open the restaurant's point-of-sale software I use that tracks daily orders, among other things. Scattered on my desk are several reports I've run, including a profit and loss for our fiscal year.

The café has done well. Not only is it favored by tourists,

but more important, it's favored by many of the Mendocino County locals. As I go over the end-of-the-year figures, I am pleased with the steady profit, which reflects a slight increase over the previous year. Even with money spent on the purchase and installation of new ovens, we're in the black.

On a good night during the high season, we turn the tables nearly two and half times, and without rushing our guests. We work long hours, but we work a short week during the winter months, Thursday through Sunday, dinner service only.

"We love you, Bella..." I know my staff respect me, but it is that love for one another that keeps us all going, working hard together to meet the end goal: satisfied customers who pay our bills.

"Thank you," I whisper. I don't take the figures lightly. This is a tough business. More restaurants fail than succeed. I click over and login to my bank accounts, personal and business. I've saved over the years, my personal expenses fairly minimal. I haven't traveled since my time in France. I haven't spent on hobbies or even much on clothing beyond my uniforms. Any profits remaining after my living expenses have gone either back into the business or into savings. The funds from my father's trust remain untouched. My needs have been simple.

I reach for the ring of keys on my desk and then unlock the file drawer. I pull out the file from Jim, flip it open, glance over the document again, then set it on my desk.

I glance back to the figures on the screen—the money I have in savings is more than enough to fund the venture I have in mind. *Venture? Really?* Yes, it is a venture, of sorts. Just because I haven't clarified all the details doesn't mean it isn't valid. *Valid? Really?*

What happened to not thinking?

I log out of the banking site, then pick up a pen. I stare at the document—a twelve-month lease on the water tower. I attempted to negotiate for six months, but Jim wouldn't budge. It was twelve months or nothing.

I put pen to paper and sign my name, but when the pen rounds the last curve of the capital *B*, I pause and lift the pen's tip off the paper. *B* for *Becker*. I'd kept *DeMoss* after we married. It's been my name for nearly fifty years. It's the name I'm known by professionally. But I added Becker after DeMoss because I love Miles. Because I respect his name. *Because, if your mother could help it, you'd never have any other name than the one you were given at birth. You showed her.*

No, that wasn't one of the reasons, was it? No. I took Miles's name because for 101 reasons, at least, I am proud to be his wife, and because there's something I like about the timeworn tradition of a wife assuming her husband's name.

But...didn't I do more than assume his last name?

I also made vows to Miles, before our friends and family, and most importantly, before God. Those vows did not, however, include never making a business decision without Miles's knowledge. That would be like him refusing to diagnose a patient without my input. Ridiculous. I lower the pen and complete my signature, date the document, then place it back in the file folder.

"What are your plans?" Jim had asked me when he dropped off the lease.

When I saw that large island in the remodeled kitchen, I thought *cooking classes*." Or maybe a B and B, although plenty of those exist in the village already, but maybe a B and B with a twist? Cooking classes spread over a weekend—participants come, stay, and cook their own gourmet meals, or at least one gourmet meal a day. The possibilities are—

"It's not zoned for commercial use, you know."

"What? Oh."

"Listen, I don't much care what you do with the place as

long as you're making the payments, but I don't have time to do the footwork involved in getting it rezoned, so if you plan to use it for commercial purposes, factor in that time, not to mention moolah, into your plans. I'm not paying to have it rezoned."

"For now, I just want to secure it. Ensure it's available when I'm ready to make a...move."

"It's your money, Ellyn." He shrugged. "You want to sign that now?" He gestured to the file he'd handed me.

"I'll drop it by your office in the next few days. I don't have time to review it right now."

He seemed satisfied with my answer, and I needed time to think. Or to not think, maybe. But now—I lower the pen and complete my signature—now that I've signed the lease, I'm eager to get the keys to the water tower.

I'm eager to go home.

CHAPTER NINE

If you want to identify me, ask me not where I live, or what I
like to eat, or how I comb my hair, but ask me what I am
living for, in detail, ask me what I think is keeping me from
living fully for the thing I want to live for.
Thomas Merton

ia

As I'm dressing for my walk with Twila on Saturday morning, a steady *rat-a-tat-tat* begins overhead. I go to my
bedroom window and pull back the blind. Raindrops slide
down the glass of the window and beat on the roof. I pick up
my phone and text Twila:

GoodLife instead?

She responds a few minutes later:

Sure. Does 10:00 work instead of 9:30?

Perfect. That gives me a full hour before I have to leave. I text Twila back and then go to my art table where I've primed a large round, a top I removed from an old bistro table I found through an online marketplace. It was listed for $7.50, but I talked the owner down to $2.00 telling him the many deep scratches on the top made the table worth almost nothing, not to mention the loose legs, one of which was cracked. What I didn't tell him was that I planned to remove the legs and cover the top with primer, ceramic pieces, and grout. The thirty-inch round will be my largest project yet and the one I've been collecting pieces of broken dishes and pottery for over the last several months.

I've chosen the pieces intentionally from those given to me, based on color, pattern, and texture. Pieces from Auntie Ellyn's platter from France are scattered on the table, along with some of the pieces from the thrift shop in Willits and pieces from the Portuguese pottery sold at Mendocino Jams & Preserves. Most of the shop owners in the Village who sell dishes or pottery know to call me when a piece breaks— they're more than happy to give them to me.

I pick up a pie-shaped piece of ceramic tile—the red clay visible on the broken edges—hand-painted in bright colors immediately recognizable as a Mexican mosaic pattern. I run my finger across the smooth painted surface of the tile, careful to avoid the sharp edges. Several more tiles of the same pattern are stacked on the table, those unbroken. I will break them as I need them.

The tiles were a gift from Manuel. He found them in a shed on the winery property and asked the owner if he could buy them from him. The owner was happy to get rid of them and gave them to Manuel. I finger the sharp point of the piece I hold—broken, it is sharp enough to cut, to wound, to maim. Like Manuel's lie, or his parents' lie, as I'm coming to see it—wounded him. Wounded us.

Yet the broken tile, all the broken pieces laid out on the table, will, when I am finished, become part of something beautiful again.

While I'm confident there is a way to reimagine my relationship with Manuel, to make it beautiful again, I haven't figured it out yet. I take a deep breath and hope rises, but it falls again as I exhale. It all seems impossible. But I can't let my mind go there. I can only consider the possibilities. I'm just not sure what those possibilities are yet.

What I do know is that I need to talk to Manuel, and I will, after my time with Twila this morning. I told him I'd text him when I'm free. My heart flutters at the thought of seeing him, of sitting next to him. We will find a way, won't we?

The other thing I know, or think I know, is that I need to talk to someone else. A friend. But my friends, at least those I'd want to talk to, have all moved on, gone to college or jobs elsewhere, and I haven't really maintained my friendships— they weren't deep to begin with. I haven't always shared a lot in common with people my age. Maybe because I've spent, literally, so much time around adults, so much time with Mama and the café family. Or maybe it's just something wrong with me.

I think of Twila. Could my mama be right? Could we become friends? I rarely want her to be right, but this time feels different.

RAIN SPATTERS my windshield as I pull into a parking spot just down from GoodLife Café, then make the dash from the car to the front door, the hood of my jacket pulled up to keep me dry. I push the hood back as I walk into the warmth of the café. The rich, nutty scent of freshly brewed coffee and the hiss of the steamer on the espresso machine are a warm welcome. The scent of freshly baked breads and pastries makes my stomach growl. Twila, already seated with a cup in front of her, waves me over.

"Sorry, I'm late." I pull my jacket off. "I got involved in a project and lost track of time."

"No problem. I've only been here a few minutes. Sorry I changed the time. I needed to... It was my mom. I just..." She takes a deep breath. "Long story."

"No problem." I smile. "I've got a mom too, remember?"

Twila offers her first smile and the knot of anxiety in my chest begins to unravel. "I'm going to get a coffee. Watch my stuff?" She nods and I hang my jacket on the back of the chair and grab my wallet out of my purse.

When I come back to the table, I sit across from Twila and take in her appearance. It's not like I haven't seen her before. She was around the café last year with Auntie Ellyn. But it's the first time I've sat across from her and really looked at her. Her dark hair, long and straight, shines against her clear, pale complexion, and the small tattoo on her cheek rather than stand out seems to fit somehow and even accentuates her natural beauty.

"Do you mind me asking about your tattoo?"

"No, not at all." She raises her hand to her cheek and runs one finger over the tattoo. "The thorns represent those who suffer—it's a reminder to stand with them. Support them."

"Why did you put it on your face?"

"So each time I look in the mirror, I'd see it and remember."

"Wow, that's so brave."

A blush colors her face and she shakes her head. "I guess it sort of felt brave at the time."

"But not anymore, or what?"

"I just, I don't know. I don't look in the mirror all that much anymore."

"Why not? You're gorgeous."

As she looks across the table at me, her face flushed, a storm seems to gather in her gray eyes, then she looks at her mug, picks it up, and takes a sip of what seems like tea.

"Sorry. Did that bother you? I mean, you are beautiful. It's just a fact."

She sets her mug down and looks back at me. "Do you ever, like, look in the mirror and wish someone else was staring back at you?"

I consider her question and decide to answer honestly. "Not really. But why? I mean, why would you want to be someone else?"

She shrugs. "I don't know. Sometimes, like, I don't know if I want to live the purpose it seems like God's chosen for me. You know?"

"Purpose?" I think for a minute but come up empty. "I guess I haven't thought much about whether or not I have a specific purpose. Do you think we each have a unique purpose?"

"We all have the same purpose—to be in relationship with God. But I guess some people have a specific purpose or a specific gift they're supposed to use. I don't know. It's just, like, something I've been thinking about lately."

I still want to understand the tattoo, understand her. "So, the tattoo, does it represent your purpose or a gift or…? I mean, when you see the tattoo, what do you do? How do you stand with those who suffer?"

"Yeah, it sort of represents one of the gifts God's given

me. I stand with others who are suffering by empathizing, I guess."

"What else? I mean, what do you *do*, literally?"

"Do? I sort of feel their pain. It's hard to explain. But the pain leads me to pray."

I stare at her a minute, thinking of Manuel, thinking of all the pain. Of his suffering. And mine.

"You pray? That's what you do?"

"I don't know what your beliefs are, so maybe that sounds weird."

"No, I get it. I just haven't prayed much lately, but I believe. And…" I shrug. "There's stuff going on that I should definitely pray about."

She tucks a piece of hair behind her ear. "Some people think prayer is passive, but"—she leans forward—"it's really one of the most active and powerful things we can do for others."

"So, what have you suffered? I mean, you must understand what that's like in order to care, to want to stand with others, as you put it." I lean back in my seat and raise my hands. "Whoa, sorry, I didn't mean to get all personal. I'm not very good at small talk, the surface stuff."

"You ask a lot of questions."

"Yeah, I know. Sorry."

"No, it's okay. It's refreshing." Twila sets her cup down, and her shoulders seem to relax. "And yeah, me either. About the surface stuff, I mean."

"So, go deep or go home?"

"Totally."

~

TWILA PUSHES the rest of the quiche she ordered to the other side of her plate. She's taken only a few small bites and eaten those slowly as we've talked. The omelet I ordered is gone. The only thing left on my plate are a few pieces of crust left from the sourdough toast that came with the omelet.

"You can't eat anymore?" She told me about the anorexia and I don't want to push her, but I'm curious because she said she was better.

She glances from me to her plate, takes a deep breath, and spears a piece of potato with her fork and lifts it to her mouth. She hesitates but then eats it. She repeats the action, then sets her fork on her plate and wipes her mouth with her napkin. "It's like...when things feel out of control, I can control the food. I can control..." She shakes her head. "But that isn't...it isn't real. It isn't the truth, so I have to choose what's true—I have to chose to eat, to fuel my body. But...it's hard to explain."

"So things feel pretty out of control now, I guess. With Will. And your mom."

She nods. "You get it, right? I mean, not the food thing, but—"

"Your mom, and the stuff with Will? Yeah. Weird how much we have in common, right? Different, but so much the same. Only children, single moms—just that, the mom thing, that's huge. The responsibility I feel for my mom, the pressure—no one understands that. I feel like I'm the only one, the one who has to take care of her, be there for her, even though she'd never say that. And our situations with Will and Manuel are totally different, but the hurt is so much the same." I nod. "Yeah, I get it. And I'm really glad my mama— I mean, she's pushy, she's controlling, but she was right about us."

"So, what are you going to do? What are you going to say to Manuel?"

I sigh and lean back in my seat. "The only thing I can say, the same things I've already said. I have to make him understand." Then I lean forward again. "What about you? Your mom. And Will? What are you going to do?"

"I don't know. I guess, I'm doing it. I have to be here. I can't leave."

"Yeah." I may not understand her gift, but the mom thing, yeah, that I understand.

CHAPTER TEN

Place no hope in the feeling of assurance, in spiritual
comfort. You may well have to get along without this.
Thomas Merton

erissa

MOTHERING an adult child is more difficult than I ever imagined. The issues an adult grapples with are deeper, emotionally challenging, and can be so painful. When Twila was a
baby, a toddler, a preschooler, my primary focus was keeping
her safe and healthy. The wounds she experienced were most
often physical—a tummy ache, a skinned knee, even a broken
arm, once. But things began to change once she entered
elementary school. Then she'd occasionally come home with
something more than a scrape or scratch. Instead, her feel-

ings were bumped and bruised. Another child called her a name, or a harried teacher corrected her harshly.

I shutter the kitchen windows against the gray afternoon and then pull my sweater close as memories play. As a child, Twila was highly sensitive, emotionally and physically. She had an awareness of others that seemed to exceed that of other children her age. If she was upset about something, her stomach roiled. If she was especially upset, a bout of hives might accompany the stomachache. There were many visits to her pediatrician and few answers. But through observation, I finally linked the physical reactions to her emotional state. So when the eating disorder began, perhaps I shouldn't have felt surprised, but I did nonetheless.

Overall, in retrospect, my job as a mother was easier when she was young. And as much as I loved those early years of parenting, they were tiring, and I looked forward to her growing and maturing. I thought then that motherhood would only get easier. It wasn't long before I realized my misconception.

Parenting through the emotional wounds life inflicts was more challenging and fraught with my own heartache as I watched my child suffer. I had no idea how to care for her psyche, her soul. I read books, talked with other mothers, and in the end, as the one who knew her best, I mostly listened to my own instinct. And I prayed. A lot.

None of that has changed. There's still heartache coupled with the joy motherhood offers. And I still pray a lot.

By Sunday afternoon, Twila hasn't said anything about her engagement ring. It's very possible she simply forgot to put it on after taking it off for one reason or another. But I suspect there's another reason she isn't wearing it, and instinct has little to do with it. No, it's circumstantial evidence leading the way this time. Each time I've mentioned wedding plans, she's evaded the conversation. She hasn't, as far as I know, spoken to Will since her arrival here. Typically, I hear her on the phone, even if her door is closed. I don't listen in, but it's evident by the glow on her face afterward or the snippets of information she shares that she's spoken to him. This time, she's silent, and her silence is speaking volumes.

She's also eaten little. Picked at her food. Yesterday, she said she ate something while she was with Pia, and I hoped that was true. Because she ate nothing else all day, at least not that I saw.

And now I glance at the clock on the kitchen wall. It's nearly 4:00 p.m. and she hasn't made a move to load her car or mentioned when she's leaving. She seems restless. She's ridden her bike to the headlands and back, walked around the village, and now she's going through things she left in her closet when she moved out.

I've given her space and assumed that if she wants to talk, to tell me something, she'll do so. She is an adult and I respect her and her desire for privacy, if that is what she needs. But another truth niggles. I also haven't asked her what's going on because of the relief I felt when I saw she wasn't wearing her engagement ring, and what that could mean for me—financial relief. And I've hated myself for that sense of relief. I've grappled with those feelings all weekend.

If Twila and Will have called off the wedding, it's caused them both great pain, I'm sure of that. How could I possibly find relief in their pain? I won't. Now—I glance at the clock again. Is giving Twila an opportunity to talk, opening a door for conversation, what she needs?

I dry my hands on a kitchen towel, then go down the hallway and tap on her partially open bedroom door. "Honey?" I open the door and step into her room, where she's sitting on the floor in front of her closet, a small pile of clothes folded in front of her. Her closet door is open, and the few clothes she'd left when she moved out are even fewer now.

She looks up at me. "I'm going to donate these."

"Okay. I have a bag of items you can add them to."

She doesn't move to get up; she just stares at the clothes. So I go into the room and sit on the chair at the desk. "I've sensed you've needed some space this weekend. But you know I'm always here to listen."

She looks up at me, swallows, and then tears fill her eyes.

"Oh, honey…" I get down on the floor next to her and put my arm around her. She leans her head on my shoulder. "Are you ready to talk?"

I feel her shrug but she says nothing, so I wait.

Finally, she pulls away and looks down at the floor. "We're taking a break," she whispers.

"You and Will?"

She nods. "We have to… We're trying to work through some things."

"That sounds wise. What kinds of things are you working through? Anything I can do to—"

"No." She looks at me again. "I quit my job and I was hoping, I mean…can I stay here? For a while? I'll work, see if I can get some hours at Corners, or something."

"Of course. This is your home—will always be your home." Her words, her request, the heartache emanating from her, rend my heart, but I can't process my feelings now. This is her time. "What about the wedding? What's your—?"

She shakes her head. "No. It's off. I can't…I don't…I can't…" Her tears flow now.

I put my arm around her again. "Shh. It's okay. You don't have to say more. It's okay." I sit with her for a long time. I let her cry. I let her feel the grief that's so evident. I don't press her for more.

When she finally pulls away again, head hanging, hair

covering her face, I reach out and tuck long dark strands of her hair behind one ear.

She looks at me then. "I'm sorry I didn't tell you. I just needed...time, I guess. Saying it makes it feel real."

I consider her words a moment. "I understand." And I do understand. I know exactly what she means. How voicing truth seems to solidify that truth in our minds and hearts. That's why, though I haven't known it until this moment, I didn't speak truth to Miles the other day about my financial issues, why I've done my own evading with Twila, and why I haven't shared with her about her father's decision.

I put my hand on her arm and give it a gentle squeeze. "I'm here for you, for whatever you need. If you need to talk, I'll listen. If you need time to contemplate and process, know that I'm praying for you."

"Thanks." She lifts her head a little higher and looks me in the eyes, her gaze intent. "So, what's going on with you?"

Understanding comes again. "You know, don't you?"

She shrugs. "I don't know what. I just know something's going on."

I nod. "Yes. I should have known you'd know—you'd sense something. I'm sorry. Like you, speaking it out loud made it real, and..." I take a deep breath. "Your father has filed a motion to stop paying spousal support, so that leaves me in a financial crunch."

I smile, and oddly, the smile is genuine. "You know, sometimes saying something out loud makes it feel real, but other times it takes the power out of it, doesn't it?" It's my turn to shrug. "A financial crunch isn't the worst thing in the world."

She doesn't respond. Instead, her expression urges me on. "I've let myself worry. But I trust God will provide." And I do trust, and as I speak it to Twila, my heart calms. Why have I worried? Trust and worry can't coexist—I know that. It's something I'll process with God later. "Anyway, it's time to stop worrying."

"There's more," Twila whispers.

When I look at her again, her gray eyes have darkened, like a storm has rolled in, and I shiver. "What? No, that's all. I'm trying to figure out what to do, what to change in order to bring in more income, but that's all." I hesitate. "Isn't it?"

Twila's eyes are filled with knowledge of something I don't understand, and fear slithers into my soul. "What do you mean by more?"

"I don't know, exactly, but..." Twila's quiet for a moment as though listening for something, or someone. "God is here." Her declaration is sure, and final. She knows nothing else. And truly, what more do any of us need to know other than God is with us?

"Yes. Always. He's here for both of us." But my verbal assurance does little to still the vortex swirling beneath the surface, pulling me in, deeper and deeper, into what, I don't know.

I HADN'T REALIZED when Twila arrived that her car was packed with all her things—she'd not only quit her job, but also given up the place where she was staying. She's a minimalist in many ways, so what she had fit in the backseat and trunk. After I helped her carry in her things, I went back to the kitchen and opened the refrigerator, then the freezer to see what I could offer her for dinner. I'd run to the grocery store after Twila arrived on Thursday, but only purchased enough food to get through Sunday lunch.

I found a container of vegan curried butternut-squash soup I'd made a couple of weeks ago. I added a small salad and gave thanks when Twila ate a large cup of the soup and the salad. As she ate, it occurred to me that I'd have to plan meals for two now, and I'd need to budget for the extra expense, extra expenses, actually—electricity, water, and other sundry items. Not much, but some. Twila would help as she could, but as my income was set to plummet, my expenses, it appeared, would climb, whether there was a wedding or not.

As Twila said, God is here. He knows. I trust Him. I won't succumb to worry.

Now, as I go through the house and turn off the lights, Twila already in her room for the night, the financial concerns return, taking up residence in my neck and shoulders. I roll my shoulders back as I stop at the thermostat in the hallway. With Twila here, I haven't turned the heat down as low as I had been after learning of Daniel's intent. Again, I think of the wedding and relief—financial relief—breezes through me again. Just as quickly, guilt rears its head.

"No," I whisper. I won't allow guilt to turn to shame. Feelings aren't right or wrong. It's what we do with them that matters.

I give this to You, Lord. Twila's wedding, her relationship with Will, whatever it is they're struggling with, and my financial situation. All of it. I trust You to provide exactly what each of us needs.

With that, having done my part, I determine to let go of the thoughts working to capture my mind.

As I wash my face and brush my teeth, I wonder if Will has spoken to Miles yet. Do he and Ellyn know of the change in plans, the issues the kids are dealing with? What would Miles say to Will? What wisdom would he share? As I have so many times before, I wish for a strong, godly father for Twila. Or, more accurately stated, I feel the pain of her loss, the loving father she never had.

Although, Miles did fill that role for her in some ways last year, his presence in her life, his willingness to engage with her, his genuine care for her, were a gift to Twila. And to me. I was thrilled by Twila's choice of Will as her life partner because of Will's character, because of the ongoing relationship she'd enjoy with Miles when he became her father-in-law, and with Ellyn, as they've shared a special friendship, too.

If Twila and Will can't work through their differences, she isn't the only one who will grieve.

When I climb into bed a half hour or so later, I turn off the lamp on my bedside table and then roll onto my side, intent on sleep. But as I lie here, the conversation with Twila plays again—what she shared, and what she didn't share. Her tears told me enough—she's in pain, hurting, and this time, a kiss and a *Little Mermaid* bandage won't offer the comfort she needs.

Oh, Lord, only You can comfort her... Comfort Will. Give them wisdom, Lord, Your wisdom. Make their paths straight.

What are they struggling with? I roll onto my back, open my eyes, and stare into the dark. What is so challenging that they can't work through it? I was so certain, we were all certain this relationship between Twila and Will was ordained by God, His perfect plan for both of them.

Lord...?

I wait for a response of some sort. Not answers to my questions, specifically, but rather an assurance of His presence. A sense. A feeling of some sort. His words of love whispering in my mind. Anything.

When silence slices through me again, I roll back over, pulling the covers tight around me. *Have I become too dependent on my senses? On my experience of You, God? Maybe so. Whether I sense You or not, I know You are here, within me, always.*

I determine, again, that I will act in spite of what I feel. I will operate on faith—what I can't see but believe to be true. I will continue to seek Him and follow Him, regardless.

As I make that vow to myself and to God, an ache, a growling longing, settles within me, the pain almost physical. I rest my hand on my chest and breathe deep, hoping in some way to alleviate what seems bent on consuming me.

I lie in bed wide awake as the minutes, the hours tick by, darkness looming, enveloping me. Loneliness crests on the shore of my soul, but I won't let it overwhelm me. I will feel the loneliness, the longing, but I won't allow it to rule. I will coexist with it.

I wait for the feeling to ebb, I will it to ebb, but again and again waves crest and crash, until the sorrow of my aloneness threatens to drown me. Tears rise and fall with each wave.

All the while an image fills my mind. A man in a lifeboat bouncing on the waves. He reaches for me. Arm outstretched, he calls my name, "Nerissa..."

I push the image away. Again and again.

I open my eyes in order to rid myself of the image in mind.

Darkness surrounds me.

Silence.

I close my eyes. *No... You Lord, only You.*

Suddenly, the silence is broken. *"Nerissa. Nerissa. Nerissa."*

Real or imagined? I don't know.

I no longer know anything.

Fog hovers over the water as waves slosh against the small boat.

"Nerissa..."

Through the fog, he reaches out his hand to me and waits for me to grasp it. *"Nerissa..."*

$\sim$

A BRIGHT LIGHT strobes in the dark, yanking me from sleep. I cover my eyes, sit up, heart pounding, mouth dry, sure the light will flash again, blinding me. A lighthouse maybe? I wait. Nothing. Was it a dream?

I lower my hands from my face and open my eyes. There is no light. I'm in my bed, the room still veiled in darkness. I turn toward the nightstand: 3:17 a.m. I fall back onto the mattress, then kick at the sheets tangled around my legs. As my heart rate slows, the memory of the man in the boat returns, and then I remember trying to rid myself of the image. But I failed. The man, the one who reached for me, who was there to rescue me, filled my restless, tangled dreams.

I finally reached for him. His grip strong as his hand grasped mine. His presence so real. So close. His breath warm against my skin as he whispered in my ear, *"Nerissa... Nerissa..."*

Only with my hand firmly held in his did I finally succumb to rest.

In my dreams.

Dreams of Miles.

THE MIND IS MORE powerful than we know. Neuroscience offers evidence of the mind's power to affect physical change, to overcome habits and addictions, to cure the body of ailments in some cases, and to manifest expectations. As I had told Miles, if you expect the Green Giant to taste bad, it's going to taste bad. There's science to support my claim. They've only just scratched the surface of one of the most intricate of God's creations: the human brain.

I find science fascinating. It's something I'm continuing to study and beginning to employ with a few of my clients who are willing to practice changing their mindset regarding nutrition: the food they put into their bodies, the desires that fuel those choices, and how they can learn to change those very desires. It's the practice—the work of changing our minds—that creates new neural pathways in the brain, new tracks for our habits to follow.

So when, in the light of day, I awake again to thoughts of Miles, I know I can't allow my mind to linger on those thoughts. I cannot entertain what my subconscious presented, what is not mine to entertain.

But again, as I've noted several times over the last week, my emotions are not in line with my thoughts. And if what I think impacts what I feel, then I need to work harder at dwelling on truth, on replacing the troubling thoughts with thoughts that will lead me where I need to go, where I believe God wants me to go. I want Him to be my focus. Now. Always.

I sit up in bed and then bow my head and close my eyes. "'Do not be conformed to this world, but be transformed by the renewal of your mind, that by testing you may discern what is the will of God, what is good and acceptable and perfect,'" I whisper the familiar verse. "Lord Jesus, renew my mind..." My prayer begins in earnest.

After some time, I'm not sure how long I've prayed, and my body shivers in the cold room. I open my eyes and then ease out of bed, my muscles still, my gait awkward. I make my way to my closet for my robe. As I slip my left arm into the downy sleeve and my hand comes out the armhole, I notice something. Or the lack of something. I gasp.

The silver band I never remove from my ring finger is gone.

I slip my other arm into the robe and tie the belt at my waist, then turn and flip the light on in the closet. I search the floor for the ring and come up empty. I trace my steps back to the bed, pull back the blankets one by one, running my hand over the bed, looking and feeling for the ring. Then I do the same with the top sheet—pull it back and run my hands over the fitted sheet.

Nothing.

I turn to the nightstand, panic rising, and scour the top, moving books and my Bible aside, lifting the lamp, but it isn't there. I pull the nightstand away from the wall and look behind it, and then underneath it, and finally, on my hands and knees, I check under the bed, even grabbing a flashlight from the nightstand drawer and shining it across the floor beneath the bed.

The ring isn't there. Nor is it in any of the other places I search in the house, and I scour every square inch, except Twila's room where she is still asleep. Did I have the ring after I sat with her on the floor of her room last evening? I'm sure I did.

I go to the kitchen and search the countertops, the sink, and even check the garbage disposal. Finally, I step out into the damp, cold morning, my slipper clad feet leaving imprints on the wet lawn as I cross to my car in the driveway. I click the fob and unlock the doors, then tear the car apart.

But the ring is gone.

Standing in my driveway, I lift my left hand. My ring finger is as bare as Twila's. And again, her loss, her grief crashes over me, this time coupled with my own.

Lord? Why? What is happening?

This time, I don't bother waiting for, listening for, a response.

It won't come anyway.

CHAPTER ELEVEN

We live on the brink of disaster because we do not know
how to let life alone. We do not respect the living and fruitful
contradictions and paradoxes of which true life is full.
Thomas Merton

llyn

ON MONDAY MORNING, I tell Miles I have an interview with a
potential employee and I make the drive into the village
again. But before the interview, I meet Jim at his office to
exchange the signed lease for the keys, then I drive straight to
the water tower. I pull into the gravel driveway, then dash
through a deluge to the front door. I insert the key in the
lock, turn it, wipe my feet on the mat on the porch—a mat I
bought, by the way—and suddenly I'm standing in the small
foyer of the water tower.

I close the front door behind me, switch on the overhead entry light and then just stand there. I close my eyes, and my heart rate, which is usually racing like a harried rabbit, slows. Rain patters on the rooftop, and the rattle of the windows facing the headlands testifies to the wind. Familiar sounds. The soundtrack of the last decade or more of my life.

I smile and then open my eyes, but what I see isn't what I expect. In fact, it's disorienting, like a bad case of vertigo. I suck in my breath and put a hand to my chest. "What...?"

The monochromatic color scheme—white on white on white, with touches of gray—is cold, as though all the lifeblood was drained from the home. The house is empty, void of any other familiarities, even the footprint has changed. And—I sniff—it smells like plastic or something equally toxic—the aromas of new carpet and fresh paint.

I slip out of my work clogs and pad across the newly carpeted living room—a nubby, tightly woven, light-gray carpet—to the kitchen, now fully exposed. "Open concept." I survey the space—white marble with veins of gray on the island and countertops, white subway-tile backsplash, white cabinets, and hardwood flooring, stained gray, then whitewashed.

I don't dislike the space, but... I do a full turn, taking in the whole bottom floor with the exception of the powder bath and mudroom, which aren't visible from this vantage point. I cross my gaze over the living and what was the dining spaces.

"Does nothing stay the same?" The question echoes through the hardscaped kitchen. I run my hand over the smooth, cold marble of the new island. *Cooking classes?* Since when have I wanted to teach cooking classes? It was the first thing that came to mind when Jim asked what I planned to do with the place. It had been a reasonable question, one I didn't have an answer for.

A question I still don't have an answer for. Not that I'm against teaching cooking classes, but...

I walk around the island and look at the open spaces for a range and refrigerator. The fridge space is fairly large and could, possibly, accommodate a Sub-Zero built-in. When I talked with Jim about the lease, I told him to hold off on ordering appliances, that I'd like to make those decisions. He gave me the budget he'd allotted and told me anything above his numbers would be on me. A Sub-Zero and Wolf range would double his allotment, at least. For now, neither are needed.

And later?

Cooking classes? A B and B? Do I want to take on more work? Spend more time away from Miles? Away from the café? A business venture? *Who were you kidding, Big Girl?* I haven't even taken the steps to add brunch service for the café.

I wander over to the stairs that run along the back wall of the living area and lead to the second- and third-floor bedrooms, each with their own bath. I plop myself down on the stairs, the only place to sit in the unfurnished space, and look around again.

Why am I here?

Whatever I'd hoped to feel by coming here, by securing the place as my own again, isn't what I feel. What do I feel? "I'll take Emotionally Inept Women for one hundred dollars, Alex."

But then I remember what I assumed I'd feel and what I wanted. To come home.

I grasp for the strands of shag carpet that used to cover the stairs but come up empty. The new rough wool carpet is scratchy and unforgiving. This is no longer my home. Miles's house doesn't feel like home, either. And the house of my childhood where my mother still lives, that hasn't been my home since I left after I graduated from high school. Nor have I returned since visiting my mother just over a year ago on Christmas Day. I don't expect an invitation anytime soon, either.

I want to go home, but I no longer have a home. Or I no longer feel at home. Or something.

There's always the café, but oh, how I loved leaving the café after a long night and walking into the embrace of the little converted water tower, the embrace of *home*, the comfort of home, the familiarity of home. The warm colors, soft and supple textures, even the small kitchen all spoke of home, representing me in some way.

I consider the lease I've signed, the money spent, the secrecy of my actions...

What have I done? And why? And what if Miles finds out? Do I tell him? But how would I explain?

A dull ache settles between my eyes.

I let my mind wander back to last week, to what preceded the call to Jim. The conversation with Sabina, followed by Rosa's declaration of motherhood and her not-so-subtle suggestion to call the *"head doctor."* How did those events lead me here?

"A large, insecure, married woman who rents a house behind her loving husband's back."

I hit the virtual buzzer in my mind. "What is *Clueless,* Alex?"

"Bingo!" Oops, wrong game. I sigh. It isn't funny and I know it. What I don't know is what I should do next. Or, maybe I do know. Maybe it's time to make the call I was supposed to make in the first place.

~

AFTER THE TIME spent at the water tower and the interview for the line cook position with the young man who, it turns out, counted his time placing precooked chicken wings under the warming light at his local mini-mart as cook experience, I spent the rest of the afternoon going through more applications, making calls to set up interviews, and considering dishes for the spring menu. A stop at Harvest Foods for groceries on the way home delayed me further.

It's nearly 6:00 p.m. when I finally walk into the house, a bag of groceries in each arm. So much for a day off. "Miles?" His car is in the garage, so I know he's here, but the house is dark. I set the bags on the kitchen island and then, flipping lights on as I go, cross the large great room to Miles's den. Because the den is also dark, I pass it, thinking he must be upstairs. But before I reach the stairs he calls to me.

"I'm in here."

I go back to the den where I find Miles sitting at his desk, his chair swiveled toward the window that looks out over the cliffs.

"What are you doing?" Concern nips at me. Miles, when he's home, typically meets me in the garage when he hears the garage door go up. It's a sweet habit I've grown accustomed to. "Are you alright?"

"I'm just thinking." His tone is flat, lacking his usual energy. He turns the chair back around and reaches for the lamp on his desk and pulls the chain.

I cross the room, turn on another lamp, then go to Miles, lean down and place a kiss on his forehead, and then knead his shoulders. Knots give way under my fingertips. "What's going on?"

He sighs and then is silent a moment. "I had a message from Will this afternoon. We finally connected about an hour ago."

I wait a moment, but he says nothing more. "And...?"

"He and Twila have called off their engagement—the wedding."

My hands still on his shoulders. "Oh. No. Oh. Wow." I give Miles's shoulders a squeeze. "How's he doing?"

"Not too well. He's pretty broken."

Platitudes rise to my lips, *He'll be fine. He'll get over it. It's probably for the best.* Fortunately they fall away before I utter them. As I look down at Miles, I can barely imagine the pain he's feeling for his son. I'm not a parent. I don't know that depth of devotion, but I at least know enough to know what I don't know. "What happened?"

"I don't know much. I'm not sure Will really knows either."

I walk around the desk and sit in the chair across from Miles. "Twila broke the engagement?"

"Apparently they've been discussing over a period of time the gifts God's given each of them and how best to use those as a couple moving forward." He smiles, though the attempt is weak. "Pretty mature of them. I don't think we had that conversation, did we?"

I shake my head as I recall Twila's question about purpose.

"Evidently, they haven't always agreed, but it hasn't caused any real friction, until last week. Twila told Will she felt like she needed to come home, to spend some time with Nerissa, and that she'd quit her job, so she was free to go. When Will questioned her, she wouldn't or couldn't explain why she needed to come home. Will was baffled, it sounded like, and then they argued. That's where he was a little vague, so I'm not sure what really happened. But part of the issue, for him, was that she'd quit her job without discussing it with him."

"Well, that was her prerogative, don't you think?"

"Sure. But it was a pretty big decision, and I think Will

felt left out or shut out of whatever Twila was going through."

An elephant has taken up residence on my chest as we've talked. No surprise. But now isn't the time to consider the similarities between Twila's actions and my own. "I'm sorry, Miles. Is there anything we can do to help? We've both been close to Twila. Should we talk to her?"

"That's what I was thinking about when you came in."

"Any conclusion?"

He nods. "Yes. Let's give it a few days. Pray about it. See how God leads." He looks past me, then sighs again. "There's no pain like watching your child suffer."

I get back up and go to Miles again. This time I bend down and wrap my arms around him. "I'm sorry." As I hold him, I think of Sarah, Will's mother, Miles's wife. How Sarah and Miles would have weathered this together. What advice would Sarah have offered Miles? What comfort would they have offered one another and Will?

And Nerissa? If Twila's told her, she certainly shares Miles's pain.

What can I offer? Empathy, but not true sympathy. Miles, Sarah, Nerissa, and me. Which of these things is not like the other? I've rarely felt my own ineptness more than I do in this moment, my own loss at never having parented a child. I have nothing to offer Miles to help him through his pain.

Nothing? Well, maybe something. I pull back from him so I can see his face. "May I cook you some dinner?"

He reaches out and places his palm on my cheek, then chuckles. "Food, the cure-all?"

"Welcome to my world."

Long after Miles's breathing has become rhythmic, I slip out of bed. Sleep has bypassed me and doesn't seem to have any intent of visiting anytime soon. I pad my way to the kitchen, pour some milk into a pan on the range to warm, then go to the pantry and pull out a container of butter cookies I made for Miles after dinner this evening—the same cookies I made when we had that first awkward coffee date. Food may not cure all the ills, but it does make them more bearable, of that I'm certain.

Once the milk is warm, I settle on one of the bar stools at the island, two cookies on a napkin, along with the mug in front of me, the container of cookies safely stowed away in the pantry again. I take a bite of one of the small, melt-in-your-mouth, if I do say so myself, cookies and savor the sweet-with-a-hint-of-salt, buttery delight. I wash it down with a sip of milk. And then pop the second half of the cookie into my mouth. As I do, it occurs to me that the cookie is made with enriched, bleached, all-purpose flour. "Can you say gluten?" I whisper. Then I look at the milk. "And dairy?"

Is it possible Nerissa is right and gluten, dairy, and let's not forget the radishes are the cause of my aches and pains, my GI issues, and—I look down at the way my thighs are spilling over the bar stool—so much more? More of me? I pick up the second cookie, lift it to my mouth, then hesitate. I set it back down as another question pesters.

Why am I sitting in the kitchen eating cookies at 2:00 a.m.?

Because I couldn't sleep. *Duh, Big Girl*, as Earl would say. Or just did say. Maybe I didn't completely exterminate him the way I'd hoped.

And why couldn't I sleep?

Because of the parallel between what Miles said about Twila quitting her job and not telling Will and me making an equally big decision without telling Miles, obviously. What had Miles said? Will had felt left out. Shut out.

And that's exactly what I did to Miles by not telling him about the water tower.

Why had I shut him out? Why would I ever want to shut Miles out of any part of my life? And while I recognize that I have, in fact, shut him out, I'm not sure what I've shut him out of. I don't understand my own feelings or actions.

Maybe I've shut myself out of my own thoughts and feelings. Is that even possible? I pick up the second cookie, break it in half, and eat one half, then the other. The container in the pantry lures, but...

No. I reach into the pocket of my robe and pull out my phone. I scroll through the contacts until I find Shauna's number, and I do what I should have done days ago. I call her office and leave a message requesting an appointment.

Before it's too late.

Before I do permanent damage. Or maybe in hopes of repairing damage already done.

As I rinse the mug, switch off the lights in the kitchen, and make my way back upstairs, all I can think about is the lease I signed, the decision I made without discussing it with Miles. Had it been a true business decision, it might be different.

My steps slow as I reach the landing. What is wrong with me? How could I be so stupid? And why am I even thinking about myself and what I've done when Twila and Will are suffering? Along with Miles, and Nerissa, too, I'd imagine.

It's always about you, isn't it, Tubby?

I stop on the landing, a familiar urge, magnetic, pulling me back to the kitchen.

I turn around and head down the stairs again, ignoring the waving red flags and alarms blaring in my mind. I retrace my steps back to the kitchen, to the pantry, to the container

117

of cookies. Once there, I open the container and, standing in the pantry alone with my thoughts, stuff the thoughts. With cookies.

All the cookies.

It's only when I've eaten the last one that I realize Miles will look for the cookies, will want another one or two with a cup of coffee, most likely before breakfast even. But they'll be gone. All gone. And he'll know.

Way to go, Fatty. You're hopeless, you know that, right?

"Shut up." But the words lack conviction. I know Earl is right, at least he's right this time. What have I done? Certainly more than binged on an entire recipe of cookies, as if that isn't bad enough.

I walk out of the pantry, set the container on the island, and then go to the refrigerator to get two cubes of butter and an egg, then return to the pantry for flour, light-brown sugar, baking powder, salt, and vanilla. Arms loaded with the ingredients, eyes heavy, feet aching, and stomach cramping, I set the ingredients out next to the mixer, then I turn on the oven, set the temperature, then return to the mixer.

I can't let Miles know what I've done.

My hands shake as I unwrap the cubes of butter and level the measure of sugar to dump into the mixing bowl. I need to hurry. What if he wakes and misses me? What if he comes looking for me? How would I explain?

What would he think?

My face heats with the thought.

What is wrong with me?

CHAPTER TWELVE

True faith is never merely a source of spiritual comfort. It
may indeed bring peace, but before it does so it must involve
us in struggle. A "faith" that avoids this struggle is really a
temptation against true faith.
Thomas Merton

ia

THE DEFROSTER WHIRS, pushing warm air into the car and
clearing the windshield, though there's not much to see.
Parked on the headlands, where the spaces are typically filled
with tourists or locals who've come to walk the trails in the
park, today I'm mostly alone. Rain spatters the windshield
and the view, all gray, is uninspiring. But I don't need inspiration. I need space and time and…what?

I swallow the ache in my throat and then whisper into the

solitude of the car, "I don't know…" It is the first prayer I've prayed since Manuel had told me. A tear slides down my cheek and I wipe it away. "I don't know what to do."

There is one simple solution to the problem Manuel faces, the problem we face. It will solve everything. Two simple words is all it will take. It's been a full week since I sat in Manuel's truck and he spoke the truth that changed everything.

The heater had been on in his truck, and we'd parked here, on the headlands, before he took me to work. I scooted next to him on the bench seat, his arm around me. We stared out at the ocean, saying little, just enjoying the time together. Then he turned and leaned down and kissed my forehead, then my lips. His kiss was soft, slow, and he lingered. After a few moments, I pulled back and stared into his dark eyes, then reached for his face and pulled him close again. My kiss more demanding, hungry.

But he didn't respond. Instead, he resisted and finally pulled away from me. He leaned back in his seat, his head against the glass of the back window, eyes closed.

"What's wrong?"

He said nothing, just sat there. His Adam's apple bobbed as he swallowed, then he took a deep breath and opened his eyes.

"Baby…what?"

He stared straight ahead, still saying nothing.

Finally, he turned and looked at me. Something glimmered in his eyes, something I'd never seen before, and my stomach clenched. "Manuel, you're scaring me. What's going on? Tell me."

He nodded. "I will. I have to. I should have…" He looked away again. "I'm sorry, Bebe." He cleared his throat. "I'm sorry," he whispered.

"What? What's wrong?"

He looked back at me and tears filled his eyes. I'd never seen him cry. He's always so strong, so sure. "Tell me." But even as I demanded he talk to me, I didn't want to hear whatever he had to say. Somehow, I knew that whatever he said would change everything. Had already changed everything.

"Pia, we can't do this anymore. I can't do this to you."

"Can't do this? Do what?" Despite the warmth blasting from the vents, I shivered. Mind, body, soul. Cold. "I don't even want to know what you're talking about," I mumbled. "I don't want to know."

"I should have told you. I should have. But at first I didn't think it mattered. And then, when it did matter, it was already too late. I loved you already. It was too late."

I look at him, eyes wide, tears swimming. "What, Manuel, what? Just tell me. Say it!" Whether I wanted to know or not, it was too late.

He took another deep breath, and as I watched the words forming on his lips, I wanted to run, to hide, but there was nowhere to go. "Say it!"

"I'm un—"

"No!" I pounded my fist on the seat. "No! Don't say it. Do not tell me that!"

"I don't have papers—"

"No!"

"I have nothing. I'm undocumented, Pia." He leaned his head back again, eyes closed, and a tear slipped down his cheek. Then he opened his eyes and banged his fists on the steering wheel. "Nothing!"

My mouth filled with saliva as my clenched stomach threatened to revolt.

"Nothing! Nada!" His words came out as a ragged sob.

I clamped my hands over my ears and closed my eyes. "I can't..." I gasped for air. "It can't be true. This can't be happening. How? How did this happen?" I open my eyes, push away from him, and shove open the truck's door.

He grabbed my arm. "Pia!"

I yanked my arm away and got out. The cold slapped me in the face and filled my lungs as I gasped for air. I stumbled past the front of the truck, stepped over the curb of the parking lot and onto the headland's uneven terrain.

A door slammed behind me and within seconds, Manuel was next to me.

"No! Leave me alone." I pushed him away again and ran toward the cliff.

"Pia!"

When I could run no farther, when I'd reached the edge of the world, I collapsed on the ground, head buried in my knees, and I sobbed until I couldn't breathe. I don't know how long I sat there before I realized Manuel was next to me, his arm around my shoulders. He pulled me close to him and held me there.

When I finally looked up at him, he gently unwrapped the scarf I'd worn around my neck. He lifted the scarf to my face and wiped the tears from my cheeks, then he held it to my nose. "Blow."

I shook my head.

"Blow, Pia. You can wash it later."

I took the scarf from him, blew my nose, and then tossed it aside. I sat for a long time, staring, seeing nothing. When I turned back to him, his jaw was set and a vein in his neck throbbed. He stared straight ahead.

The words that had been screaming through my mind finally came out, "You lied to me!"

He looked at me and shook his head. "No. You assumed."

"But you knew what I assumed, and you didn't tell me the truth."

He said nothing.

"My mama knew. She knows. That's why she doesn't approve. That's why. How could I be so stupid? How—?"

"I should have told you, but...I couldn't lose you, Pia. I can't lose you. It was selfish. I see that now. I'm sorry. I just"—he hung his head—"I didn't want to lose you." He whispered, "I'm sorry."

"How did this even happen?"

He took a deep breath. "I didn't know—for a long time, I didn't know." He shrugged. "I didn't understand until I wanted to get my driver's license." He lifted his hand to his mouth and bit at a nail.

I reached over and pulled his hand away. How many times had I done that since meeting him? I suddenly understood his nervous habit.

"My father sat me down and handed me a card. He said, 'You'll need this to apply, but you'll have to wait until January.' It was an ID card from the Mexican consular—it had my photo on it. 'Why?' I asked him. I didn't get it—didn't understand. I'd gone online and knew what I needed to get a driver's license or a permit, at least—a birth certificate and social security number. I didn't even know what the card was. And then..."

Manuel stared out at the sea again, then sighed. "And then I did know. I thought about how they'd kept telling me—my parents—that I had to wait to get my license. I had to bring my grades up, even though I already had good grades, so I worked harder. Then I had to wait because of the insurance cost, so I saved up, then... It doesn't matter. I knew. I finally understood."

"They lied to you all those years?"

"No, they just didn't tell me."

"They lied. That's a lie, Manuel. They didn't tell you the truth. They withheld the truth."

"It doesn't matter, Pia. It doesn't change anything. Don't

you understand? It doesn't matter whether they lied or not. That's not the point now."

"How did they...?" I didn't even know what to ask. I knew so little.

"They had work visas when they first came. I was only a few months old. When the visas weren't renewed, they stayed anyway, like so many others. They had nothing to go back to—no home, no jobs, no money. Even illegally, they knew they could provide a better life for us here."

"But the card, how'd they get it for you?"

He said nothing, just looked away.

"Is it—?"

"I don't know, Pia. I didn't ask."

"Wait, January? Why'd you have to wait until January?"

He said nothing, just kept looking out at the ocean.

"Look at me."

He turned and when his eyes met mine, the anger was there again.

"What happened in January?"

"I got a license. There's a new law, as of January 15. I can drive legally now."

"What? Manuel, you've been driving without a license? What if something happened, what if—?"

"You don't understand, Pia. You're not going to understand. You haven't had to live this like I have. Your life is different." He shook his head and laughed, but the sound was bitter. "Governor Brown introduced a bill—AB 60—it will provide a way for undocumented immigrants to get driver's licenses in California. I am a good driver. I am safe. I obeyed the laws, and now—"

Heat rose up my neck as I understood what he was telling me. "You obeyed the laws?" I spat the words at him. "How can you say that? You drove without a license but say you obeyed the laws? Is that a joke? Is it, Manuel? Because it isn't funny."

"I drive legally now."

"But—"

"Let it go, Pia!" His chin was set, his eyes hard.

"You don't—"

"Stop! I had to work. I had to drive. It's the way it is. Your life is different." He ran his hand through his dark hair and turned away from me. "This is why I didn't tell you. Why I didn't want to..." He shook his head.

"Okay, okay. Just..." I inhaled and took a minute to think. "Okay, what about that plan—the deferred...whatever it's called, the one President Obama implemented that gives undocumented immigrants some rights or protection? It allows you to..." What did it allow? I didn't even know. I hadn't needed to know. "Have you applied for it?"

"It's called DACA—Deferred Action for Childhood Arrivals. And no."

"No? What?"

"No, I haven't applied. I won't apply."

"Why not? That makes no sense."

"It makes sense, Pia. This is my home. It is my family's home. This is where our lives are. There is nothing in Mexico for us. Nothing. If I apply for DACA, I have to give the government my address, my parents' address. I have to expose my parents in order to cover myself. I won't do that— I won't take that risk. I won't. They've sacrificed too much. You can't possibly understand. You were born here. Your parents came legally. They had opportunities we didn't have."

"You could be deported, Manuel."

"You think I don't know that? And what about my parents? How could I live with myself if they're deported?"

I thought of my mama and shook my head. "I don't know," I whispered. "So that's why you work at the winery?

They'll pay you cash—under the table, right? My mama was right about that, too?"

"I work hard, Pia. I love what I do, you know that. Someday I'm going to—"

"I know what you want to do, Manuel. But how? How do you think you'll go to school, learn viticulture, get a job legally? Own a vineyard?" I laughed, but there was nothing funny about it. "How?"

When he looked at me again, the anger was still in his eyes. I'd seen that look before but hadn't known what it meant.

"I don't know."

Then something occurred to me, and I reached for him. I put my hands on his face, leaned in, and kissed him quickly. "There is a way. Manuel, there's a way! Marry me. That's how it can all work. If you marry me, then you can get a green card, right?" I looked into his eyes but didn't see the excitement I felt. "Manuel, that takes care of everything."

He stood and started back toward the truck.

"Wait!" I got up and followed him. "What? What's wrong? We want to get married. I mean, we haven't said it, but we both know. Right?"

He stopped, the anger throbbing again in his eyes, his neck. "I will never marry you for that reason. Never. Your mama, others, they'll assume that's why I married you. No, Pia. I won't do that. That's not an option."

"It's the only option!"

"No. I won't talk about it. No."

"You're making this impossible, Manuel. Do you want it to be impossible? You have options, but you won't take any of them."

"You don't understand."

"No, you're right, I don't," I shouted.

I jump at the tap on the car window. It takes me a second

to realize where I am. I turn to the window where Manuel stands, bent down, looking in at me. I unlock the car doors and he walks around the front of the car to the passenger side. He opens the door and gets inside, his flannel shirt dotted with raindrops.

I breathe in the scent of him—soap and damp flannel and wine—and all of me reacts. My heart both races and aches. Without thinking, I grab his hand, lace my fingers with his, and hold on so tight, I'm afraid to let go, ever.

"Thanks for calling." His voice is thick with emotion.

"I'm sorry. I'm sorry I didn't understand."

"How could you, Pia? It's not your fault. I'm the one who's sorry. I never should have...gone out with you."

"How can you say that?"

"It's true. I knew. But I..." Tears fill his eyes and he looks away from me.

"Manuel, don't. I love you." The words are lodged behind the lump in my throat, so I say nothing more. I just squeeze his hand tighter.

We sit like that for a long time, holding hands, saying nothing. Words, it seems, have nothing to offer us, least of all solutions. Though I know I will speak the only possibilities I see, again. And again, if necessary.

Finally, I feel him looking at me and I turn to face him.

He is the first to break the silence. "Bebe, someday I will marry you, if you will still have me. It's all I want. All I think about. But I won't do it until it's right. I won't let your mama think I'm marrying you for any other reason than because I love you."

"It doesn't matter what she thinks."

"Doesn't it? It's been just the two of you most of your life. You love her, Pia. You respect her. So I respect her, too."

"Then you have to apply for—"

"And I need you to respect my desire to protect my family."

"I do, Manuel, but I looked it up, the information about DACA. The information they collect from you is protected— it won't be disclosed to Immigration and Customs Enforcement. So you can apply and—"

"No, Pia. I know what they say, but how can I trust? I can't take that risk. If you can't respect that, then…" He shrugs. "It is what it is."

I turn back to the view and stare out, considering Twila's words this morning about standing with others. And about praying. So I begin again, I try because I don't know what else to do. This is impossible.

Lord, please… Help us. Show us what to do.

CHAPTER THIRTEEN

We have the choice of two identities: the external mask
which seems to be real...and the hidden, inner person who
seems to us to be nothing, but who can give himself eternally
to the truth in whom he subsists.
Thomas Merton

llyn

FOLLOWING my middle-of-the-night gorging and baking
spree, Miles has left me alone—left me to my own devices—
silly man. Although we typically spend Tuesdays together,
one of our mutual days off, he left early to go hit a bucket of
balls. The physical action of swinging at and smacking the
golf balls is an emotional outlet for him, and he needs one
after the news Will shared last night.

That's called a healthy outlet, Ellyn. Right.

After he left, I showered, and while I was in the shower, my cell phone rang. Now hair dripping, body wrapped in a bath sheet, I sit on the edge of the large soaker tub in the master bath, phone in hand. I recognize the number of the caller—Shauna. If I wasn't sure I needed to see her, last night cemented the necessity. Good grief. I put the phone to my ear to listen to her message:

"Hi, Ellyn, it's so good to hear from you. I would love to see you, but I'm going out on maternity leave in two weeks—taking three months away from the office. I am thrilled, as you can imagine, but so sorry I won't be available. I'm referring clients to..."

I end the message without listening to the rest of it. The idea of starting over with a new therapist—well, no thank you. Okay, maybe starting over is what I need to do, but I require a few minutes, or a few hours, to let that idea rise. It's definitely not ready to bake yet.

Maternity leave? I do the math—she must have gotten pregnant just after I saw her last. I'm happy for Shauna. I am. But couldn't she have just adopted? Maybe an adult child? Really, that would have been so much more convenient for me. Because, as Earl reminded me last night, it's all about me, isn't it?

I wait for Earl's snarky retort, but it doesn't come.

Maybe last night—the cookies—was just a slip. A return to an old habit. And the lease for the water tower? What was that? As I stand up, my feet and knees scream in protest. Even after a shower, the hot water usually soothing, my joints ache. My stomach has also been staging a protest since the cookie escapade.

Head hanging, my bare feet and ankles draw my attention. They're puffy. Fat. As is the rest of me. I pull the bath towel tighter around my bulging midsection, but the ends barely meet.

God, I'm sorry. I must be such a disappointment to You.

I hobble from the bathroom to the closet where I trade the towel for my robe, then go to the bedroom, throw back the covers on the bed, and climb back in. I am so tired. So, so tired. How is it even possible to feel this tired?

And the cookies may have been just a slip—okay, a total flat-on-my-face smackdown—but it's proving something I've refused to deal with. The gluten and dairy issues are real. Why would I eat something I know will cause me pain and discomfort?

"You know it's one thing to believe you're created in the image of God, but it's another to live into it, right?"

What did Nerissa mean by *live into it?* Chalk that up to one more thing I'm clueless about. But I want to learn. I do.

Nerissa... How must she feel about Twila and Will's broken engagement? Surely this can't be any easier on her than it is on Miles. And what about Twila? For the first time since last night, I shift my focus off myself for more than a second and consider Twila. What is she going through? The last time she and Will were here, they seemed so happy, so compatible.

What precipitated her need to come home, to spend time with Nerissa?

The water tower comes to mind again, and with it the desire for home. I stare at the ceiling above me, then survey the spacious master bedroom decorated in cool shades of blue, a contrast to the warm autumn hues I prefer—a space that belonged to another couple first. Again, the desire for home accosts me, as does the realization that I no longer feel at home anywhere.

What brought Twila home?

I want to ask her, not because it has anything to do with what I'm feeling—it's different, I'm sure. I want to ask her because...

I sit up slowly.

Because I can ask her.

Because I'm a neutral party. Because I'm not Nerissa. Or Miles.

Because *I'm not a parent.*

Oh.

I'm a friend.

I ROLL OVER, awake, but lingering in the cotton of sleep. I finally open my eyes to the sunlight streaming through the large windows. Whitecaps break on the ocean beyond the cliffs, a pod of pelicans, reminiscent of the prehistoric age, soar just above the waterline.

"Good morning." Miles stands in the opening between the bedroom and master bath, his grayish-black hair mussed from the breeze, I assume, his blue golf shirt the same hue of blue as his eyes.

"Is"—I clear my throat—"it?" I pull myself up and lean back against the headboard. "Still morning?"

"Barely." He crosses the room and comes to sit on the edge of the bed next to me. "You feeling okay?"

"*Okay* is"—I clear my throat—"a big word. But, I think I'll survive."

"That's good news." He bends and kisses me, then cups my face with one hand. "What's going on?"

"Well, Doctor…"

Miles leans back to listen.

I push the curls dangling in my eyes off my face, and then remember I'd climbed into bed without drying or even combing my hair. "Sorry, I must look—"

"Beautiful," he whispers. He reaches up and gives one of those dangling red curls a gentle tug. His smile is genuine and the love he feels for me gleams in his eyes.

"I don't deserve you." I tilt my head and really look at him, take in his demeanor, the relaxed shoulders, the easy smile. "Hitting balls did its job?"

He nods. "It helped. But what's going on with you? You're not feeling well?"

I sigh, then consider my response. "I couldn't sleep last night, so I got up and..." I peer past him, back out at the view, make my decision, then I take a deep breath and look him in the eyes again. "I ate cookies. The butter cookies I made for you."

He chuckles. "A worthy midnight snack."

"No. I mean, yes, but...I ate..." Oh, why does the truth so often hurt? "all of them."

His eyebrows rise, just slightly, the change in expression almost imperceptible. Almost.

"Don't worry. I made another batch for you."

"In the middle of the night?"

I nod. "I didn't..." I stare down at my hands clenched together in my lap. "I didn't want you to know."

"But you decided to tell me." His tone is gentle, thoughtful. "Why?"

"Because. I called Shauna," I blurt out.

"The therapist you saw?"

I nod again.

"And that made you want to eat cookies in the night?" His brow is furrowed now as he works to understand.

"No, I ate the cookies, then I called. I thought it was—I mean, it was, definitely, a setback or a return to..." I close my eyes and shake my head. "I just thought... But she's going on maternity leave, so... Anyway, this morning, I'm paying the price, physically, for the gluten and dairy, I guess."

The corners of his eyes crinkle, an expression I've grown to know so well, as he smiles. "So, there was also milk involved in the Great Cookie Caper?"

"Miles, I'm serious."

He chuckles. "I know you are. I'm sorry. So, what are your symptoms this morning?"

I explain what I feel physically, and he nods as he listens. "Well, based on what you learned from the test results, and from Nerissa, it sounds like you've made an accurate diagnosis. But what made you—?"

I hold up one hand. "Wait. I'm getting to that." As I take another deep breath, what Miles shared last night about Twila quitting her job and Will's reaction come back to me. I want to tell Miles the truth—all of it—but my brief sense of resolve crumbles like the proverbial cookie. I exhale, deflated. "Maybe I'll make another appointment with Nerissa. Deal with the dietary issues."

He watches me, his expression expectant. But I say nothing more.

"Is there anything else? Something more you wanted to say?"

Unable to meet his gaze, I pull the covers back and move to get out of bed, which also necessitates him getting up. He stands, and I swing my legs over the side of the bed—well, swing would be a bit optimistic. I tend to lumber more than swing. "No, that's all." I get up, a lump the size of a matzo ball in my throat. "That's all *for now*. Okay?" I glance up at him.

"When you're ready, I'm here to listen."

I nod and move past him toward the bathroom. Who was I to think I could talk to Twila? That I'd have anything to offer her? I can't even talk to my own husband. Can't tell him the truth.

Way to go, Fatty. Blew it again.

As much as I want to squash my inner critic once and for all, I have to agree this time. I blew it, and I don't have the courage to confess.

"Ellyn?"

Here it comes. He's going to ask for more. *You'll have to tell him the truth.* I straighten, steeling myself for what's to come, then I turn back and look at Miles.

"I had a thought while I was at the driving range. I spent some time praying about Twila and Will. About talking to Twila?"

I nod.

"You've shared a special friendship with her. I think you're the perfect person to support her. At the very least to let her know we're here for her, whatever happens."

"Me?"

He comes to me, leans in, and kisses me, then pulls back and looks me in the eyes. "Absolutely. God's placed you in Twila's life and He'll continue to use you."

He turns and walks out of the room, and I stare after him.

Did God place me in Twila's life? "But..."

"What?" he calls from the hallway, then comes back to the bedroom door and leans in.

I shake my head. "Nothing."

"Okay." He turns to leave again but stops. "Hey, how about going for a drive this afternoon, if you feel up to it? We could go down the coast, have dinner at the Heritage House on our way back—you'd mentioned wanting to check out their new menu and chef."

"Sure." He acts as though nothing is wrong, as though the cookies make no difference. "What about...?"

"What?"

"The...cookies?"

"What about them?"

"You don't think, I mean, you don't seem like... I need to see a therapist, right?"

He shrugs. "If you want to see someone, if you're bothered by the choice you made and you think talking it through with a professional might be helpful, then sure, see someone.

Or, maybe as you implied, you just took a step back. You don't have to stay there. We all make a choice we regret now and then."

"Oh."

After he's gone, I stand for a long time trying to make sense of his actions, the ease or the respect with which he accepted my response that I didn't want to tell him more now. And then his suggestion, *even after* hearing of my failure, that I talk to Twila. And his lack of a reaction to the cookie thing. *"If you want to see someone..."* Like it wasn't a big deal. *"We all make a choice we regret now and then."*

But if he knew the truth, all the truth, he'd feel differently.

Of that I'm sure.

CHAPTER FOURTEEN

You do not need to know precisely what is happening, or
exactly where it is all going. What you need is to recognize
the possibilities and challenges offered by the present
moment, and to embrace them with courage, faith and hope.
Thomas Merton

ia

AFTER MY CLASSES on Wednesday I head to the library to do
some research. Not for a school project but for my own
knowledge. To figure out what I don't know. What I don't
understand. To find a way to change things. There has to be a
way for Manuel to become a citizen—some loophole he
hasn't thought of—a way for him to stay here, for his family
to stay here, within the bounds of the law. And if there is a

way, I will find it. Seeing him on Saturday fanned that ember, and I won't let the flame die. It's keeping me going.

Without something to do, a direction, I don't know... I'd cease to exist. Without Manuel... No. That's not going to happen. It's just not. But then I think of Twila and the decision she made, and the pain of that choice. A choice I had told her I didn't understand. But what I do understand is the ache she feels. How could she choose that ache? How does she have that strength?

I think again, as I have several times since we met, of her comment about our purpose—relationship with God. She believes God's given each of us gifts that He'll use for His purpose—His purposes become our purposes; His desires become our desires. She's still learning how to use the gifts God's given her. And I'm trying to figure out what gifts He's given me and how He might use them.

For now, my purpose is to figure out a way for Manuel to become a US citizen, or at least get a green card. *Is that your purpose, too, God?* It's the first time I've thought to ask God, to pray to seek His desire rather than my own. But as I pray the short prayer—the question for God—I'm not sure I want to know His answer. Because what if His purpose is different than my own? Would he change my desires to match His?

What if God's plan doesn't include my relationship with Manuel? I can't even go there, not now.

Twila and I had spent hours together on Saturday, sitting at the table at GoodLife, telling each other our stories. When I told her about Manuel, the lie, the words poured out of me. I'd had no one to talk to, no way to get the anger and hurt out. When I was done, and I glanced at the time, I was shocked. *"I'm sorry. I talked nonstop. I totally took over the conversation."*

"No, you needed to talk. It helps. Anyway, I talked a lot, too.

And thanks. Things seem, like, easier somehow, just sharing them with someone."

She was right. Circumstances haven't changed, but now there's a friend to share the load.

I enter the library, pass the information desk, and find a cubby where I can work. I slip my backpack off my shoulders, set it beside the chair, and pull my laptop out. I set it on the desktop and as it powers up, I settle into the quiet space. Students around me read or look at computers, some typing as they do. There's a welcome hush here, conversations are few, and most are quiet. I've come to love the library, the wealth of knowledge available, the time to search and study and learn.

Talking to Manuel on Saturday made me realize how little I know about our federal and state immigration policies. Since he told me, I've spent hours online reading articles and documentation and viewing videos of young Latinos who've applied for DACA—the immigration policy implemented last year by President Obama.

I also now understand AB 60, the Program Information Assembly Bill signed by Governor Brown that will allow for issuance of a driver's license for those Californians unable to provide proof of legal presence in the United States. Another program is underway, too—the Low Cost Auto Insurance Program implemented by the state insurance commissioner. Following the implementation of AB 60, the program will offer affordable insurance to the many undocumented immigrants, and others, unable to afford traditional auto insurance.

I return to the website with the information I've read about AB 60 and the insurance program and scribble more notes on a pad of paper. The information fascinates me.

Both the bill and the insurance program have their opponents, I learn, but it seems that both will provide a measure of safety for residents of our state. Applicants will have to pass both the state's written test and driving test, ensuring they are familiar with the laws and can drive safely. And a provision for auto insurance, which includes basic liability coverage, protects all of us. I also learn the licensing fees and taxes on gas will feed the economy.

None of that information will keep Manuel here, but once I started doing the research, I couldn't stop. And I've just begun to scratch the surface. There's still so much I need to learn.

There are, I've discovered, so many young people who were brought to this country as babies or young children who are, by no fault of their own, undocumented immigrants. They know nothing but life in the United States, and the idea of deportation to a country many of them have no connection with, no memory of, can be nothing but terrifying.

The thought of leaving everything I've known, the people I love, to have my entire life uprooted... My breath catches as I consider what that would feel like. And I can only begin to imagine the fear so many live with.

The fear Manuel and his family live with every single day.

Did Manuel's parents lie to him so he wouldn't have to live with that fear? So he could grow up experiencing the same freedoms others enjoy? It's the first time I've considered why Manuel's parents did what they did. But does that excuse the lie?

"You always tell de truth, Pia. Always. You understand?"

Is there ever a time when truth isn't best? When a lie is justified? Maybe even better than the truth? It's a question I want to ask my mama. What would she have done if she were in Manuel's parents' circumstances? Staying here illegally made their whole lives a lie. Would going back to Mexico have really been that bad?

Manuel is right. I don't really understand. I haven't lived what he's living. I'll never know that type of fear for myself. And as he reminded me, his parents didn't lie. But they did withhold the truth, which is the same thing. But maybe, as he said, they believed the laws would change. They hoped there would be a way to make things right.

The words on the screen blur as does my mind. I can't make sense of it all.

My own parents left Mexico, too, and I've heard Mama's stories of her childhood, a life I try to envision when she speaks but one I can barely imagine. Mama has spoken of the time and money it took to first secure their legal entry into California from Mexico, then the years and the cost it took to finally become citizens. They only had the means because my father came from Mexico City, his family had money. What did they do? And what made my father and mother decide to leave their families to come here?

There is so much I've never asked. Never thought to ask. But they spent the money and did the work to become citizens. There is a photo of my mother and father smiling, heads held high, at their naturalization ceremony in Sacramento, the state's capitol. My father wore a shirt and tie, and Mama a maternity dress.

I sit back in my seat, my hands still on the keyboard. I made these issues about me, about how I feel. About the pain I'd experience if I lost Manuel. But the impact is so much bigger than me. It affects so many lives. So many who live in fear, who stand to lose all they've known and loved. I have to do something. After 9/11 attitudes changed, and fear of illegal immigrants set it. I see both sides. But we can't let fear rule, can we? There are no easy answers.

Is there an answer for Manuel? If I can find an answer for Manuel, then there is an answer for others.

I turn my attention back to the laptop screen. Is what I

was sure I'd find, if I worked hard enough, here? Is there a solution? Why do so many risk coming here illegally only to live a life of lies? The one person, besides Manuel, who might answer that question is the one person I don't want to talk to about this.

But I want to understand. I need to understand.

My stomach clenches at the thought of telling my mama the truth about Manuel.

But it's a truth I have to tell, so maybe it's time to tell that truth.

It's already dark when I pull in next to my mama's car in the driveway. The lights in the cottage are on—the little house warm and welcoming. Mama will have something in the oven or on the stove for dinner, and she'll want to hear about my day. *"What did you learn, Pia?"* The question she's asked me almost every school day since kindergarten will be asked again tonight, most likely, over dinner at the table, where the two of us have sat together for so many years, unless we're at the café.

Does she drive me crazy? Yes, a lot of times. But I respect her, the hard work she's done as a single mother, the way she's raised me, the values she's instilled in me, and the sense of security, stability she's created. Partly, because she could. She didn't have to hide. Didn't have to worry about who might knock on the door and rip us from the life she made for us, to send her back to a country she no longer knows, one that holds nothing but hardship for her.

What did I learn today, Mama? Too much to put into words. But I need to know more.

As much as I respect her, she also wants control. Of most things. Including me. Tonight if I decide to tell her the truth about Manuel, she will freak out. Totally. *"I told you, Pia. Din't I tell you?"* I can hear her already. But there will be more than her anger. There will probably be boundaries, too. *"As long as you live here, there are rules you obey. Understand?"*

Will she tell me I can't see Manuel?

I grab my backpack out of the passenger seat and get out of the car. All the way home, I considered everything she might say and prepared a response for each supposed reaction. I will argue Manuel's case. And my own. Our case.

And the case of so many others.

But can I win? Can I convince my mama? That's where the argument falls apart. Convince her of what? To let me continue seeing a man with no guarantees? Someone who is here today but could be gone tomorrow? A man who comes from a family who lives a lie?

As I reach the front door, the assurance I'd felt as I waged the battle in my mind vanishes, and instead of one adult woman confronting another, I stand at the door of my home, a little girl who just needs her mama's love. Who just needs to hear that everything will be okay. Tears prick my eyes. I want her to make everything all better, like I used to believe she could do.

But now I know. There are some things not even she can fix. Some things that seem impossible. *"In America, with God, all things are possible."* How often have I heard her say those words? But are they really true?

MAMA SPOONS the pork tomatillo stew into bowls and sets them on the table, fragrant steam rising from each bowl. I take a warm homemade tortilla from the basket on the table as she takes her seat across from me. I set the tortilla on my plate as she bows her head.

"Jesus, thank You for de food You give us. Thank You for de freedom we enjoy. Amen."

It is the same prayer she has prayed at every meal since my memories begin, but tonight the prayer bothers me. Why do we enjoy freedom while others are bound by poverty and all it leads to? Including the laws and the lies that bind them. None of it makes sense.

I open my eyes to the food in front of me but want none of it. I'm not ready for her questions either, so I pick up my spoon and dip it into the soupy stew. Eating is the easier option. The spicy broth warms me, and I take a second bite, and a third, then I set the spoon down.

Across the table, Mama watches me. "Dat all you eat?"

I look up from the bowl and meet her gaze. "I want to talk to you." I lower my hands to my lap and grab the paper napkin there, crumpling it in my fist. "I want to tell you something."

Her eyebrows rise. "Dis about *him*? About why he make you cry?"

My heartbeat throbs in my ears and I hesitate. But no, I won't let her intimidate me. I sit up straighter and square my shoulders. "This is about me."

I take a deep breath, the words I'd planned to say run through my mind, but a question, like a sliver, irritates. "Why do you always say that in America, with God, all things are possible?"

"Why? Because dat true, of course."

"But..." I let the words form so I can voice the feeling that's bothered me. "Aren't all things possible with God in Mexico, too?"

She shakes her head. "It different there."

"God's different there?"

"He..." She hesitates, and her forehead creases slightly. "No. He de same there. Everywhere."

"So, all things are possible with God in America and in Mexico?" This was not part of the conversation I'd rehearsed on the way home, but it suddenly seems important.

"With God all things are possible. Everywhere."

"So, it's about God, not about the country?"

Her eyes narrow. "What you asking?"

I'm not sure what I'm asking, exactly, or why I'm asking—it's something I'll have to think about later—so I return to my mental script. "Is there ever a time when a lie is better than the truth?"

"Why you questioning everything I tell you? No. Truth is always best."

"What about during World War II when people hid Jews to protect them from the Nazis? They lied to protect them." It's a question I've wondered about as I did my research in the library today.

"Dat different." Her spoon is suspended halfway between her bowl and her mouth.

"How is it different?"

She lowers the spoon back to the bowl. Like me, it appears she's finished eating. "Why you asking me? What got into you?"

I take a deep breath. "I'm trying to understand—I need to understand some things. I need your help to understand." I watch as she takes in my words, words I planned, yes, but words that are true.

She nods just once. "I help you."

"Thank you." I twist the napkin in my lap. "Okay, I want to understand why some people are willing to live a life that isn't true—a life that causes them to lie. I want to know why some people come here, from Mexico, from other countries, illegally. They come because America is free, but how can they be free if they live a lie?"

"They can't be free and live a lie at de same time."

"So why do they come? Why do they stay?"

I watch as she gets where my questions are leading. I twist the napkin again and again.

"Because, maybe some freedom better than no freedom. Corrupt government, poverty, *drugs*."

I know how she feels about drugs without her emphasis. She's made it more than clear as I've grown up.

"It no good for many people in Mexico and many other countries. They hope for something better here. It's not right if they don't do it legally, but what they live with, dat not right either." She leans forward. "So, he undocumented, just like I said. I was right."

Tears prick my eyes, but I blink them back. "He's undocumented, yes, but I didn't know. And now..." I look down at the table, the lump in my throat aching.

"And now it too late?"

Her tone is gentler than I expect. Does she understand? I look up and her expression answers my question. She will never understand. "Mama—"

She points her finger at me. "I tell you, Pia. I tell you from de beginning he not good for you. I tell you, but you won't listen. Maybe now you listen. You walk away. He has nothing to give you. Nothing. You hear me?"I push back from the table. "You're wrong." I try to keep my tone level, but my voice shakes.

"Oh, I not wrong." She places her hands palms down on the table. "I not wrong at all."

I stand, "You won't even talk to me about Manuel. You won't listen. I love him, Mama. I love him!" It's the first time I've admitted to her what I feel for Manuel.

"You get over him."

"Get over him? It's not that easy, Mama. I don't want to get—"

"Dat's your only choice." She gets up from the table too

and comes to stand in front of me. "There no other choice for you. You think you love him. But there no future with him. You have opportunities, Pia. You a smart girl and you work hard. You make something of yourself. But with him, you have nothing."

I swipe at the tears running down my cheeks now. "You just don't get it." The arguments I'd planned, the facts, the information about DACA, the possibilities—all of it is gone from my mind, replaced by a desperation to make her understand.

"Oh, I understand. I understand much more than you think. Not only do I understand, I know—"

"You don't know everything! You don't! It's arrogant to think you know everything."

The lines around her eyes and mouth deepen, and the heat in her eyes cause me to take a step back.

"You the one who don't understand." She turns back to the table, takes our bowls still filled with stew to the sink, where she dumps the contents, turns on the water, then the garbage disposal.

I have been dismissed. Conversation over. At least in her mind. I wait until she's turned off the garbage disposal and the water, then I go to her. "Mama, I'm sorry. But you've always listened to me and supported me. Won't you just—"

"No." She turns and looks at me and points beyond me to my room.

I know she thinks she has spoken the final word on the topic, but she's wrong. I turn and go, but only for now. I will make her listen to me. I will make her understand.

I SIT ON MY BED, back against the wall, knees pulled to my chest. I'm nineteen years old, an adult, yet she still sends me to my room. And I go. As I came in, I shoved the door closed, intending to slam it as hard as I could, to make the house shake, the windows rattle, but I caught it just in time, almost slamming my own hand between the door and the jamb. I closed the door, firmly, but without the slam. If I'm adult, I must act like one.

My anger found its release in tears and in the thoughts that took over my mind. *She is so stubborn! So arrogant! She thinks she knows everything!* Until the anger waned or was at least contained. Contained? Yes. It's still smoldering, embers still crackling. It's a fire I can't let die. Won't let die.

It's a fire I need. Though I'm not sure why. But there will come a time when I will need to fan the flame, when I will need it to blaze again.

For now, nothing has changed. The boundary I expected wasn't set. She didn't forbid me to see Manuel. She may have thought the boundary was implied when she told me to get over him, but she didn't specifically tell me not to see him. Because I still live with her, it may come to that, but for now, I am still free to see him.

Mama is wrong—she doesn't know everything despite what she thinks or says. Manuel has a lot to offer me—love and respect and shared interests and beliefs. And that's just the beginning. What he can't offer me is a guarantee. I get that. The future is uncertain, but isn't that true for everyone? For every circumstance? Why can't she see that?

She knows there are no guarantees. If there were, my father, her husband, would still be alive, wouldn't he? Mama thought she had a guarantee, but she was wrong. None of us have that kind of control.

And if all things are possible with God, then all things are possible with my relationship with Manuel.

Why can't she see that?

Or is it that she won't see it?

CHAPTER FIFTEEN

Causes have effects, and if we lie to ourselves and to others,
then we cannot expect to find truth and reality whenever we
happen to want them. If we have chosen the way of falsity we
must not be surprised that truth eludes us when we finally
come to need it!
Thomas Merton

llyn

I MAKE the turn from Highway 1 onto Lansing and follow the
road along the cliff, past the north entrance to the Headlands
State Park and into the village. But rather than go straight to
the café, I turn toward the water tower. Pulling into the gravel
driveway feels as natural as breathing. The key to the front
door is in the glove compartment of my car for safekeeping.
Safekeeping? Who am I kidding? It's hidden there. I was afraid

Miles might notice the key on my key ring and ask me about it, or come across it in my purse if he was looking for something.

And the fact that I felt the need to hide it? That kernel of truth wrapped in the big fat lie I've told, or at least the omission of truth I've chosen, sits like a stale bagel in the pit of my stomach. Whatever I'd hoped to gain by leasing the water tower has instead led to… What? Whatever it is, it feels familiar. Like my GPS led me somewhere other than where I thought I was going. And now that I've arrived, the landmarks are unsettling. Paralyzing, actually.

I stare at the house, my former home, but make no move to get out of the car. What's the point? The house holds nothing for me, I know that now, except, of course, a large monthly payment.

As I sit parked in the driveway, a dark cloud overhead gives way and raindrops pelt the windshield. There's no point sitting here so I back out of the driveway and turn back onto the lane. When I reach the road, I stop, begin to pull out, then hit the brakes.

A few paces off the left fender of my car, a young woman, head down, hood covering her head, hands tucked in the pockets of her hoodie, is walking, and it's clear she hasn't seen me. Twila. If I hadn't seen her, well, I'd hate to think what would have happened. I roll down the car window to ask if she wants a ride, then hesitate. How will I explain why I'm here?

She looks up, sees me, and stops. Then she pulls one hand from her pocket and waves.

I lean my head out the window. "Hop in. You'll get soaked out there."

Twila jogs in front of the car and then over to the passenger side, opens the door, and slides in. "Thanks." She pushes her hood back, then turns and looks at me. The storm swirling in her gray eyes rivals the one moving in from the Pacific. When she looks away, she wipes her eyes on the sleeve of her hoodie, but I don't know if they're tears or raindrops. "I didn't know it was supposed to rain."

"Were you walking to the Headlands?"

"Yeah." She stares out the passenger window.

I turn right toward Headlands State Park, the entrance just a block or so down the road.

She turns and looks at me. "Where're you going?"

"Might as well go where you were headed. How about we park and watch the storm for a few minutes?"

"Sure. Thanks."

I drive the short distance to where a row of parking spaces face the ocean. I pull into a space and leave the engine running to keep the heater going. We sit without saying anything for a few minutes, rain pattering on the roof and windshield of the car, creating a safe, intimate environment I hope will put Twila at ease.

What will put me at ease? Twila hasn't asked me why I was at the water tower. She's clearly too lost in her own thoughts to have considered why I was there. I exhale, the muscles in my shoulders pulled taut like yeast dough being stretched begin to relax.

"So, you were at the water tower?"

The dough is stretched tight again. Come to think of it, the stretching and folding process for dough is done to orient the gluten. Does everything come back to gluten?

"Ellyn?"

I glance at Twila. "Oh, sorry, I was thinking about... Never mind." I look back out the windshield. "No. I mean, yes, I was there, but just in the driveway."

"Do you miss it?"

"I do, or I did, or I thought I did. But, no." I owe her the truth, so I look at her again and shrug. "I don't know. I'm trying to figure that out."

"It's a cool place and you lived there a long time. I could see why you might miss it."

"Really? Well. Maybe." I shift in the seat so I'm facing Twila, at least as much as is possible in the tight space of the car. "So, girly, how are you? I was going to call you today to check on you, to let you know we're thinking about you, and we love you, and…"

As Twila's eyes glisten with tears, I reach over and give her arm a gentle squeeze. "I'm sorry. This must be so hard."

"So…" She wipes her eyes. "When did you find out? Did Will…?"

Her tears fall freely now and I reach into the console and pull out a packet of tissues and hand it to her.

"Thanks," she mumbles.

"He called a few of nights ago and told Miles."

"How'd he seem? Is he, like, okay?"

"From what Miles had shared with me, I'd say he's confused and, like you, hurting." Twila's tears tell me she's hurting and I don't sense that the postponement of the engagement, or the breakup, offers her relief in any way. But then, I don't know, do I?

"Honey, do you want to tell me what happened? I'm here for you, to listen, if talking will help."

"I just…I felt like…I had to come home. And he didn't understand. But it's bigger than that, and I'm just, like, I'm not sure, you know?"

"Not sure about Will, that he's the right one?"

"No! I mean, I love him, I totally…" She covers her face with her hands.

"Oh, girly," I whisper as I reach for her again. I put my hand on her shoulder as she cries. "I'm so sorry you're going through this."

When she calms again, she wipes her eyes and blows her nose. Then she looks at me. "I've only told Pia."

"What about your mom?" Twila had shared how much she loves and respects her mom. Why wouldn't she talk to Nerissa?

"I can't. Not this. Not now."

"Why not now?" As soon as the question leaves my mouth, it feels intrusive. "Sorry, I don't mean to pry. Well, actually, I guess I do. Not pry, but...I just care."

She says nothing, doesn't respond to either my question or my bumbling statement. "Okay. Well"—I glance at the clock on the dash—"I have time to listen to as much as you want to tell me." The rain on the roof and windshield pounds now instead of patters, and I have to raise my voice. "Sometimes it helps to say things out loud to someone else. Right?"

"My mom said the same thing over the weekend—that sometimes talking about something robs it of its power." She seems to weigh whether or not she wants to tell me more.

Lord, help her, whatever she needs.

Twila shifts in her seat so she's facing me, and as soon as she's made that move, the beating rain causing the ruckus inside the car lightens to a sprinkle, quieting the din. She wipes her eyes one more time, then takes a deep breath. "So, you know how I sort of know things sometimes? Like we talked about the other day at the café?"

I just nod, not wanting to disrupt her train of thought.

"I felt like, I mean, I kind of had this strong sense that my mom was going through something. I didn't know what, and when I called her, she seemed okay. But, like, I couldn't let it go. And I kept telling Will that I knew something was wrong, but he thought I was overreacting, and I get why he thought that, but I...I guess I just wanted him to trust me. I mean, I know it's weird, but—"

"It's not weird, honey. It isn't common—it's a special gift."

She shrugs. "Will wants to understand it and be support-ive, but when I told him I just needed to be here for my mom, we got into this big discussion again about how God's gifted each of us and how we see ourselves using those gifts. And, like, I don't know how I'm supposed to use this…this…thing. I mean, it just happens and then I respond. But Will thought I was reacting rather than responding, and…maybe, but it's my mom and I'm all she has, and I couldn't just ignore it. And then as we were talking about it, this…this…*feeling*, like, overwhelming, hit me…" She wraps her arms around herself and turns and looks back out the window.

"Twila? What? What was it?"

She continues staring out the windshield. "Darkness," she whispers.

"Darkness?"

She looks at me again. "Yeah. I didn't understand then. I just knew, I mean, I had to…come home. I told Will I was going and that I didn't know how long I'd have to stay. And he…" She shakes her head. "I mean, I get it. I was intense and insisting I had to leave, and he said that maybe I'm too attached to my mom and not ready to get married, and like, it just sort of fell apart after that." She stares down at her lap, her energy spent, it seems.

I consider what she's shared, and really, I can see both sides. But was that enough to call off their engagement? "You said you didn't understand then what was going on with your mom, exactly. What about now?"

"I know now. Not all of it, but the gist of it. I figured it out this weekend."

I'm almost afraid to ask, but we've come this far. "What is it?"

"A sifting."

"Sifting?" I'm sure my confusion shows. "Like flour?"

"Wheat."

Gluten? Again? "I don't understand."

"You know in the Bible when Jesus warns Peter, before the Crucifixion, he tells him that Satan has demanded to sift him like wheat, but that Jesus has prayed that his faith won't fail?"

"That thing with the rooster? When Peter denies Jesus?"

"Yeah."

"Okay, so your mom is… What?"

"Like, it's a spiritual battle. That's the darkness I felt. That's why I need to be here, to pray, to battle with her, for her. To…"—she shrugs—"I don't know. I just think I'm supposed to be here."

"But she doesn't know that's why you're here?"

"I don't know. I mean, I'm just beginning to understand, so I haven't talked to her about it yet. She seems okay. There's some stuff going on with my dad—financial stuff— but that's all I know right now. I'm praying and just waiting, you know?"

Do I know? I have no clue. "Okay, how can I help? What do you need?"

When she looks at me again, her eyes are wide, and the shadows beneath her eyes speak of the fatigue and grief she's feeling in the midst of whatever battle is being waged. One thing I do understand is why she wouldn't want to share the reason she and Will called off the wedding with Nerissa.

"Pray."

"You got it. What about Miles? May I share this with him? Ask him to pray?" As soon as I asked, I regret the question, though I'm not sure why. Of course, I'd tell Miles. Why wouldn't I?

"Sure. So, what about Will? Do you think, I mean…?" Tears fill her eyes again. "I can't believe it's just over, you know?"

I reach for Twila and wrap her in a hug. "I know, girly. I know."

～

AFTER I DROP Twila off at her cottage, I pull into the parking spot behind the café, the conversation with her playing on a loop in my mind. Running the same loop are dozens of unanswered questions. Questions Twila doesn't have answers for. What is it like to operate on that much faith? To walk away from so much because God revealed just enough to lead her home? I've never lived life like that—had that kind of faith. Do I even want that kind of faith? To trust so fully that I'd lay down everything to follow when nothing is clear except the invitation?

"Invitation? What kind of party is that?" I sigh. "Sorry, Lord." But as I issue yet another apology to God, is it necessary? Is it Him I doubt? Or is it Twila's discernment?

The most plausible answer is that leaving Will to come home was a big, fat mistake. Although Twila has a solid connection with her mom so unlike my fractured relationship with my own mother. To sense something was truly wrong and ignore it? Maybe Will is the one who made the mistake in not understanding Twila's need to be here.

Clearly, there are no easy answers, and that reality tugs at my heart. For both Twila and Will, but especially for... Nerissa. Huh. That's a surprise. I glance at the clock on the dash. I spent more than an hour with Twila. I reach for the phone sitting in the console, knowing once I go into the café, privacy will be nonexistent. I didn't arrive early enough to close the office door and get away with it. Who to call first? The therapist Shauna recommended? Or Nerissa?

Who was it that said, *"Keep your enemies close?"* I scroll through my list of contacts and find Nerissa's number and then pause. Nerissa's not my enemy. She never was. If anyone's the enemy, it's me. I'm my own worst enemy, as usual. Although, Nerissa does want to take butter out of my diet, so there is that.

But that's not what's bothered me most about her. It's how much I actually like her. More than that, it's that she is likable. She is a kindhearted, generous woman. And okay, moment of truth—that's what scares me and has always scared me. Just how good Nerissa is and how attractive goodness is to others, Miles included.

How's that for a moment of self-awareness? Maybe I don't need the therapist, after all.

Keep your enemies close? Where did that come from? What is wrong with me? And why do I keep asking that question? Clearly, I still need the therapist. Since I'm having a moment of self-awareness, I may as well take responsibility for myself, too.

What's the new therapist's name? I open the Notes app on my phone and search for the note I created with her name and number. "Serenity? That can't be right." I was obviously in a sugar coma when I typed her name. Maybe the number will be wrong, too. One can only hope. I key in the number next to the name, then lift the phone to my ear.

"You've reached the office of Dr. Serenity Sterling, I'm unavailable at the moment, but I look forward to talking with you. Please leave a message along with your number, and I'll return your call at my earliest convenience. I value you, and your time. I won't keep you waiting long."

From the sound of her voice I determine she's twelve, a mature twelve, but...Serenity? Really? Clearly, she had been born and raised here—a local—and her hippy parents were probably high when they named her.

When did I become the judge of the world? Good grief.

"Um, yes, I..." Am I really going to make an appointment?

Nerissa comes to mind again. "I'm sorry. I was referred by..." I leave the necessary information and then end the call.

I stare out the front windshield at the weathered, natural wood of the building next to the café, the gray tone just a few shades darker than the sandy earth the building seems to have grown out of. Beyond that, the horizon, sky, and sea are also gray. Again. "Appropriate," I mumble.

So great, I'll sit across from a twelve-year-old who will tell me exactly what's wrong with me. "Get over it, Ellyn. It was the right choice."

I grab my bag off the passenger seat and start to drop my phone into its depths when I remember the other call I was going to make.

How is Nerissa feeling about Twila and Will having called off their engagement? I assume she has friends besides Miles she talks to, but the village is small. And while I may not understand the specifics of what she's going through, I do know what the life of a single woman in this village is like. It can be a lonely life. And as much as I don't want to—

"Stop analyzing and just make the call, Ellyn. Now."

Again, the call goes to voice mail. Does no one answer the phone anymore? But this time rather than leave a message, I hang up. I'm not sure what I'd have said anyway. Maybe I just need to do as Twila asked: pray.

I STUMP my way through the alley and over the path between the garden and the back of the café. I pause at the gate to the garden. The dark greens and purples of the winter lettuces wave in the breeze, droplets of rain shivering on the leaves. Condensation dots the glass inside the greenhouse. I close my eyes and imagine the organic scent of peat and soil, mingled with the spicy scent of the potted herbs. If only I had time to lose myself for a while in the plants. Instead, I turn toward the café, lug myself up the steps to the back door, and enter what, by this time, is the fray of the day.

I cross the kitchen, head down, stride purposeful.

"There you are. It about time."

I keep walking, enter the office, and drop my bag on the desk, hoping Rosa hasn't followed me.

"We need to talk. We need to change—"

I hold up one hand. "Not now, Rosa."

"When? You tell me when."

"Fifteen minutes."

She raises one eyebrow, indicating she doesn't believe me. "I hold you to it."

"I'd expect nothing less."

The new line cook passes behind Rosa and nods to me. "Chef."

It's my turn to raise an eyebrow. "Did you hear that? That's called respect."

"He new. He get over it."

"Very funny."

"I be back." She turns on her heel, her dark curls bouncing.

"Wait." I'll regret this, I know, but she's piqued my curiosity. "What do we need to change?"

She turns back. "De wine."

I stare at her trying to make sense of what she's said. "So, now you're a sommelier, too?" Pia passes the open office door. "Oh, Pia, wait."

She comes back, leans into the office, eyes focused on the floor.

"Hi, honey, hold on just a minute. I need to show you something." I look back to Rosa. "Why do we need to change the—?"

"Nope!" She glances at Pia, then back to me. "Fifteen

minutes. Dat what you say. I come back." She skirts around Pia—they didn't look at one another or exchange words—and is out the office door before I can say anything more.

I stare after her. I've often wished I could silence Rosa, but the reality is unsettling. "What was that about?"

Pia's gaze is still glued to the floor.

"Pia?"

When she finally looks at me, I notice dark smudges under her unusually puffy and bloodshot eyes. Not unlike Twila's eyes. Heartache must be going around. "Uh-oh. What happened?"

"I'm sure she'll be happy to tell you."

I am often amazed by the respect Pia, at only nineteen, affords her mother. It is a testament to both Rosa's mothering and Pia's character. So the sarcasm or anger in her tone tells me all is not well between daughter and mama.

"Is it Manuel?" He's the one topic on which the two are divided, though I'm not sure why. Rosa has never backed up her stance that Manuel isn't good for Pia with any sort of evidence. Manuel has always seemed friendly and respectful when he's made deliveries to the café. And he works hard, a trait Rosa demands. So her assertion is based on something deeper, I assume, and it's something she hasn't shared.

Pia's shoulders droop. Her fatigue, both physical and emotional, is evident as she nods.

"Hang in there, honey."

"Easier said than done. She's so..."

"Exasperating, controlling, annoying?" I smile.

"Literally. Sorry, what did you want to show me?"

"Oh. Right." I grab a stack of menu inserts off my desk. "Here. I made a change to the menu."

"Got it. I'll replace them."

"Thank you. And listen, things will..." I note Pia's expression again, the swollen eyes, the slump of her shoulders, and

I rethink the platitude I was about to offer. "I'm sorry things are hard. Let me know if I can do anything, okay?"

Pia's eyes fill with tears and then she quickly averts her gaze as she nods.

"Take a minute, honey. The office is all yours." I give her shoulder a squeeze as I pass her on my way to the kitchen. I close the office door behind me as I leave.

Whatever has gone on between Pia and Rosa has taken a toll. I'd like to sit them both down and intervene. After all, didn't Rosa make me part of the family with her declaration of motherhood? But there isn't time now.

As I make my way to the kitchen, I think about when our next delivery from Toulouse is due—it's still two days out before Manuel will drop our shipment. I trust Rosa to behave professionally, well, for the most part. But when angry, she is a pint-sized brick of dynamite, and we don't need her ignited. I glance at my watch. The kitchen will have to wait. I better have that conversation with Rosa now.

I find her in the back room, sitting at the family table going through the laundry delivery—counting napkins and aprons. "Let's talk. What is it we need to change with the wine?"

"De order from Toulouse. Dat wine no good. We make a change."

"So their award-winning pinot noir, the one we serve, the one that sells more than any other wine on our list, is no longer good? And how do you know that? Last time I checked, you didn't drink wine."

"I hear things. You know dat. I talk to customers."

"What's the real reason, Rosa? Is it the wine or the person who delivers the wine?"

She turns away from me. "I don't know what you talking about."

"Truth, Rosa. Remember, the truth is everything, as you've told me."

When she looks back at me, her lips are pursed, but it's the look in her eyes that makes me soften my tone. "What happened, Mama? What's going on?"

"He not good for her. I tell her dat. You know I tell her dat. She not believe me. But now, now she knows de truth. He not de one. But she..." Rosa takes a deep breath. "She not listen."

"Do you want to tell me why he isn't good for her?"

"No."

"Maybe I can help."

"No. You can't help. No one can help. She need to get over him. Dat her only option. And if he come here to deliver de wine and she see him all de time..." She shakes her head.

"Is Pia in danger?"

Surprise registers in Rosa's eyes. "No. But he hurt her, dat for sure. He hurt her..." She puts her hand to her chest, over her heart. "He hurt her heart."

"I'll make a call. I'll see if someone else can make the delivery or if Manuel can come earlier in the day, before Pia's shift. Okay?"

Rosa's dark eyes soften as she nods. "Yes, thank you, Chef."

I stare at her a moment as the gravity of the situation hits me. "It's that bad?"

"It dat bad."

I step toward Rosa and give her a quick hug. "I'm sorry. Let me know if there's anything more I can do to help."

CHAPTER SIXTEEN

To enter into the realm of contemplation, one must in a
certain sense die: but this death is in fact the entrance into a
higher life. It is a death for the sake of life, which leaves
behind all that we can know or treasure as life, as thought, as
experience as joy, as being.

Thomas Merton

erissa

I STARE at the pages of my calendar open on my desk.
Thursday already? Twila's been home a full week. I flip
through the calendar—the year is still young. The thought of
having to fill each day, having to create something out of
nothing—more work, more income, more life—constricts
like a snake suffocating its prey.

I close the planner, and that simple action seems to drain

me of the last of my energy. Getting up, closing the office, walking home, cooking dinner... I close my eyes, wanting to give in, to give up, to go to sleep. Sleep? Will I ever sleep again? Sleep through the night? Wake rested?

Do I even want to wake?

The question startles me. But even as I deny the question, the thought, I sense I need to sit with it for a moment. To acknowledge it and turn it over to the One who I've trusted in my weakest moments—His strength through me. Yet, how many times have I hoped for, in spite of hardship, a new day? I've hoped, only to awaken again, day after day, to heartache. Or at least struggle.

No. That's not true. I've known true hope.

I must change my focus, my thoughts.

But I can't.

Can't? Even in my depleted state, *can't* is a waving red flag, one I don't miss.

I open my eyes. I am here. Now. In my office. I will use the last of my waning energy to fight the pull into the sulphuric pit of self-pity. If I change my thoughts, my emotions will follow, and maybe even my body.

Fight, Nerissa, fight.

I search my mind for some piece of truth, something on which to focus my thoughts. *"I will never leave you nor forsake you. I will never leave you nor forsake you."* I rehearse the memorized words. They aren't whispered within me; they aren't spoken to my soul. The voice I've heard, the presence, palpable in the past in a way I don't have words to explain, is absent. Gone.

Just like the ring.

Have You forsaken me? Abandoned me?

As I finally acknowledge the question that has languished in my soul since losing the ring, or perhaps since I read the letter from my attorney, an army invades my soul. Ant-like it crawls up and over my shoulder, a tingling irritant I attempt to swat away, but the action does no good. The army creeps and crawls over my shoulder and into my soul, where it takes up temporary residence as it mines my peace and then carts it away, bit by bit.

"No," I whisper, my mouth dry. "I believe in the peace that passes understanding, Jesus Christ." I say the words aloud, lay claim to the promise. I voice my belief so that whomever or whatever is listening knows the power they are up against. I say the words aloud to remind my God that I believe, to remind Him of the promises He's made through Jesus.

Yet, anxiety crawls.

What do You want me to do? I don't know what else to do. I don't speak my questions, my doubt, aloud.

Now my mind, like the ants, busies itself, moving, marching, searching. Solutions exist and I will find them. Twila comes to mind, her broken engagement, her pain. I must remain strong for Twila. I am, I have been, the peace in her storm for so many years. The rain of uncertainty beats on her, just as it does on me, but I must remain that calm center for her.

I must find a way to earn more income, to make up the deficit, to provide. I must work harder, work longer, work more creatively to come up with another way—

"Stop!" I must rein in the chaos. I must change my thoughts. I must—

"Mom?"

I startle at the sound, my body jumping reflexively, adrenaline coursing. "What?"

"Whoa, sorry. I didn't mean to scare you. Are you okay?"

Twila. It's just Twila. How long has she been here?

She moves from the door to stand across from me, the desk between us. I focus my gaze on her face. "Yes." I force the word out of my mouth, then try again. "Yes, I'm okay. What are you doing?"

"It's late, almost dark. You weren't home and you walked to Corners this morning, so, like, I thought you'd walk home before dark. I texted but you didn't respond."

I glance at the phone on my desk. There is a text, unread, from Twila. I pick up the phone to see if I'd inadvertently silenced it, but no. I just didn't hear the text come in. I was lost in my own mind. "I'm sorry. I didn't..." I glance around the office as though I've just walked in myself. The lights are off, the space shadowed, nearly dark. No wonder Twila asked if I'm okay. "Do you mind turning on the lights?" I point to the switch on the wall behind her.

As the office is illuminated, so is my mind. The ants settle. "I was..."—I gesture to the planner on my desk—"considering the year ahead, making a few plans, or trying to, and then I got lost...in thought."

Twila stares at me with a knowing that's unsettling. As unsettling as the nearly manic swings of my mind and mood. "I'm sorry if I worried you."

"So, do you want a ride? Home?"

"Yes. Thank you for thinking of it." I get up from the desk and take my coat off the rack in the corner of the office. I pull it on, my back to Twila. I take a moment to focus. Here. Then I turn and face her again. "How was your day? Or, more importantly, how are you doing?"

She shrugs. "I'm okay, I guess."

Her response doesn't tell me much, but I don't press for more. There will be time to talk later, to delve deeper. When she's ready. I reach for my purse, then tuck the planner under my arm and we walk out of the office together. As we step into the dusk of evening, the cold, damp coastal air offers relief from the dry heat of the office and I breathe deep, filling my lungs with the moist air. We both pause and stare out at the bay across from the office, the sky the shades of twilight, midnight blue and deep lavender, swirled with the last streaks of orange fade into the horizon.

Stillness envelops me—mind, body, and soul. Peace, however momentary, returns. Twila's shoulders rise and fall as she, too, breathes in the evening. Then she points up the street. "I parked up there, by the water tower."

The water tower is one of many in the county, one of a few on Main Street alone, that add to the charm of the area. The one she points toward is now surrounded by buildings. A wooden stairway leads to a restaurant on one side of the tower.

When we reach the car, I move to get in, then pause and look across the roof of the car to Twila. "Wait a minute. I have an idea."

"What?"

"Let's keep walking. Let's go to Ellyn's for dinner."

Even in the dim light, I see Twila's eyebrows rise in surprise.

"Um, like, that's going to cost—"

"I know." And I do, but... "Let's just splurge. Maybe it's an act of faith." I smile. "Or stupidity." Which makes Twila smile. "You're home, my bank accounts aren't empty yet, and if God's in control, then..." I shrug. God *is* in control, but that doesn't mean my actions won't come with consequences. I should save everything I have. Isn't that my part? To do what I can? To figure out how to earn more money while at the same time depending on God to lead? To save? To act wisely?

"Are you sure?"

Maybe it's the anxiety, the darkness of the last couple of hours, the last several nights, the lack of sleep, the struggle, the pain I know Twila is harboring, that makes me want to grab this moment of peace to simply be, enjoy, and live. To hold on to what I fear is fleeting. "No, I'm not sure. But let's do it anyway."

As we walk the last block, passing shops with *Closed* signs already hung, I sense the shadow of darkness trailing me. And I know, in the moments of light, I must give Twila all I have, all I can, because when the shadow overcomes me again, I will have little to offer.

For the first time since receiving the letter from my attorney, I sense more is going on than the financial stress Daniel's action induced. Twila's words had warned me, *"There's more,"* or perhaps they simply prepared me. God is allowing something. What and why, I don't know. But I will trust that whatever is going on hasn't caught Him unaware.

I OPEN the café's front door, the panes of glass sparkling, and hold it open for Twila. The last time I was here was for Ellyn and Miles's wedding reception. Tonight, as always, the atmosphere is a balm to the senses—the warmth of the lighting, including the candles flickering on each table next to small arrangements of fresh flowers, the scents of the rich fare cooking in the kitchen and served in the dining room—sizzling meats, sauces, herbs, garlic, and butter meld, offering both comfort and enticement. The clink of silverware and wine glasses, lilting conversations and laughter, provide a backdrop of welcome.

At the hostess station, Pia comes around the small counter, gives Twila a quick hug, and then smiles at me.

"Pia, nice to see you. Twila enjoyed her time with you over the weekend." A smile passes between the two young women. "Is your mother here? I'd love to say hello." At the mention of her mother, the smile fades from Pia's face.

"Yes, she's here. I'll send her over—"

"I here now." Rosa appears behind Pia, then steps in front of her. "I not see you for a while. What you think of our daughters? They friends now."

"Yes, it sounds like they enjoyed one another's company." I wrap my arm around Twila's shoulders. "It's good to see you again, Rosa."

Rosa stares at me a moment, then taps her forehead like she's just thought of something. "We have you over for dinner. That's what we do."

"That would be lovely, Rosa." Her invitation surprises me, but it would be enjoyable to spend time with Twila and Pia. And Rosa, too, of course. I smile at the thought. I could use a little of whatever it is that makes her so spunky. I'd love to get to know her better.

"I check de calendar and call you. I write your number down now." She reaches behind the hostess station and pulls out a notepad and pen.

As I give Rosa my number, Pia picks up two menus. When I've finished, she says she'll seat us.

"No, I seat them." Rosa tucks my number in the pocket of her apron and then takes the menus from Pia and walks toward the dining room. "I have special table for you," she says over her shoulder.

"I'll be right there," Twila says.

I follow Rosa to a table for two set in front of the large fieldstone fireplace, where a crackling wood fire burns.

"Best seat in de house."

"Rosa, thank you."

She pulls out a chair for me and I sit, then take the menu she offers.

"I tell Ellyn you here."

Before I can object, Rosa sets a menu at Twila's place, then turns on her heel and disappears into the dining room. I look back to where Twila stands talking with Pia. I am so grateful for the budding friendship between the two young women. *Thank you, Rosa.*

I close my eyes and inhale the comforting scent of the wood burning in the fireplace, along with the tantalizing scents coming from the kitchen. The table is set so both Twila and I can see the fireplace. The heat radiating from the fire warms me, soothes me, almost lulls me. It offers a sense of ease I haven't felt in many days, and my body responds in the same way my mind responds. It loosens. And releases the tensions it's held. For what feels like the first time in ages, I truly rest.

"Mom?"

Lids heavy, I open my eyes. "Hmm?"

"Were you asleep?"

"Almost."

"Do you want to go?"

"Go? No." I gaze around the café, then back to Twila. "I want to stay forever."

"You're sure?"

"Yes. Why?"

Twila pulls out the chair and takes her seat across from me, then shrugs. "You're tired. If you can sleep, then you should."

"It's a little early for bed, don't you think?" I smile.

"You need to sleep. And you're not. I've heard you. At night. You know?"

"I've woken you? I'm sorry. I thought I was—"

"No. I mean, you've been quiet. It's more like I wake because I know you're awake—unsettled or something."

I stare at Twila across the table, the light from the fire plays across her face and dances in her eyes. "Your intuition is so strong. You'll make a wonderful mother someday."

She drops her gaze to the tabletop. "Maybe. If I ever get that chance."

I open the menu, then pause as the meaning behind Twila's comment settles. I close the menu and set it back on the table. "Are you ready to talk about Will? About what happened? I respect your need for time, for space to process, but I'm here to—"

"I know. Thanks." She picks up her menu and seems to hide behind it. So I slowly follow her lead, my heart aching for her and the pain she's enduring. But I'm also confused. Why won't Twila tell me what's happened? It isn't like her to keep something from me. Is it just that she isn't ready to talk? A bit of the peace I've enjoyed since entering the café wings its way elsewhere. How I longed for it to perch and stay awhile.

Once we've both closed our menus and set them aside, Twila looks around the café, appearing to soak in the ambience just as I did when we entered. I hope at least she can rest this evening, find peace here.

"I'm so glad you and Pia have connected."

"Yeah, me too. We have a lot in common."

"Did I sense some tension between Rosa and Pia?"

Twila glances back at Pia, then looks across the table at me. "Yeah, there's some definite tension. Didn't you say once that anger is rooted in fear?"

"Oftentimes that's true."

"Yeah, that makes sense. So, what are you going to have?"

Whatever Pia has shared with Twila is between the two of them. "The roasted chicken with rosemary au jus, I think." I reach for the menu to glance at it one more time. "What about you?"

"Hey, where's your ring?"

I close the menu and lift my left hand, staring at the bare ring finger, again. "I lost it. I've searched everywhere, even in your room when you were in the shower this morning. It's gone."

Twila glances at her own bare ring finger, then looks back to me. "Sorry. I know it was important to you. Will you get another one?"

"I don't know."

"Why? I mean, why wouldn't you?"

It wasn't the ring itself that was significant. It's what it represented. Why wouldn't I replace it? Because I don't want to spend the money right now? No, it isn't the money. I want, maybe even need, to find the ring. The original symbol of my commitment to Christ. What I want is for Him to return it to me.

The cloud of uncertainty—or is it doubt?—descends again. *Lord, where are You?*

"Mom?"

"What? Oh... I'm sorry. I guess I'm just hoping it will still turn up."

Twila's quiet for a moment, then seems to make a decision. "So, like, after the divorce, why...?" Her gray eyes cloud over and she starts again. "Why didn't you go out? Did you think about getting married again? I mean, why did you, you know, make that commitment to God?"

"We've talked about it." But as I remind Twila of that fact, I realize she needs to hear it again or she wouldn't have asked. "I thought I might meet someone and marry again. I hadn't ruled out the idea, but I knew I'd wait until you were grown. I wanted to focus on you and your needs. The divorce brought a lot of grief into your life."

She nods. "Yeah, but it had to happen. I get that now."

"I know you do. And I'm sorry for what you've gone through in your own relationship with your father."

"So, what happened though? I mean, once I got older you didn't date anyone. For a while, I sort of thought maybe you and Miles might go out."

With the mention of his name, I'm swept back into the

dreams of Miles—recurring dreams, it turns out, and the emotional intensity that's swirled through the short hours of sleep and followed me into the days. The longing they've evoked.

I glance down at the tabletop, pick up my salad fork, and move it over a quarter of an inch or so. Something to do as I ensure my emotions are tucked in place before looking back to Twila. "I'd made the commitment to God before Miles and I became friends. That's all we've ever been, or would have been. He's a good man, but by the time Sarah had died and he was ready to..." I shake my head. "It seemed clear that God was enough. Is enough. More than enough. He had met my every need and I didn't want to divide my focus."

I was so certain of the commitment I made. "I wanted that intimacy with Him, and Him alone. Romantic relationships, marriage, can divide that focus."

"Do you still feel that way?"

I glance down at my finger where evidence of the ring is still visible, the skin worn smooth where it encircled my finger for so long. "Now, it's more than a feeling. It's a choice. Emotional love, much like the sea, ebbs and flows. Passion is a wonderful feeling, but it is the commitment, the choice to love that stands the test of time."

"So even if you met someone else and fell in love, you're committed to God. Like, you just wouldn't consider it?"

"Honey, I know the choice I made is unusual, and most people don't or won't understand. But it was right for me, at the time. It's still right for me." Am I working to convince Twila? Or myself? "If God wants something else for me, I trust He'll make that clear."

I move to twist the band on my finger as I have so many times before, a habit formed, and then I realize, again, that the ring is no longer there.

A wave of loss crashes over me. Not for the lost symbol,

but rather the loss of the emotional connection I've felt for so long. *Are You testing my commitment? Is that what's happening? Will I still choose You in spite of what I feel or don't feel?*

Is what I said to Twila true? Do I still choose You and You alone?

Even while longing for another?

"Rosa, the town crier, told me you two were here. How are you?" Ellyn stands next to Twila and drapes an arm around her shoulder in the same way Miles has so often done. And with that thought, my face heats and I look away from Ellyn. I search the café for something to focus on as Twila responds to Ellyn.

I'm grateful for their exchange of conversation—it gives me a few moments to gather my emotions. When I return my attention to Ellyn, she is looking at me, a question in her eyes. "The fire is lovely, Ellyn. I've not sat here before."

"It's a perfect night for it. Enjoy. If you get too warm, we can move you to another table."

Instinctively, I place my hands on my cheeks. "Too warm? No. It's truly lovely." Had Ellyn noticed my blush? Does she know? Oh, what is happening to me?

"Enjoy your dinner, you two. Always good to see both of you. Nerissa, I'll call soon to schedule another appointment."

Twila's wise gray eyes stare across the table at me, but she says nothing. Was my discomfort with Ellyn noticeable? Did Twila see it? Sense it? The image from that first dream flashes again, as it has dozens of times. Miles, with his hand reaching for mine in invitation, an offering. *Come to me, Nerissa.*

"Mom?"

"What?"

Does Twila know? No, of course not. There's no way she could know what's in my mind. The thoughts are mine and mine alone. And I must make them stop.

I must take control of my mind.

My thoughts.

But what about the dreams, the stories my subconscious is telling me, night after night? How do I control what is not a conscious act?

As I move through the routine of preparing for bed, I pull my mind from the dreams, from Miles, time and time again. I intentionally focus elsewhere—on the conversation with Twila over dinner, on work, on the phone call with my attorney earlier today, the information he imparted and the actions he suggested, my waning finances—all of it is punctuated by prayers that feel more perfunctory than passionate, more one-sided than reciprocal.

When memories of the dreams of Miles continue to intrude in my thoughts, I stop what I'm doing, close my eyes, and repeat a verse out loud, the act filling my mind with not only the words of Scripture, but also the sound of my own voice.

I climb into bed to face what will be yet another restless night. Another night of staring, wide-eyed, into the darkness, listening for a voice that no longer speaks to me, hoping for comfort or assurance that will not come. Fearful that when I do drift off to sleep, they'll come again—the longings, the desire, for what I don't have, can't have.

Shadows dog me. And the dark chasm that's opened within me, the valley of silence, pulls at me, vacuum-like, sucking me into its cavernous depths. Until exhausted, I can fight its pull no longer, and I succumb. Not to thoughts of

Miles, but to the chasm. I teeter on its edge, staring into the vacuous space, where I'm tempted to believe some sort of respite awaits me.

When engulfed by darkness, one's options are limited, one's responsibilities deferred. When fatigue—mental and physical—overwhelm me, I fall to what feels like the depths of Sheol.

The abode of the dead.

The valley void of hope.

CHAPTER SEVENTEEN

Souls are like athletes, that need opponents worthy of them,
if they are to be tried and extended and pushed to the full use
of their powers, and rewarded according to their capacity.
Thomas Merton

erissa

I STAND in front of the bathroom mirror and scrunch
product into my damp hair. Then I dust some powder onto
my face and tip my lashes with mascara. The reflection
staring back at me looks aged, older than my years. I reach
for the compact of powder again and dust a bit more under
my eyes, hoping to conceal the dark circles left after yet
another restless night. But a night without dreams, I am
relieved to recall.

After dressing, I cross my bedroom, open the door, but

when I move to step into the hallway, I stop and take a step back. "Twila?" I whisper.

Right outside my door in the hallway, Twila is curled on the floor, an afghan covering her. She is cocooned in sleep. On the hard floor. She must be freezing. I bend down and place my hand on her shoulder, "Honey..." When she doesn't wake, I gently shake her. "Twila." I speak her name a little louder and her eyelids flutter, then open.

She gazes at me through the haze of sleep. When her focus clears, she slowly sits up and looks around.

"What are you doing out here, in the hallway?"

"I...fell asleep, I guess."

"Yes, I see that, but why here? Honey, are you okay?"

She pulls the afghan off herself and then moves to stand— her movements stilted. When she gets to her feet, she rubs the back of her neck.

"You didn't even have a pillow. And it's cold out here. What were you doing?"

"I just...I was..." She looks away from me and says nothing more.

"Why don't you put the afghan away, use the bathroom, and then meet me in the kitchen. Okay?"

She nods and heads back to her room. I head to the kitchen, where I make a pot of tea, strong tea. We'll both need the caffeine this morning. But I want more than the caffeine. I also want an explanation from Twila. As much as I enjoyed our dinner at the café together last night, the conversation revealed little.

It's time for honesty. I've respected her privacy, her silence on what happened with Will. But it's time for more. I need to know she's alright. And there's something else I need to know.

When she joins me in the kitchen, I fill two mugs with the steaming tea. I motion to the table where Twila takes a seat. I set the mug in front of her, then take the seat across from her. We both wrap our hands around the mugs for warmth.

I give Twila a few moments to sip her tea and give myself time to do the same while also considering the questions I want answered. But before I can pose my questions, she offers a piece of what I want to know.

"I was praying. Last night. I was praying for you and then decided I'd sit outside your door for a while. To pray. For sleep, you know? That you'd sleep peacefully. Did you?"

"You did that for me?" I set my mug on the table. "Thank you, Twila." Her act moves me deeply. "I slept. Not as much as I'd like, but"—I'm careful with my response—"more peacefully than I have recently. So, yes. Truly, I'm grateful."

I consider again the questions I want to ask her. "Twila, why are you here?" The question startles me as much as it seems to startle her. "I'm sorry." That was not what I'd planned to ask her, and yet, it is the core of what I want to know, isn't it? "You're always welcome here, you know that. I'm just wondering why now?"

"I told you. Will…the wedding…"

When she doesn't say more, I read the pain in her eyes. Is probing for more cruel? Yet I sense it's time. "Yes, I know. But you haven't told me what happened, and that's not like you. We've always shared open, honest communication. I wanted to give you some time, but…" I stare down at the tea cooling in the mug, then look back at her. "What happened with Will? Between the two of you?"

Her eyes wide, she stares across the table at me. As I wait for her response, her pale complexion flushes, and then she fixes her gaze on the tabletop. "We just disagree on some things. And we couldn't figure it out."

"What about doing some counseling? Surely it's something you can work through together."

She shrugs but offers nothing more.

I want to respect her privacy, she is an adult, but for reasons I don't understand, I feel compelled to get a direct answer from her. "What's the issue? What couldn't you agree on?"

When she finally looks back up at me, tears swim in her eyes. She slowly shakes her head.

"You won't tell me?"

"No," she whispers. "Do you want me to leave? To go stay somewhere else?"

"What? Oh no, honey, of course not." I suddenly want nothing more than to close my eyes, rest my head on the table, and fall into sleep—to escape the darkness that seems to constantly hover now. To sleep until it's gone, all of it—Twila's pain, her obvious heartache, her silence, God's silence, and the always-present financial burden. Although, even sleep isn't safe any longer. Even there I feel haunted by something I can't control.

"All shall be well...and all manner of things shall be well." Will it? I'm no longer sure. I no longer know if I believe that's true. If I believe—

"Mom?"

I inhale and sit up straighter, though the effort is taxing. "What?"

"Are you okay?"

I stare at her a moment. "What did you mean when you said there was 'more'? The other night, when I told you about the financial issues. What did you mean? What has God revealed to you?"

I wait for her response, but again, she is silent and my patience is waning.

"I'm praying for you," she finally whispers.

"Thank you. But..." I sigh. "Twila, I'm tired. I just need an answer. Please. Straight answers."

"It's a battle."

"A battle? Spiritual? Yes, I know. But—"

"That's all I know. Really."

She gets up from the table, takes her mug, and heads out of the kitchen toward her room. "Wait."

She stops in the hallway and turns back and looks at me.

"Is that why you're here?"

She stares at me for a moment, then turns and walks away.

"What is going on?"

There is no response. No one is listening.

CHAPTER EIGHTEEN

It is not that someone else is preventing you from living
happily; you yourself do not know what you want. Rather
than admit this, you pretend that someone is keeping you
from exercising your liberty. Who is this? It is you yourself.

Thomas Merton

llyn

I FOLLOW Nerissa from the small waiting area into her office,
where the shutters are folded back and the cool light of the
day filters in through the windows. The view beckons, as it
does from most places in the village. A dense forest of
cypress and redwoods meets the road encircling the top of
the cove. "The views never get old, do they?"

"No. We're certainly blessed to live here."

"Well, I no longer actually live here, but yes."

"You and Miles have stunning views, too."

"Definitely. Sure. He and Sarah did a beautiful job designing the house to take advantage of those views."

Nerissa's expression softens, and it's that softening that makes me regret my words, which isn't unusual. Why'd I have to go and mention the first wife?

"I've wondered if it's been hard on you living in the home Miles shared with Sarah."

"No. Of course not." The words are out of my mouth before I can catch them, but the heat that sears my face likely gives me away. "Well, I mean… I don't know." I do know. I really know. But… "Would it be hard on you, you know, if…?" If you'd married Miles? "You know what? Could we just talk about diets? Because you know how much I love a good diet."

Nerissa laughs. Bless her. I do like her, which is sort of inconvenient, isn't it?

"Have a seat, Ellyn." She gestures to the chair across from her desk as she takes the seat behind the desk. "We can discuss whatever you'd like. But for the record, yes, if I remarried it would be hard, I'd imagine, to live in a home my husband shared with another woman. It seems like a natural struggle."

"Oh. Well. It may have crossed my mind once or twice. But it is a beautiful home and the views are incredible." There, full circle. "Speaking of Miles, I've wondered, we've wondered, how you are? We were so sorry, I mean, the breakup, it's just so… Well, they'll work through it, don't you think? Anyway…" I take a deep breath. "How are you?"

Nerissa's gaze leaves mine and shifts back to the view outside her window. When she looks back at me, her brow has furrowed. "I pray they'll work through it. I was so certain their relationship was meant to be. Does Miles…?" She stares down at a file sitting on her desk as she speaks, then she opens it and shuffles through the contents. "Does he have any insight?"

The friendship Nerissa and Miles have shared, much like Sarah, is never far from my mind. But it would probably be helpful for both Nerissa and Miles to share with one another the confusion and pain regarding the hardship their kids are going through.

"You haven't talked to Miles since they called off the engagement?"

She looks from the file, which seems to fascinate her, back to me. "No, I haven't."

"Maybe you…" The one time I'm going to say something right, the words get stuck. I clear my throat. "Insight? No, not really. He only knows what Will shared with him, which wasn't much."

She nods. "Yes, Twila hasn't told me much, either. I've wanted to give her time to process. I assumed she'd share more when she was ready, but I'm beginning to wonder."

"I'm sure she will."

"I hope so. Has she talked to you? You've had an important role in her life."

"Um—"

"Oh, Ellyn. I'm not asking you for information. Truly. I'm just concerned for Twila and I'm hoping she is talking to someone."

"We've talked some. She's a wise young woman, which isn't news to you."

Nerissa smiles, though the concern remains in her eyes. "No, it isn't news to me. She's wise in spite of me. Thank you for making yourself available to her." She returns her attention to the open file on her desk, mine I presume. "So, Ellyn, you wanted to talk about the elimination plan I'd mentioned?"

"Yes, thanks for getting me in on such short notice. No

time like a Monday to start a diet, right? And yes, I do want to talk about it. I mean, I don't, but yes, let's just deal with the issues. What do I have to do? What do I need to give up? Everything good, right? Gluten, dairy. Just cut it all out. That's how it works?" I glance at my watch. "It's almost noon and I haven't had either dairy or gluten today."

"Actually, I recommend a cleanse before you begin the elimination process."

"Like a juice cleanse? I did one of those last year, or I tried to anyway. It didn't go too well."

She smiles. "I recommend a fast first—just liquids—water with lemon."

"Water?"

"Yes, with lemon. You can drink it warm or iced."

"Well, at least there are options."

"It's just twenty-four hours."

"*Just* twenty-four hours? Right. Okay, then what?"

Twenty-four hours? Without food? Nothing? I lean forward and try to take in what she's saying, but...twenty-four full hours? I hold up one hand. "Wait. I'm...I'm sorry to interrupt, but couldn't I just sort of gradually, you know, ease into this? Maybe give up one thing at a time and see how it goes?"

"I recommend the fast, then I suggest you remove foods that are common culprits: dairy and gluten, yes, but also nuts, soy, corn, nightshades—I'll give you a full list. It isn't as bad as it sounds, really. I've had many clients—"

"Again, I'm sorry, I don't mean to interrupt. It's just that food is my work, it's what I do, it's... Nightshades even? I don't know if I can. I thought I was ready, but I don't, I mean, how? Just...how?"

Nerissa stares at me, her look patient, thoughtful. "Ellyn, remember when I said it's one thing to believe you're created in the image of God, but another to live into that image?"

"Yes." But please don't ask me to explain what you meant.

"Part of that practice, a large part, is a mindset. It's the practice of changing our thoughts. What we think impacts what we do and even how we feel."

"Right. So…"

"Likewise with our habits. What we think impacts what we do. So when you think about food, what goes through your mind?"

"What do you mean?"

"What are the thoughts? When you eat something, what thoughts precede the action of eating?"

"Oh." I consider what I was thinking before I ate the entire batch of cookies the other night, and my face heats like the bottom of a sauté pan. I look down, unable to hold Nerissa's gaze. My bag sits on the floor next to my feet, so I busy myself reaching for it, pulling it onto my lap, and digging through it as though looking for something.

"Let's see… Thoughts? That depends, I guess." I pull out a pack of gum, old gum. Or maybe it's just aged like a fine… Who am I kidding? I pull a piece out of the package and then gesture to the pack. "Would you like a piece? It's sugar-free."

"No, thank you. Ellyn, are you willing to try something?"

"Something other than the water plan?"

Nerissa smiles and there's something so pure about the gesture. Again I realize how much I actually like her. We might become friends if it weren't for the Miles thing. Well, that and the torture she seems bent on inflicting. Water with lemon? Who does that?

"Yes, something other than the fast. A place to begin."

I toss the pack of gum back in my purse without taking a piece. "That's a relief. What is it?"

"Start keeping a food journal. Just for a few weeks, maybe a month. Write down everything you eat and—"

"Wait. Everything? Do I have to turn it in?"

"Turn it in? To me? No, you don't have to give it to me. Although, sometimes it's helpful—I might identify patterns you miss. But no, keep it for yourself. Write down what you eat and what you were feeling at the time. Begin paying attention to what you feel before you eat something—what precedes the act of eating. Are you hungry? Or frustrated? Upset, maybe? Whatever the feeling, make a note of it. Write about it, if you'd like. Also note what you're thinking. Identify the thoughts and how those thoughts make you feel. Then after you've eaten, pay attention to your body, its signals, what it's telling you. Do you feel full? Bloated? Nauseated? Tired? Energized? Whatever the feeling, note it."

"Okay, so it's that or the water diet?"

"It's just a twenty-four-hour fast before the elimination process."

"Right. The journal it is."

"Great. After a few weeks or so, you may see some patterns. If you'd like we can discuss those. See if we can identify anything that isn't agreeing with you, but also, perhaps it will offer you something more."

"More?"

"Insight, into your own mind. When we make changes, those changes begin with our thoughts. While there's some truth in the saying that we are what we eat, we're really what we think—our thoughts direct our actions. The mind-body connection is so strong. And, by the way, there are no wrong answers when it comes to the journal—this isn't about what you think you should or shouldn't have eaten."

"Oh. Okay." I consider what she's said. "Wait, no right or wrong answers?"

"You're just collecting data."

"Data? Huh. Okay then, I'll stop at Gallery Books on my way back to the café and buy a journal. That's easy enough. I'll just keep track. Great. Then we can talk about it? But we have to wait a few of weeks?" Not that I mind waiting, but I'd hoped to schedule weekly appointments with Nerissa. After my conversation with Twila about Nerissa's financial struggles, I hoped maybe I could help in some small way. And, who am I kidding? The appointments can only be good for me, too.

"Not necessarily. Would you like to set another appointment?"

"Sure. I may as well figure all this food stuff out once and for all. But I like starting with the journal and progressing to the water diet. Maybe in between you could educate me about how gluten and dairy may be affecting me. I know a lot about food, obviously, but that's new territory."

"I'd be happy to do that, Ellyn."

"Do you offer packages of appointments?"

"Packages? No, just individual appointments."

"A package might be good marketing, you know. Offer a small discount for five or more appointments scheduled at once. That would also hold clients accountable, right?"

"I've never thought of that. Thank you, Ellyn. That's a wonderful idea. Oftentimes, someone will schedule an appointment or two, then when the work gets challenging, they disappear. If they've made a financial investment, maybe they'd continue, which would be so helpful for them."

"It's good business all the way around. So, how much for five appointments?"

After I've written Nerissa a check and we've scheduled my next appointment, I get up and gather my coat and bag. The idea that almost slipped out my mouth as Nerissa and I talked about Twila and Will hasn't vacated the premises as I'd hoped it would. But I make it all the way to her office door without heeding its pull on me. "Okay, see you next week."

"Good. Thank you, Ellyn. If you have any questions in the meantime, just call."

I reach to open the door, wrap my hand around the knob, turn it, and actually get the door open before I turn back and open my mouth. "You know, Nerissa. We'd love for you to come for dinner one evening when the café is closed. Maybe tomorrow evening? I know Miles would like to see you and the two of you, well, Will and Twila are your kids and I know you're both concerned, and you're friends, good friends, and... Dinner, it's just dinner, just..." I shut my mouth. Finally. And wait for Nerissa's response.

And wait.

And watch.

Her face flushes, and she opens her mouth as though she's going to say something, then stops, looks away, then opens my file again and shuffles the contents again. "Thank you, but I'm busy tomorrow evening. How about a rain check?" She glances up at me and her expression tells me... What? It tells me something, that's for sure, but I have no idea how to interpret what I see beyond Nerissa's obvious discomfort.

"Rain check it is. Maybe we can set a date when I'm in next week?"

"Yes, maybe."

"Okay. Then I'm off to buy a journal." I walk out of the office, through the waiting room, and out the front door. When I've closed the door behind me, I stop, open my jacket, and let the breeze cool me because, maybe it's just me, but things seemed a little heated at the end there. What just happened? What would make Nerissa so uncomfortable with my invitation?

She's going through a hard time, as Twila shared, so maybe she's just off. But she was fine before the invitation.

I let the conversation with Twila play through my mind again—Nerissa's financial struggles, and the darkness to come for Nerissa, what Twila sensed or, as she said, knows. She described it as a battle, warlike.

I didn't offer opinions to Twila; I listened. That's what she'd needed. But had she asked, I'd have told her—okay, hopefully I'd have been wise enough to simply have suggested—that perhaps she was creating drama where none existed. I mean, a battle? Really?

What I did ask Twila was whether she was comfortable with me telling Miles what she'd shared. Miles is so much wiser and has a much better grasp on the Bible and spiritual matters. I haven't had a chance to talk with him yet, but now an image of Miles, always so willing to help others, setting out to rescue Nerissa? That doesn't sit well.

Thoughts lead to feelings? Okay, what does the thought of Miles swooping in to save Nerissa make me feel? Nothing good, that's for sure. What I do know is how it feels as a single woman to need help, to feel all alone, with no one but yourself to depend on.

Send in a knight in shining armor, and…

I roll my shoulders back, hoping to loosen the tension that's gripped them. *"I'm busy tomorrow evening. How about a rain check?"* Tension releases its grip and is replaced by relief, which does nothing to bolster the image I hold of myself.

I AM DETERMINED to leave my thoughts on the sidewalk as I walk through the door of Gallery Books, just a block up the street from Nerissa's office. The store offers a warm embrace against the cold, damp day. As the door clicks closed behind me, I stand for a moment and take in the maze of bookshelves, along with racks of artsy greeting cards, and shelves and tables laden with gifts. Near the front door, I spy Catsby, the store cat, curled in a patch of sunlight. I've learned disturbing him is not worth the glare he'll inflict, so I leave him and head toward the back of the store, where, if memory serves, I'll find an array of journals.

An array is right. "Wow." I pick up a journal and run my hand over the embossed cover, then I lift it to my nose. Leather. I open the cover and flip through the pages, which aren't lined. Does that matter? It might. As I set the journal back down, I note the size of it—pocket-sized. Nerissa said to write down everything I eat, which means I'll need something larger. Much larger.

I scan the selection and my gaze lands on a larger, amber-colored journal, the cover also leather. The color reminds me of honey, which reminds me of a flaky, buttery croissant, which is luscious when drizzled with lavender honey, and that thought makes my stomach growl. Seems appropriate based on the purpose of the journal. The color is also part of my preferred palette—the fall tones I love so much. Which makes me think of the water tower, the way it was before *Jim* stripped it of all color and personality.

I flip through the journal again. It's just right. Job done. I tuck it under my arm and head for the register. But before I reach the register, a basket set on a shelf catches my attention —it's filled with pieces of sea glass engraved with words. I smile at the memory of the pieces Miles and I had exchanged with one another. The piece he gave me was a declaration of *Friendship* early in our relationship. The piece I gave him was inscribed with the word *Love*, given to him the night I made my own declaration.

I pick up a piece of the glass, the edges worn smooth, its surface cool. I set it back in the basket, but as I do, another piece beckons. I pick it up and stare at the word engraved on its surface, and all those thoughts I left outside on the sidewalk come flooding back.

Trust.

I run my thumb over the engraving.

I trust Miles. I do. He is, above all else, a man of integrity. A godly man.

But that doesn't mean he isn't harboring feelings for another woman, right? He wouldn't act on them, but...

"Has that man ever given you any reason, even a hint of a reason, to believe he is not completely in love with you? And devoted to you? You, Ellyn. Has he?"

No, Sabina, he has not. But...

What about Nerissa? Do I trust her? I wish I could say no, but the fact is, I do trust her. She has, it seems, as much integrity and genuine care for others as Miles does.

The water tower, just a few blocks over, comes to mind, and with it my stomach roils like a bubbling cauldron of newt eyes and frog toes.

I look at the piece of glass again.

Trust?

I'm the one who can't be trusted.

I set the piece of glass back in the basket. Facedown.

CHAPTER NINETEEN

Despair is the absolute extreme of self-love. It is reached
when a person deliberately turns his back on all help from
anyone else in order to taste the rotten luxury of knowing
himself to be lost.
Thomas Merton

llyn

I DROP my purse and the bag from Gallery Books on the
counter in the laundry room when I come in from the
garage. Then I remember I set my phone to vibrate before
my appointment with Nerissa and forgot to turn the ringer
back on afterward. I dig through the purse until I find the
phone, then see that I've missed a call from *"de head doctor."*

"It's about time." I'd almost given up on Serenity Sterling.

I lift the phone to my ear. *"Hi, Ms. DeMoss, I apologize for the delay in returning your call. I recently closed my practice to new clients. I'm referring people to Mitchell Sander—"*

"Mitchell?" I pull the phone away from my ear and hit End. A man?

I glance at the phone to check the time, then slip it into my pocket. I look at the bag with the journal in it. Tomorrow. I'll write down everything I eat tomorrow. And my thoughts. And did she mention feelings, too? Good grief. All of it. Tomorrow. Including Mitchell.

Right now, I have just one thought: croissants. Buttery croissants. And what I feel, what I woke up feeling, was the need to bake. With Miles covering for Courtney this week, I have a rare Monday to myself. Not that I don't love my Mondays with Miles. I do. But lately...

No.

No thinking. No feeling. No writing things down.

Today, I bake.

I walk through the living room, past the sleek, ice-blue, leather sofas that sit atop the plush, silver-toned area rug. The brushed-aluminum face of the fireplace catches the sunlight streaming through the large windows, the gleam blinding.

The first time I saw Miles's home, he told me with restrained pride, which I'm sure I didn't imagine, that Sarah chose the contemporary, minimalist decor in cool tones so they wouldn't compete with the stunning views of the crashing surf and craggy rock outcroppings.

Mission accomplished.

I go to the kitchen and don my favorite apron for the long process ahead. A process that will fill my afternoon and evening and will also fill my mind. That's the plan. It's also a process that will have the house smelling like heaven when Miles walks through the door after his rounds at the hospital tonight.

Typically, croissants are made in the spacious, well-equipped kitchen of the café, by Juanita, the Mexican American *maître pâtissier* who is also Le Cordon Bleu trained and spent many years working in France. The croissants, along with other traditional French and Viennese-style pastries and desserts, are sold to coffee shops and restaurants in Mendocino, Fort Bragg, Eureka, and even Santa Rosa.

I had begun making the pastries for that purpose—as a way to supplement the café's income in the early years as I built the business. There was always a preferment in the refrigerator. I'd mix dough after the dinner service each night, let it rise, then place the trays in the walk-in fridge before I went home to sleep for a few hours. Then I'd return to complete the multiple steps in the process before I finally baked the croissants, or whatever pastry I was making.

I was younger then. A lot younger.

It turned out the baked goods purchased elsewhere were also a great marketing tool. When people asked where the goods were baked, they wanted to try our other offerings. Before long, I could afford to hire someone to assist me, then finally to take over. Now Juanita and her small crew come in after the dinner service and work through the night.

But today, croissants will be baked in Sarah's kitchen.

My kitchen.

I glance around the stark kitchen and realize, for the first time, that it's similar to the water tower's remodeled kitchen only larger—white marble countertops, white subway tile, white cabinetry. White on white on white on... It's a clean look. Trendy, I suppose. And, I know. It doesn't compete with the view. But...

My kitchen?

No, this is definitely Sarah's kitchen.

In Sarah's house.

And the kitchen in the water tower? Technically mine now, but it isn't the kitchen I loved when I lived there.

Why does every thought lead me back to the water tower? "Don't think about it, Ellyn."

I wipe down the marble on the island, disinfect it, then sprinkle a handful of flour on the surface. I don't know if this was Sarah's intended use for the island, but it's the perfect surface for rolling dough.

Chalk one up for Sarah.

Ugh. Sorry, Lord. I know Sarah isn't the problem. I'm the problem. We established that in the bookstore.

Anyway, it's just decor. It's meaningless. What matters are the people in the home and the love that fills the home.

But what if that love is hampered by the memories that also occupy the house?

Whose love is it hampering, Big Girl? Yours or his?

I pick up one of the sticks of unsalted, high-fat, European-style butter I've left on the counter to soften and look at it. "What happened to you filling my mind? Do your job, will you?" I unwrap the butter, reach for a knife, and cut a sliver off one edge. The sweet, cold butter melts on my tongue. *Heavenly.* "That's more like it."

I had made the preferment early this morning, and then mixed the dough, let it rise, and rolled it into a rectangle before leaving for my appointment with Nerissa. I covered it and then placed it in the refrigerator. I pull the tray out of the fridge and set it on the island. Then I rip a couple of large pieces of parchment paper from a roll in the pantry and lay the paper on the island next to the floured surface. I'll roll my butter sheets on the pieces of parchment.

I spend the rest of the afternoon rolling and then laminating the dough with the butter sheets, refrigerating the dough again so the gluten can rest, and then doing the whole process over again. I roll all my angst into the dough and then fold that angst—namely the nagging lease on the water tower—into the dough.

In twelve months, the lease will be up. I won't re-sign, and the worst that's happened is that I made a bad business decision. End of story. No one need ever know. Especially Miles. It was business. Nothing more.

But even as I fold the dough on top of itself, I know I'm not only lying to myself, but I've lied to Miles, or at least omitted the truth.

I've shut him out.

Why?

By the time I pull the last tray of croissants from the oven, the sun has set. As the tray cools, I go to the pantry for a jar of local, lavender-infused honey. I take a still-hot croissant off the tray, plate it, then break it open to cool. The soft, buttery layers are paper thin, the exterior flaky.

I drizzle honey on the croissant, then pick up one half and take my first, long-awaited bite. I close my eyes as I savor the flavor, and my heart rate, I'm certain, slows. Is there anything better than a fresh, warm croissant? I take another bite, and another.

As I reach for a second croissant, I catch a glimpse of my reflection in the darkened window. I pause and stare at what I see—my hair, which looks darker in the reflection than its natural carrot color—is a bush of curls. My complexion is pale and splotched, my face round, and chins doubled. Body tripled, which I know without having to see it reflected back to me.

Emotion rises like bile.

I lower my gaze to the tray of croissants.

What did I think before I ate the first croissant?

I don't know.

What did I feel?

I don't know.

But what I do know is what I feel now.

Disgust.

Tears blur my vision. I don't know what to do. I don't know how to… What? I don't even know what I don't know. I rip off the apron and toss it onto the counter, grab a napkin, and wipe my eyes. Then I reach into my pocket, pull out my phone, and punch in a number. *Please, let her answer.*

I wander into the living room and curl up on one of the sofas as the phone rings on the other end.

"Hey, Sister, what's up?" Sabina's voice, a hint of the south still in her tone even after all her years in California, soothes almost as much as the croissant.

"I need help, but I can't see a therapist."

"What? Why not?"

"Because he's a man."

"Who's a man?"

"Mitchell."

"Who's Mitchell?"

"He's a man."

"Yes, I believe we've established that."

"He's a therapist. A referral from a referral. I can't. I don't have to, do I?"

"Ellyn, there are many wonderful male therapists, obviously. Maybe he's exactly what you…"

When she trails off without finishing her sentence, I insert, "Need?"

"That's what I was going to say, but…"

"But? I love you, but I need help here. Could you finish a sentence?"

Sabina's laughter draws my own smile, despite my tears.

"Ellyn, you're always so resistant to what's good for you. This is your decision to make, not mine."

"Really?"

"Really. Listen, I wouldn't have said this a year ago, or

even six months ago. But maybe God has a different plan. As much as I believe in the value of therapy, I'm also learning to recognize that God works in myriad ways. Maybe you have all the tools you need to work through the issues you're struggling with. Maybe the Divine wants to lead you Himself."

Mouth agape, words fail me. A rare moment.

"Ellyn? Are you there?"

"Wait. I don't *have* to see a therapist?"

"I never said you *had* to see a therapist. I simply suggested it might prove beneficial to work through some ongoing struggles."

"Suggested?"

"Okay, strongly suggested. But you've made the effort and clearly, those doors aren't opening easily. Maybe it's time to employ what you learned when you worked with Shauna, then be still. Listen."

"Listen? To who?"

"Yourself. Your heart. Those in your life. And God, of course, above all."

"Oh."

"Oh, what?"

I shrug. "I don't know."

"What are you feeling?"

"Feeling?"

"Yes, you know, those emotions that rise within. What's going on inside you?"

"You mean that overwhelming sense of relief that's washed over me and momentarily cleansed me of disgust and self-loathing?" Though I can't see her, I know Sabina is shaking her head in agitation, and that vision makes me smile.

"Don't think you're off the hook. You have work to do, girl. Being still and listening is work, believe me. That's not going to happen without some intention on your part. So, I suggest you make a plan."

"You strongly suggest, I assume?" I raise an eyebrow.

"Don't you start with me. You go take care of yourself."

"Yes, Doctor." I move to end the call, then think of one more thing I want to say. "Sabina?"

"Yes?"

"Thank you."

Maybe I do have all the tools I need. I get up from the sofa and cross the living room and go into the laundry room, where I left the bag from Gallery Books.

I stare at the bag for several seconds before I finally open it and pull out the journal. I run my hand over the supple leather cover as questions form that, I'm sure, have nothing to do with what I've eaten.

What was I thinking before I signed the lease on the water tower?

What was I feeling?

Is this the tool I need?

It's just before 11:00 p.m. when I hear the garage door rise. I settled on one of the sofas after I cleaned up the kitchen, a lengthy process. I set the journal and pen on the coffee table, the pages still blank. In a reversal of roles, I go to meet Miles at the back door. I open the door and when he steps inside, I kiss his cheek, the stubble from a day's worth of growth tickling my lips.

He takes off his jacket and hangs it on a hook by the door and then loosens his tie.

"Long day?"

"It was long, and one I'd rather have spent with you. But all in all, not a bad day."

"Are you hungry?"

"I grabbed something at the hospital, which I regret now. Something smells incredible. You baked?"

"Croissants. How about a cup of chamomile tea?" I ask over my shoulder as he follows me to the kitchen.

"With a croissant?"

"If you'd like."

"Sure thing. I don't need to be hungry to eat one of your croissants."

Once in the kitchen, he perches on a bar stool as I fill the kettle, set it on the range, and pull mugs from the cabinet. The chamomile tea was Miles's habit with Sarah. One I rarely join him in because, well, Sarah. But tonight I need something that will help me sleep, or I'll stare at the ceiling all night, my mind categorizing my foibles, faults, and failures, all of which I'm more than aware of today.

We make small talk as we wait for the water to boil, then for the tea to steep.

"One of Courtney's patients came in today for a follow-up—lab and test results. I was pleased to tell her she's healthy."

I nod, not sure why that's newsworthy.

"She beat cancer, at least for now. Complete remission." Miles looks past me, his expression thoughtful, his mind filled with thoughts of Sarah, I assume, who lost her battle. When he looks back to me, he smiles. "Did I ever tell you why I asked you out for coffee that first time?"

"My skills in the kitchen?"

He chuckles. "That was definitely part of it." He takes the mug I hand him and takes a sip of the hot tea, then holds up the mug. "It was Sarah's idea." He smiles at a memory I know nothing about, then sets the mug down.

"But Sarah was already..."

"Gone. Yes. A few weeks before she died, she made me

promise I'd keep living, and that eventually I'd consider dating and marrying again." His eyes take on that faraway look again.

"So, you asked me to have coffee."

He looks back at me and nods. "When she made me promise to keep living, she said, 'You could ask Ellyn DeMoss out. You've always enjoyed her company.'"

For the second time tonight, I'm rendered speechless.

"We were regulars at the café before Sarah got sick, remember?"

I nod.

"She saw something in you, or maybe something in me when we'd speak to you, and"—he shrugs—"she thought we'd make a good match. As I drove home tonight, I gave thanks for her foresight. If I hadn't made that promise to keep living, and if she hadn't mentioned you, I might have missed out on life with you."

I work to assimilate the idea that I owe my marriage to Miles's first wife, the one I've... I shake my head, unable to make the information fit. "Miles..." I turn away from him, unable to look at him, to internalize the love I see in his eyes. Love I don't deserve.

I busy myself getting his croissant. "Sometimes...I'm not sure I'm...who you think I am." I reach for the jar of honey, and as I unscrew the lid, I hear the bar stool scoot back and Miles come around the island.

He nestles up behind me and wraps his arms around me. He rests his head against mine. "I don't think you know who you are."

"No. I know who I am." *It's just that I've fooled you.*

He turns me toward him, takes the jar of honey from me, and sets it aside, then looks me in the eyes. "You are intelligent, creative, and caring."

Heat crawls up my neck to my face, and I take a step back but hit the counter.

"You're wise and compassionate and—

"Miles…"

"More talented than anyone I know."

Tears prick my eyes and my chest tightens. "Please…"

"And you're beautiful."

"Stop." Unable to breathe, I step around him and then inhale sharply. "You don't…know. You don't…" A sob catches in my throat.

"Ellyn?"

"I'm…sorry, Miles. I'm sorry." I walk out of the kitchen, through the house, and into the laundry room where I just welcomed Miles home. I pull my jacket off one of the hooks by the door, shrug into it, then walk out the side door onto the deck. I cross the yard and trudge toward the cliffs, head down, hands jammed in the pockets of my jacket. In the ink of night, I'm reckless on the path, caring not whether I trip and fall or not.

When my lungs burn, I slow, then stop for a moment. I turn back toward the house and see Miles watching me from the deck. I plod on toward the thundering sea. The closer I get to the cliffs, the more the clamor and crash of the waves drowns all else fighting for my attention. The noise fills my mind and dulls my senses.

It deafens me, inside and out.

I walk until I can go no farther. Until there is no land left. Until the next step would be my last step.

CHAPTER TWENTY

There is in every weak, lost and isolated member of the
human race an agony of hatred born of his own helplessness,
his own isolation.
Thomas Merton

ia

"How could you invite them for dinner without even
talking to me about it first?"

"What? She your friend. Of course I—"

"It's not the best time. I mean, literally, you're barely even
talking to me."

"I talk to you just fine. It you who don't talk."

"Mama—"

"It good to have them here. You see."

"But—"

She holds up her hand. Conversation finished. I know. I grab my backpack and head for the door.

"They come tomorrow night."

"You already called her?"

"Yes. I call de next day. I know your schedule. Tuesday not a work night, and you not going anywhere else, so dat a fine time for you."

I turn back, ready to tell her I'll go somewhere if I want to, but the truth is, I don't have any plans to see Manuel. After our last conversation, there isn't much to say. It isn't that I don't want them to come, it's just *her*. "Fine." I turn to go.

"Pia, you wait."

I stop and turn back again. "What?"

Mama takes a few steps toward me, then stops, her expression serious. "I love you. Dat why I do what I do, why I say what I say. Because"—she puts her hand on her chest, over her heart—"I love you. I want de best for you. And it my job to protect you. It always my job."

"I know you love me, Mama. I love you, too, but I'm an adult now—you have to let me make my own decisions, even if I make mistakes."

"No." She shakes her head. "Not this time. Not this."

I COME straight home after my last class on Tuesday afternoon rather than go to the library as I'd like. Twila and her mother are coming at six o'clock, and though Mama didn't ask for my help, I know there will be things to do. Even leaving right after my classes will give me little time before they arrive.

When I walk in the front door, the sweet, spicy scent of mole greets me, and with it comes memories of my papa.

Mole is what Mama always makes for company, and it was Papa's favorite traditional dish. How would things be different now if he were here? Would Papa understand how I feel about Manuel? Would he have ideas of how to help him? Help us?

Though I have many good memories of my papa, in the last couple of years, I've realized I only knew him through the eyes of a child. I didn't really know him, the man. Now, more than ever, I wish, as an adult, I could know him. Understand him. What he believed and what he stood for. I have a sense of those things, but they've come from Mama.

I make my way through the house to my bedroom, where I drop my backpack on the bed and hang up my jacket. As I leave the room to go to the kitchen, I stop at my art table and pick up one of the broken pieces of the Mexican tile Manuel gave me. Last weekend, after I'd seen Manuel, after he opposed every idea I offered, I came home and took several of the nine-by-nine tiles to the workbench in our small garage. I put on goggles and then picked up the hammer. One by one, I broke what was whole. But I was careful not to destroy the tiles. Only to hit them with enough force to break each into large pieces. Later, I will cut the individual pieces into smaller tile-like pieces.

I look at the piece I hold, then back at the pieces I've laid out on the table and search for just the right one. When I find it, I pick it up and match its sharp edge to that of the piece in my other hand. The two halves fit together perfectly, the crack between them almost invisible. Is it possible the break between Manuel and me will someday be nearly invisible?

"Please, God…" I whisper.

"You home?" Mama calls from the kitchen.

"Coming." I set the tile pieces back on the table, side by side. Then I head for the kitchen where I find Mama pulling ramekins of custard from the oven.

"You let these cool, then dust them with cinnamon."

"Okay."

She takes off the oven mitts, tosses them onto the counter, then turns and looks at me. "You have a good day?"

"Not really." What does she expect?

"What did you learn?"

"Nothing, Mama."

She glares at me, then her expression softens. "Well, tonight we enjoy." The reprimand I expect doesn't come. She picks up a stack of plates from the counter and goes to our small table, already set with place mats.

I count out settings of silverware and pull cloth napkins from a drawer where they are kept, perfectly pressed and folded. We set the table in silence, Mama moving between the table and the food in the kitchen. I place the glasses and fill a pitcher with water. We busy ourselves as we ignore each other.

When a knock sounds on the front door, Mama wipes her hands on her apron, takes it off, and hangs it on a hook inside the pantry door. "Go." She points toward the entry hall. "Welcome our guests."

As I walk toward the front door, I work to adjust my attitude. When I open the front door, Mama right behind me, my breath catches.

"What you doing here?" Her tone is terse as she pushes past me. She points her finger at Manuel's chest. "You go! You have no place here."

"Mama!"

Manuel glances from Mama to me, then back to my mama. "Mrs. Sanchez, I'd like to speak to you." He removes the baseball hat he's wearing and runs one hand over his thick, dark curls.

I want nothing more than to reach for him, to hug him, to hold him. To tell him, over and over, how much I love him.

Instead, I say nothing, braced for whatever it is he's come to say and for my mama's response.

"You have nothing to say dat I want to hear."

"I love Pia—"

Mama holds up her hand. "No. I don't want to hear—"

"I respect Pia, and"—Manuel talks over Mama—"I respect you."

Mama stops talking and he continues. "Someone else will be making the wine deliveries to the café for now."

"What? Why?" I step toward Manuel, but Mama puts her arm out to block me.

She lowers her arm—she's made her point to me and she knows it. "If you respect Pia and you respect me, then you leave. You leave here. And you leave Pia alone. You have nothing to offer her."

A vein throbs in Manuel's neck and his hand tightens around the hat. "You're right, I have little to offer Pia, except love. I am a good man, Mrs. Sanchez. But until I have your permission to see Pia, I will stay away. I came to tell you that —to tell you that I will respect your—"

"Manuel. No! What are you—?"

"Dat all you have to say?" Mama raises her voice over mine.

"Yes, ma'am."

"I am an adult! I will make my own choices!" I choke back a sob. "Mama!"

"Pia." Manuel's tone is firm. "This is the choice I'm making. Because I love you, I will respect your mama's wishes."

As he steps off the porch and walks back down the stone pathway, Twila and her mother stroll up the path.

"Excuse me." He steps out and around them. Twila stops and turns and watches him, then looks back to me. Then Manuel disappears into the shadows of the redwoods.

I wipe the tears from my cheeks. "Mama..." I whisper, "please."

"We have guests, Pia."

"Have we arrived at a bad time?" Nerissa takes the last few steps to the porch.

"You come at de perfect time."

I offer Nerissa and Twila a weak smile, and Nerissa gives me a quick hug. When she steps back, she looks me in the eyes, her smile reassuring. Then Twila does the same. "Was that Manuel?" she whispers in my ear.

I nod. She pulls back and looks at me. "Are you okay?"

My eyes fill with tears again, and I shake my head.

"Come, come in." Mama ushers them into the house ahead of us. I follow them in, but Mama stays on the porch. When I look back, I see the headlights of Manuel's truck. Mama watches until he backs out of the drive and turns onto the road. Then she turns, comes inside, and walks past me to Nerissa and Twila.

I CLOSE MY BEDROOM DOOR, lean against it, and exhale. I thought dinner would never end.

"What happened? Like, it seemed pretty intense when we got here." Twila stands next to my bed.

"Yeah. He just showed up. Here..." I pull the chair out from my art table. "You can sit here."

Twila glances at the pieces of china and pottery spread across the table. "What is all this? It's beautiful." She picks up a piece of the broken Mexican tile, sets it back down, then picks up a piece of Ellyn's broken tray.

"I collect broken things—pottery, china, tile." I point to the thirty-six-inch round tabletop, now covered with fiber-glass mesh. Some of the pieces I've chosen to use are laid out on the round. "I'll glue the pieces to the mesh, then fill the spaces with grout, like you would with tile. It's just something to do."

"It's more than that. It's art. Wow…" She picks up a piece I cut from the center of a plate, a bouquet of delicate pink roses painted on Limoges porcelain. "Haviland?"

"It's French. The pieces are from all over. Portugal, Mexico, England. I'm using the heavier pottery pieces for that, since it's so big."

"Cool." Twila looks around the room, then sits in the chair.

"Sorry dinner was so awkward."

"Probably more awkward for you than us. It was good. I know you and your mom aren't getting along, but I'm glad we came. As much as we have in common, our moms have the same things in common. Maybe they can, like, support each other."

"Maybe. But your mom seems so much more chill, you know? Mine is just so…" The emotions I worked so hard to contain during dinner erupt now. "She's so infuriating! And controlling! She thinks she knows everything, and she…" I swipe hot tears from the corners of my eyes. "She's impossible. It's all just so impossible. First, *her*. Then Manuel. They act like I have no say, no voice. Like I have no choice in what they decide for *my* life. *My* life!"

"Sorry," I mutter, pressing my palms to my eyes.

"What did Manuel say? Why was he here?"

I sigh as I drop onto the edge of my bed. I tell Twila the details of the brief conversation, but as I do something occurs to me. "Why would he have told my mama he won't make the deliveries to the café? Did she call the winery? Did she tell them not to send him? She better not have gotten him into trouble."

"Would she do that?"

"I don't know." I get up and pace the room. "I feel like I have no control over my own life. First, she tells me I have no choice but to get over Manuel. Then he comes here and tells her he will respect her wishes. Basically, that he won't see me. When do I get a say?" I stop at my nightstand, grab tissues from the box sitting there, wipe my eyes, and blow my nose. Then I turn back to Twila. "I'm sorry. I'm really glad you're here."

"Stop apologizing. I'm glad I'm here, too. This is what friends do for each other, right?"

I sit back down on the bed. "He didn't even talk to me before coming here."

"Maybe by showing respect for your mom, he's really showing how much he cares about you. I mean, like, that's what I wanted from Will. For him to get how important my relationship with my mom is to me."

I consider Twila's words. "Maybe. But it won't change anything. They're both too stubborn." I lie back on the bed and stare at the ceiling for a minute, hoping that fire inside me will burn itself out, because there's nothing I can do about anything. I sit back up. "There's literally nothing I can do to make this better. I can't figure out a way for Manuel to become a citizen. And he won't listen to anything I suggest that might give him a chance to stay here legally. I can't change the way my mama feels about him. And now, I guess I can't even make the choice to see him."

I shake my head. "I can't fix anything. I can't *do* anything. I'm completely powerless!" But even as the words leave my mouth, fueled by my anger and frustration, I know I have more power than so many others. Those like Manuel who, by no fault of their own, live without benefit of legal status and the rights I take for granted.

For the first time, I have a glimpse of what Manuel might feel. But not just Manuel. To have no control over your circumstances, no power to change things. The faces on the videos I've watched, the young Latinos who are brave enough to speak out about the hardships they face, those willing to work for change, but with so few options—

"You can't control it."

"What?"

"You feel powerless because you're not in control."

"I'm not a control freak. I'm not like *her*."

"That's not what I mean."

"Then what do you mean?"

"Like, it's all bigger than us. God is the One in control."

"How does that help? Because, honestly, I'm not sure He's doing a very good job right now."

"That's what faith is—believing, trusting what we can't see. He's working, Pia."

"Do you believe that for you and Will? I mean, look where you are." I motion around the room. "You should be with him."

Pain glints in Twila's eyes, pain I understand, but her presence, something about her, is totally peaceful, too.

"I didn't say it was easy—it's hard sometimes, to believe. Faith is a choice, not a feeling. You know?"

"I guess. Maybe this is the first time I've really had to make that choice, to decide to believe when everything seems so impossible. You seem so sure. How do you know you made the right decision? How did you just let go? I mean, you love Will, so how...? I don't get it."

"I don't know that I made the right decision. I'm trusting that God is working."

"Working everything out?"

"Yeah but, like, that doesn't mean it'll work out the way I want it to. Instead, I guess I trust He'll work things out for the best—He'll do what's best for me. And for Will, too. But I hope..." She looks down at her lap. When she looks back at me, tears pool in her eyes, and one slips down her cheek, past the small tattoo of thorns. "I hope He'll work it out the way I want."

"And you pray."

"I pray."

"I'll pray, too. But..." Again, that sense of powerlessness returns, and with it the anger—it smolders in my chest until it bursts into flames, a consuming fire I can no longer ignore. I stand up and go to my art table and pick up one of the pieces of Mexican tile, then the piece of Haviland Twila held. I look at the pieces and then those scattered across the table —pieces from all over the world. Here. Broken. The flames spread... "I'm going to do something else, too. I'll pray. And I'll fight."

"Fight?"

I look at Twila. "Something has to change. It has to."

CHAPTER TWENTY-ONE

Let no one hope to find in contemplation an escape from
conflict, from anguish or from doubt. For every gain in deep
certitude there is a corresponding growth of superficial
doubt. This doubt is by no means opposed to genuine faith,
but it mercilessly examines and questions the spurious faith
of everyday life...
Thomas Merton

Nerissa

ROSA SETS a small dish in front of me, and the sweet scent of
cinnamon rises to greet me. I relax into the warmth of Rosa's
home—candles flicker on the table, and russet-colored place
mats cover the smooth oak tabletop. Mementos from Mexico
are placed throughout the cottage, pointed out by Rosa after
our arrival. She provided a feast for the senses with the rich,

spicy scents of the meal she prepared, and the tantalizing flavors we enjoyed.

I relax more than I have in days, more than I have since having dinner at Ellyn's several nights ago. I must grasp these moments, enjoy them, and give thanks. For they are fleeting now.

Having Twila and Pia decline dessert and go to Pia's room also relieved some of the tension—tension between Rosa and Pia. "Thank you so much for having us, Rosa. Your home is lovely, and dinner was delicious. It was a treat to have someone else cook."

"I glad you come. De mole was my Raul's favorite dish. I use his *abuela's* recipe—his grandmother's. Twila eat it. She look healthy."

"Yes, she seemed to enjoy it. She is doing better, though I've had some concerns lately. Perhaps you've heard that she and Will have called off their engagement."

"I heard. I sorry. He seem like a nice young man. Maybe they work it out?"

"I do hope so."

"Or maybe she be like you—she commit to de One." Rosa points heavenward, then puts her hand over her heart.

I shift in my seat. Is it Rosa's comment that unsettles me or is it just my unsettled state of late poking at me? Reminding me of all that isn't right?

"Where de ring?"

The ring... I hold out my hand and look, as I have dozens of times over the last few days, at my bare left ring finger. "I lost it. I don't know what happened to it."

"Well, dat not change anything. It's what in your heart dat matter."

"I hope you're right. Lately, well, I've wondered."

"Wondered? Or doubted? Wondering fine, but doubting?" She shakes her head. "Dat no good."

"You're right, of course."

"I am right. 'De one who doubts is like a wave of de sea, blown and tossed by de wind.'"

"Thank you, Rosa. I needed that reminder." I dip my spoon into the dish for a bite of the custard. "So tell me more about you. When did you and Raul come to the US?"

"In 1988. Dat so many years ago now. We take all the right steps—we get our green cards, we get jobs, and after we wait de necessary five years here, we apply to become citizens. We study, we take de test, we interviewed. But de process begin even before dat. I had to learn to speak English —I didn't have much schooling, but I pick it up. Raul, he already speak de language. He come from Mexico City. He had a good education. Wait"—she scoots back from the table and gets up—"I show you."

When she comes back, she holds out a framed photo. I take it and smile at the photo of a much younger Rosa, and her tall, handsome husband. "Rosa, Raul was so good looking." I glance over my shoulder and look at Rosa, who is staring down at the photo.

"Yes. Dat taken de day we pledge our allegiance to the United States. We make dis country our home, for ourselves and for Pia. I was pregnant then."

She takes the photo from me and sits back down, her gaze on the picture, of the husband she loved and lost, I assume.

"You must miss Raul terribly."

She sets the photo down. "Lately more than ever. It not easy being a single parent. You know dat."

"Yes, I do." The photo piqued my curiosity further. "How old were you when you left Mexico?"

"Too young. Several years older than Pia now, but too young."

"Why did you leave? Do you mind me asking?"

"No, I don't mind. Opportunities, dat's one reason we

come here. But also…" Rosa, who always seems so assured, hesitates.

I wait as she seems to consider her words, and her already-dark eyes seem to darken more, as though shadowed by painful memories.

"It's okay…" I encourage.

She nods once. Her decision made, I take it.

"It no longer safe in Mexico. For Raul. He leave to protect himself. To protect me. I not usually talk about dis, but it's been in my mind lately."

"Why wasn't it safe?"

"His family—they in a business dat… It doesn't matter. He didn't want to be involved, but he wasn't given a choice. He wasn't willing to leave me because he love me, and because he afraid of what his family might do to me. I wouldn't have let him leave without me anyway, so de decision was easy."

"What about your family? Do you still have family in Mexico?"

She holds up her hand. "Dat enough for now. You want coffee? I make coffee."

"No, thank you. I haven't been sleeping too well. So I won't risk it."

"I have coffee." She moves to get up.

"Rosa…"

She stops and looks at me. "Thank you for sharing some of your story with me. Your decision to come here may have been easy, but starting over in a new country… I can't imagine the challenges. You're a strong woman."

"Yes. But dat strength not come easily. It was earned."

"I'm sure it was."

When she comes back with her coffee, she sets the cup on the table but doesn't sit down. Instead, she points at me. "You and me? We be friends?"

Her question makes me smile. I would have expected a statement, a declaration, or a demand. "I'd like that."

"Good. Me too." She sits back down and takes a sip of her coffee, the aroma wafting across the table, as comforting as the cinnamon. Then she leans forward. "Those girls in there give us plenty to talk about." Her tone is hushed.

"That's true. How is Pia? It seemed there was some tension when we arrived." I keep my voice low, too.

"Tension is right. And I right, too—dat young man not good for her. You remember I tell you dat at de reception last summer. So I tell her she have to get over him. Dat her only choice. I tell her he only have pain to give her, nothing else. I won't allow it."

"Can you stop it? Pia is young, but she is an adult. I know it's hard for us as mothers to realize sometimes, but—"

"I stop it" Rosa shakes her finger at me. As long as Pia live under my roof, she have to respect de rules I set."

"You've told her she can't see him?"

"I not have to. He take care of dat. He come here tonight, uninvited. He knock on de door and we think it you and Twila. When Pia answer, it him. He tell me he love her and dat he respect me. He say until I give permission, he leave her alone."

"Did that change the way you feel about him?"

"He try to earn my respect, but who can believe him? He already lie to her once. But I hope he keep his word and not see Pia. Why you not sleeping?"

"What? Oh…" It takes me a moment to shift my focus. "Just some recent struggles—financial, mostly." How much should I say? "Honestly, I'm not sure I really understand what's going on."

"You pray?"

"Yes. But…"

"But God is quiet?"

"How did you know?"

"I know things. And I know things because I experience a lot of things. Ellyn, and even Pia, they think I'm arrogant. But de reason I know is because I live a lot of life. Hard life. Just like you. We learn things. We talk to God and He make us wise. We know things." She picks up her coffee cup. "You keep praying."

"'Never give up prayer, and should you find dryness and difficulty, persevere in it for this very reason.'"

"Who say dat?"

"Saint John of the Cross."

"He sound like a smart saint."

For the first time in weeks, I sense God's presence. Or maybe I don't sense it as much as I see evidence of it. Through Rosa.

Through the friend I didn't know I needed.

One other thing I sense—there is more to Rosa's story. And one day, I hope she'll trust me with more of it.

As TWILA and I pull out of the dense forest of redwoods surrounding the property where Rosa and Pia live and cross over Highway 1, we chat about the evening and I ask Twila the question I've wondered about. "Do you know why Rosa is so set against Pia's relationship with Manuel?"

"He's undocumented. Pia didn't know until recently."

"I see." Although, I don't really see. I don't know all that implies, except that the potential consequences are weighty. "I guess Rosa wants to protect Pia. Perhaps it's better, in her mind, for Pia to end the relationship now rather than later."

"Yeah, but shouldn't that be Pia's decision?"

I glance over at Twila, her profile silhouetted against the window. "I suppose. But as a mother, you always want to protect your children. You asked me the other night, while we were at Ellyn's, about anger…"

"Yeah, you said most often it's fear based."

"Right. You were talking about Rosa and Pia."

"Rosa seems angry, right? About Pia and Manuel?"

"Yes, she does. Now I know how to pray for her."

"Yeah, for Pia, too."

As I PULL BACK the comforter and climb into bed, I reflect not only on the evening, but on its impact on both Twila and myself. While we enjoyed our dinner at the café last week, tonight was different. We both were focused on others rather than just ourselves. Work has afforded me that opportunity as well, but not in the same way.

I'm reminded of the importance of community and how darkness tends to breed in solitude. I will invite Rosa for coffee soon. And tonight I will pray, whether I sense God's presence or not. I will not give up the fight.

The battle has already been won, the enemy defeated for all time.

As I turn my mind to prayer, my eyes grow heavy. *Lord Jesus, I ask for Your mercy for Pia and Manuel, for Twila and Will, and Lord, for Rosa…* As I pray for Rosa, something nags at the corners of my mind. What is it? I still my prayers, my mind, and wait…

My breathing slows and for the first time in weeks I'm certain, my mind and body will surrender to the pull of sleep.

"Or maybe she be like you—she commit to de One."

That's it. Like me? Twila? No, that's not her path, I'm sure of it. Yet I was also so sure God had brought Twila and Will together, and it seems I was wrong. But just as it did when

Rosa made the comment earlier this evening, the thought unsettles me.

I roll over and pull the down comforter up around my shoulders, a cocoon of warmth. I breathe deep. *Lord, whether I sense You or not, You are present. Thank You.*

"'De one who doubts is like a wave of de sea, blown and tossed by de wind.'"

I will not doubt You. I believe. You are perfecting my faith. I will persevere.

As my mind stills, words are replaced by images of the sea and the gentle lapping of waves carry me to sleep, but just before I reach that longed for, blissful state, a gale of wind howls through my mind and the sea begins to churn. The waves no longer gentle rollers, instead they toss and crash.

And on that tossing sea is a boat, with a man leaning over its side, his hand outstretched, reaching for me. *"Nerissa, come...come to me..."*

I fall. I am falling, tumbling through the air, headed for the sea... My body jolts and I bolt upright. Eyes open. Heart pounding. I open my eyes and see nothing but darkness.

Engulfing, suffocating darkness.

"No."

"No!" I hiss. I reach for the bedside lamp and turn it on. "No. I will not succumb. Jesus Christ is my Lord and Savior, and the enemy has no power over me." I speak the words over and over. "Jesus Christ is my Lord..."

I throw back the comforter and climb from the bed and kneel. I bow my head, and do what I know to do. What has eluded me before now. "Lord Jesus, I take every thought captive to Your obedience. I submit my every thought to You." As images flash in my mind, I interrupt them with prayer. When the images persist, I open my eyes and pray aloud. "Every thought, I give to You, Jesus..."

With eyes open, the room illuminated, the small boat

tossing on the sea remains in my mind's eye, Miles reaching out to me…

"I give it to You, Jesus."

I must replace the image. I must fill my mind. I get up from my stance of prayer and reach for the Bible on my nightstand. I hold it to my chest, then climb back into bed and open the Bible. I turn to the Psalms and let the words soothe and reassure.

"Where can I go from your Spirit? Where can I flee from your presence? If I go up to the heavens, you are there; if I make my bed in the depths, you are there. If I rise on the wings of the dawn, if I settle on the far side of the sea, even there your hand will guide me, your right hand will hold me fast…"

I read the passage over and over and over. I read until my eyes are heavy and the words run together on the page. I close my eyes, the words, memorized, filling my mind, their assurance my companion. *Even on the sea, you are there…*

You are there…

You are there…

CHAPTER TWENTY-TWO

There is only one problem on which all my existence, my peace, my happiness depend: to discover myself in discovering God. If I find Him I will find myself and if I find my true self I will find Him.

Thomas Merton

llyn

ON WEDNESDAY, I lumber from the kitchen into the café's office, then wedge myself into the desk chair. I lean back in the chair to ease the ache in my lower back. But rather than easing the pain, the gentle stretch stabs like a butcher knife shoved in my lumbar region. I suck in my breath determined not cry. Then I try leaning forward in the chair, bending at the waist, but nothing relieves the pain.

After the debacle I had created Monday night, I woke

Tuesday morning on one of the lounge chairs on the deck under the warmth of an electric blanket. I traced the cord of the blanket to an extension cord, which was plugged into one of the outside outlets. Miles must have seen me land in the lounge after the hour or more I spent on the cliffs. I was exhausted, and if I'm honest with myself, a novelty, I know, I was also humiliated. How could I go inside and climb into bed next to Miles after that *display*? I must have fallen asleep on the lounge.

A few minutes after I woke Tuesday morning, Miles came out, already showered, shaved, and dressed. He handed me a mug of steaming coffee. "I filled the tub. I figured a hot bath might feel good this morning."

"Thank you," I mumbled. I sat up and winced, the muscles in my back unforgiving, my entire body aching. I gritted my teeth, not wanting Miles to see my pain. "I'm, sorry. I…"

He waited, but I didn't know what to say, how to explain what was unexplainable even to myself. When I said nothing more, he leaned down and gave me a quick kiss. "Take the day. Rest. We'll talk later." He stood back up and headed for the garage, then slowed and turned back. "I love you, Ellyn, whether you choose to accept my love or not."

By early afternoon, the pain in my back was unbearable, and I finally texted him and asked him what I should do. He prescribed a muscle relaxant and had the medication delivered to the house. I slept the rest of the afternoon and through the night.

Thus far, I have successfully avoided talking to Miles about what happened. I've avoided the man who claims he loves *me*. What is wrong with him?

I sigh. That's the wrong question, I know. The right question is the all-too-familiar question: What is wrong with me? It's a question I'm sick of asking. More than that, I am sick of myself. The disgust I felt on Monday has only intensified. As the memory of my image reflected in the window returns, so does Nerissa's question, the one I was too proud, too arrogant to admit I didn't really understand.

"You know it's one thing to believe you're created in the image of God, but it's another to live into that image, isn't it?"

My image bears little resemblance to the image of God.

That's because you're so self-focused, Tubby. Get your eyes off yourself already.

For once, Earl's right.

But as I declare the accuser right, something nags. What was it Shauna taught me?

The muscles in my lower back spasm and I bite my lip to keep from crying out. I breathe in and out, slowly, intentionally, as I work to relax my back. Although working to relax seems oxymoronic, doesn't it? But there's too much to do, and I need to do it. I can't take another muscle relaxant and sleep my life away, however tempting that particular escape may be.

When Pia passes by the office, I call out to her.

She leans into the office. "Hey…"

"Honey, would you please bring me a large bag of ice? Fill one of those gallon-sized Ziploc bags. Also a cup of coffee."

"Sure. Your back is bothering you?"

"Understatement. And wait, make it an espresso. A double."

"Are you sure?"

"Do I look unsure?"

"I'll be right back."

As I wait for Pia to return, I gently bend at the waist and rest my head on the desk.

Pain and fatigue gang up on my mind and fight for control, but I can't let them win. I have to think. What was it Shauna taught me? The memory takes a moment to break through the haze in my mind. *"Agreeing with Earl's voice is a waving red flag."* That's it. It's a warning that I'm off track. But isn't it true that I am entirely too focused on myself?

"Here, Auntie Ellyn." Pia hands me the ice pack she's made and I tuck it behind my back.

She sets the espresso on my desk.

"Thank you."

She tilts her head and seems to asses me, which is disconcerting. "What?"

"You look totally wiped out."

"Hence the espresso."

"Are you sure you're okay?"

I take a sip of the near-scalding espresso and sigh. "I will be, honey, I will be."

After Pia leaves, I let the ice and caffeine do their work. I lean back against the ice and endure the cold discomfort knowing soon my back will be numb to it, and to the pain. And with each sip of espresso, my mind clears a bit more, and with clarity comes a decision.

I will do as Sabina suggested: use the tools I have. And… what else did she say? Be still and listen. Listen to the people in my life and listen to God.

I don't know where to begin, but I have to begin. Wallowing is getting me nowhere except more disgusted with myself by the moment.

Miles was right in a way. I don't know who I am. I know what I do. I know the labels I wear: chef, businesswoman, employer, friend, and the new label: wife. But I sense I don't really know the woman beneath the labels. And it's time to get to know her, as distasteful as that idea seems.

Just as I begin to relax, a tornado whirls into the office.

"What wrong with you? Pia say you don't look good." Rosa assesses me. Like mother, like daughter, I guess. "She right, you don't look good. You look terrible." She comes to me, reaches behind me, and adjusts the ice pack, then she places her hand on my forehead. "You not hot."

"What are you doing?" I push her hand away. "I'm fine."

"You *not* fine. What happen to you?"

"Nothing."

"You lie to me? Your mama?"

"My mama? Rosa, you're not..." But as I spit the words at her, my irritation gives way to need, and tears as well. If there was ever a time I needed mothering... Listen to the people in my life? I wipe a tear from my cheek as she hovers. Even Rosa?

"You talk to me." Her tone has softened. "You tell me what wrong."

I nod and point. "Close the door. Please."

She does as I ask, then sits in the chair next to the desk. I swivel the chair so I'm facing her. "Okay." I gather whatever courage I have, which isn't much. "Mama..." I whisper.

A look of surprise registers on Rosa's face but is quickly replaced with her usual assurance. "Dat right—I your mama. Now, what wrong?"

I swallow, my mouth suddenly dry as flour. "I'm going to tell you because, I need... I need to know...Because, I don't know—"

"Because you don't know what to do, so I tell you. You just spit it."

"What?"

"You hear me, you spit it."

"Spit? You mean spill it?"

"Spill? What you spill? No, spit. You know, say it out."

"Spit it out?"

"You just tell me!"

"Right. Okay, I did...something."

"You make a confession?"

"Yes, I'm confessing."

"Dat good, because otherwise what you keep inside grow. It get bigger and bigger, and it fester. It make you sick in de head, and in de heart, and in your back, too. Okay, I listening."

"Oh." I stare at her a moment. "I think you're right."

"Of course I right."

"Rosa—"

She purses her lips and holds up her hand like she's directing traffic.

"Mama…"

She nods. "You confess now."

"Okay. Um, I…did something. Without telling Miles. I made a decision. A big one, and I didn't tell him. I didn't include him."

"What you do?"

I take a deep breath. "I leased a house."

Her dark eyes harden. "What house?"

"The…water tower," I whisper.

"Why you do dat?"

"I…I don't know."

"You dig"—she taps on her chest—"inside. You dig and figure out why you do dat."

"It doesn't matter why I did it. I just need to figure out what to do now. How to undo it."

"No."

"No what?"

"No, you dig, otherwise you do it again in some other way. I know why you do it."

"Why?"

"Same reason you always do stupid things."

I push back from the desk and start to stand, but pain keeps me down. "I don't know why I thought—"

"Same reason *everyone* do stupid things."

I pause. "Okay, why?"

"You scared."

"No, I just wanted to go...home. I wanted home. My home."

"Because you scared."

"Of what?"

"How I supposed to know. You think I know everything?"

"No, *you* think you know everything."

She waves off my comment. "You tell me why you scared."

I exhale and lean my head back and stare at the ceiling as I consider her words. Why had I gone to the water tower that day? It seems so long ago. Was it really just a few weeks ago? What was I feeling? It was after my appointment with Nerissa, and...

I look back to Rosa. "I was afraid I wasn't...enough. For Miles. That I wasn't, I'm not, who he really wants. That..."

Rosa pulls a tissue from the box on my desk and hands it to me. "You afraid, so you go home before he send you home. Dat what you do."

"What?"

"You hear me. You leave him before he leave you. Dat's what in your mind, right?"

Like a piece of a puzzle, Rosa's words fall into place and I see what I couldn't see before. "Oh."

"I right, right?"

"Maybe."

"No maybe. I right."

"Okay, you're right. But what do I do now?"

"What you mean 'what I do now?' You do the only thing. You tell de truth. Dat's always what you do. You tell de truth. Otherwise, like I tell you, it fester. It make you sick."

"Tell Miles...the truth? But..." Even as I stare at Rosa with what I'm sure is the gaped-mouth look of a dead fish, I know she's right. The only thing to do is tell Miles the truth. Tell him, the one person I least want to tell. "But what if...?"

"No what if. You tell him. Without de truth, there no real relationship. It all a lie, and that no way to do marriage. But first, you have to tell yourself de truth."

"Tell myself the truth?"

"Why I have to keep repeating myself? You dig, you do de digging work. You figure it out inside you. Now, go. You got work to do. You go."

"Go where?"

"Home. You go home."

"I can't go home." I point toward the kitchen. "I have to—"

"No. We all take care of all dat. Paco run the back, I run de front. You go home and take care of yourself. You do what you need to do."

"You might be my mama, but you're not the boss of me."

She gets up and heads for the door, then turns back. "De mama always de boss. You go. You tell yourself de truth."

"Wait."

"What you want now?"

I hold her gaze for a moment as I weigh my words. "What are you afraid of?"

"Me? I don't know what you talk about."

"I think you do, Mama," I whisper. "I'm not the only one who needs to tell herself the truth."

Her eyes narrow and she points at me. "You go home."

I MAKE the short walk to my car parked behind the café, carrying the plastic bag filled with fresh ice and a bag Paco packed for me before I left. I ease into the driver's seat and once the ice pack is in place, I pull out of the parking spot. *"You go home."* I make a U-turn and in less than two minutes, I pull into the driveway of the water tower, as I have thousands of times before.

I sit in the driveway and let memories of the house I called home for so many years play through my mind. While the exterior of the house is unchanged, the inside is completely different. It's all new, and it's no longer mine. Yes, I hold the lease. But the lease and my memories are the only ties I have to the water tower now.

I back out of the driveway, make my way out of the village, then turn north on Highway 1.

I'm going home.

CHAPTER TWENTY-THREE

God Himself begins to live in me not only as my Creator but
as my other and true self.
Thomas Merton

llyn

WHEN MILES WALKS into the house after work, he finds me
sitting up in bed, a bag of melted ice next to me, pillows and
a heating pad behind me, the shutters on the window adja-
cent to the bed opened wide. The sun hangs just above the
horizon, tingeing the bank of puffy clouds in hues of orange,
coral, and lavender. Scattered around me on the bed are the
journal I purchased, my Bible, and an assortment of pens.

Miles sits on the edge of the bed but keeps some distance
between us. "How are you feeling?"

"Better. Alternating between ice and heat, with an occasional ibuprofen thrown in for good measure, and rest. The perfect recipe."

"Or prescription." He turns and looks out at the sunset for a moment, then looks back to me. "So..."

"Miles, I'm..." My heart starts doing the mamba and I struggle to hear myself think above its rhythm playing in my ears. My mouth is as dry as day-old bread. I reach for the glass on the nightstand and take a sip of water. "I'm...so sorry. For walking out the other night, and for so many other things, one of which, you don't..." I put my hand on my chest. Is it possible I'll have a heart attack as I try to tell Miles the truth?

"Ellyn?"

I hold up my hand. "Just give me a minute." I take another sip of water. "I'm sorry."

"It's okay. Take your time."

"No, I mean I'm sorry for what I'm about to tell you. For what I..." I can't hold his gaze, those blue eyes staring back at me, reflecting his love, and so often filled with laughter. And now there's a good chance I've ruined everything, or at least done significant damage. But I have to do this. Rosa, as much as it pains me to admit it, is right. "I made a decision without you. Without discussing it with you." I shift my gaze to the view outside the windows where the sea, darkening as the sun sets, is calm. "Like Twila did with Will."

I glance back at him and see an expression I don't recognize, then return my focus to the view outside the windows. "I'm really..." My breath catches and my heart seems to trip over itself a time or two. "I'm really sorry, and I know feeling sorry doesn't make it better, but I am, I really am."

Miles says nothing and his silence does nothing to ease the tension I feel. But then, I deserve the tension, and more. So much more. I finally look at him again. "I don't know what that expression means. On your face. I don't know..."

"I'm not sure I know either." He runs his hand through his hair. "Are you going to tell me what decision you made?"

"Oh. Okay, yes, I'm getting to that. "I was...I mean, I had... I don't know, exactly. I mean, I know, but I don't know why, but I..." I close my eyes and take a deep breath, then open my eyes. I make myself look at him. "I signed a lease—a twelve-month lease."

The rise of his eyebrows is almost imperceptible. Almost.

"On a house," I whisper.

Confusion clouds his expression, but he says nothing as he, it seems, tries to assimilate the information.

Heat climbs from my neck to my face, and the lump in my throat has grown to the size of a grapefruit. I sit up straight. "Miles..." As hard as this is, I want him to look at me. I deserve whatever I see in his eyes or whatever I hear after I've told him the truth. All of it. "I signed a lease on a house, but not just any house. The water tower—I leased the water tower. I went there, I saw it—just the outside, mostly. I peeked in a few windows, and then I called Tom. I should have, I know, I really know, I should have talked to you about it. I'm...sorry."

When he still says nothing, I prompt him, "Miles?"

He nods, then clears his throat. "The water tower? Huh." He turns and looks out the windows. I assume he's processing what I've told him. Considering his response rather than reacting. He is a wise man on so many levels. So good and full of integrity and... My heart swells with love for him, my husband, and then it twists and constricts as I consider how my actions shut him out.

"Miles, I'm so sorry." Tears fill my eyes. "I didn't mean to shut you out."

He looks back at me. "Why did you?"

"Sign the lease?"

"No. Shut me out."

"Oh."

"Ellyn, are you leaving?"

"Leaving? No, we're talking. Why would I leave? Well, after Monday night, I can see why you might think—"

"Are you leaving *me*?"

"*You?* Leaving you? Oh. No. No! I would never, no, not even a little bit. Never. If anyone was going to leave..." I bury my face in my hands, but I can't just cry. I need to push through this. I need to make him understand, or at least... I drop my hands to my lap and look into his eyes. "Rosa said I was afraid—afraid you'd leave me, so I...I'm so sorry."

"Is that true? Is that how you felt?"

"Maybe." I gesture to the journal and Bible and pens. "That's what I was trying to figure out. It's true, I think. I was...I am...afraid."

Miles gets up and comes and sits closer to me. He takes my hands in his, his touch warm and gentle. Always gentle. "Ellyn, I'm not going anywhere. I'm here—I'm in this. All in. But I don't know how to make you believe that."

"I know. I mean"—I wipe the tears from under my eyes, as fresh tears fall—"I know it's me, my insecurity, my issues."

"We all have issues we need to work through." He gives my hands a reassuring squeeze, then lets them go. "So, if you weren't planning to leave, what were your plans for the water tower? What are your plans?"

"It was a business decision. At least, that's what I told myself."

"Business?"

"I thought maybe I'd offer cooking classes or..." I lift my hands, helpless to explain what I don't understand myself. "But it isn't zoned for commercial use."

"Can you get the zoning changed?"

"Yes. I just have to do the legwork—file the paperwork, pay the fee."

"So you want to teach classes?"

"No. Not really."

"Ellyn, this isn't about the water tower—the lease. We discussed our finances before we married—your money is your money and, by the way, you're very good with money. If you'd decided on a new business venture, I'd have no doubt it would succeed. I trust your business instinct over my own."

"Thank you," I whisper. "It's about me shutting you out, not including you in the decision. Not talking to you about what I was feeling."

Hurt flickers in Miles's eyes. "I don't expect we'll talk about everything."

"I know. But signing a lease is a big decision."

"It isn't even that. There's a disconnect. Between us. At least, that's what it's felt like recently. I suppose the water tower—your decision—represents what I've felt. Ellyn, are you unhappy?"

"Unhappy? No, I... I thought you were..."

"You thought I was unhappy?"

"I thought you were disappointed."

"Disappointed?"

"I'm not..."—I look down at the bed—"Sarah, or Nerissa, I'm just..."

"Nerissa?"

I shake my head and look back at Miles. "It's not about them. I know it isn't, but you loved Sarah so much, and you built this house together, and...she's here Miles, everywhere I look. She's here."

Miles slowly eyes the room as though seeing it for the first time through my eyes. "You're right, of course. I didn't realize..."

"Maybe I was afraid you'd leave me, and leasing the water tower was protection in some way. I told myself it was a business decision, but I knew it wasn't business. I'm just very adept at not dealing with what I'm feeling. As you know."

"One of your many talents." His smile is brief. "So, you were afraid I was disappointed, what else?"

"I just wanted to go...home. Not leave you but find, I don't know, the solace maybe that home offers. I wanted *my* home. And then once I had the key to the water tower and saw it, everything had changed. Renovated. It was all different. And it wasn't my home. It isn't my home. I went by there today after I left the café, and I realized that the place, the house, isn't what matters. You're"—I wipe the tears from my face again—"my home. Wherever you are, that's my home."

He leans forward, wipes the tears from my face, and then kisses me, which draws even more tears. He wraps his arms around me and holds me until my tears finally subside.

When I finally pull away from him, I ask him something that's nagged at me. "You said we all have things to work through. But you don't have any issues."

"Savior complex. Very common in doctors." He chuckles, then grows serious. "I had to deal with that while Sarah was dying, but I recognize some of the traits are still intact. It's something I have to be aware of."

I remember my concern in telling Miles about Nerissa's struggle, that he'd swoop in like a knight in shining armor, wanting to rescue the damsel in distress. Maybe I wasn't too far off the mark. "Miles, about Nerissa..."

He nods.

"Why...?" Do I want to ask? Do I really want to know?

"Why what?" His tone is patient, loving.

Suddenly, I feel foolish for even asking. "Never mind."

"I'm happy to answer whatever questions you have. Let's talk through it."

I take a deep breath. "Why...didn't you go out with her?

After Sarah, when you were ready? You obviously care for her. She's kind, and wise, and…" I shrug.

"I do care for her. I enjoy her. She's a good friend. But that's all she's ever been."

"Is that because of the commitment she made to remain single?"

"Fair question. But no. I wasn't drawn to Nerissa that way. The way I'm drawn to you. She's a friend." He shrugs. "Nothing more."

"Is it possible…?" I think again about Nerissa's discomfort with my dinner invitation but then think better of asking Miles if it's possible Nerissa has feelings for him. If that's the case, it's something she'll have to work through. "Nothing. Thank you for…just thank you."

"Ellyn, back to the lease. Like I said, it seems like a symptom rather than the issue itself. But how do we deal with the issue? You mentioned seeing someone again, a counselor, is that still on your mind? Would you like me to go too, for us to see someone together?"

I tell Miles about my attempts to make an appointment and then about my call to Sabina. I gesture to the journal and the Bible. "I think my next step has something to do with those. During my appointment with Nerissa this week, she suggested I track my thoughts and feelings—as they relate to food, of course—but maybe I'll write down other things, too." I reach for the journal. "Like this." I open the journal and read what I've written. "It's one thing to believe you're created in the image of God, but it's another to live into that image."

I set the journal aside and look back to Miles. "Nerissa said that. We were talking about Twila, and how her insight about being created in the image of God impacted me. I worked through so much with Shauna—the accusations Earl hurled at me daily, Earl who turned out to be Earleen, my mother. At least, that's where those negative perceptions of myself began. But, I'm not sure how to live into the image of God. I'm not sure what Nerissa meant."

"Your friend Sabina set you on the course for living into God's image. Be still—spend time with God, in close relationship with Jesus." He points to my Bible. "May I?"

"Sure." I pick it up and hand it to him.

He flips through the pages until he finds what he's looking for, then he looks at me. "Mankind was created in the image of God, male and female."

"Right."

"After the fall, that image was tarnished. But through Christ's death and resurrection, those who believed received new life. Paul wrote, 'And we all, who with unveiled faces contemplate the Lord's glory, are being transformed into his image with ever-increasing glory, which comes from the Lord, who is the Spirit.'" Miles closes the Bible. "We live into the image of God as we participate in relationship with Jesus, as we spend time with Him. The transformation that takes place is the Spirit's work within us."

I consider what Miles has said. "I guess for some of us that takes longer than others."

He smiles. "It takes a lifetime, for each of us. But, in my experience, the more time I spend focused on God, the more He reveals, and the more I grow." He shrugs. "Not a bad deal." He leans in and kisses me again. "I'm starving."

"Oh. Paco boxed up dinner for us. I put it in the fridge. I'll heat it up."

"I'll heat it up. You take care of your back. Want it on a tray in here?"

"No, I'm feeling better. I'll come out with you."

"I'll meet you in the kitchen." He grabs the bag of melted ice off the nightstand, then heads for the bedroom door.

"Miles…"

He stops and turns back.

"Do you…forgive me?"

"No question. Thank you for your honesty tonight. It's good to talk."

I nod. "Thank you for loving me."

"Easy to do."

I meet Miles in the kitchen and take a seat at the table in the nook as he dishes the beef bourguignon into shallow bowls and then sets them in the microwave, which really is a sin, but I won't complain.

Miles sets a dish in front of me, then takes his seat. He reaches for my hand and offers a brief prayer of thanks for the food.

We eat in silence for a few minutes, then Miles looks across the table at me. "So, what are you going to do with the water tower?"

CHAPTER TWENTY-FOUR

Our vocation is not simply to be, but to work together with God in the creation of our own life, our own identity, our own destiny…. To work out our identity in God.

Thomas Merton

ia

I WALK OUT of MacMillan Hall after my appointment with my counselor, the plan she printed for me after we talked in my hand. I cut across the grass and make my way to the library, eager to go over the plan again before my first class.

I settle at a table and then read through the list of classes I'll need to take before I transfer. Then I look at the list of colleges that offer the major I now know I'll pursue. And after I earn my undergraduate degree, I'll study for the LSAT and apply to law schools—those with the concentration I want to study are also listed. And then I'll study for the bar.

A month ago, I had no idea what direction I'd take—now I have the next six to eight years of my life planned and no idea how I didn't know this before. Didn't feel this before. The passion burning within me.

What will Mama say? Will she support my plan?

How will I ever earn enough money to pay off the student loans I'll need?

And how will any of this help Manuel?

The reality is that it won't.

I stare at the list, the flame inside me flickers. How will I ever do this? I just can't see it. I unzip my backpack and stuff the sheet of information into it, then slouch in the chair.

Then I remember. I don't have to see it. That's what faith is, like Twila said, believing what we can't see. "I will believe," I whisper as I sit up straighter. And then louder. "I believe."

ON FRIDAY AFTERNOON I sit at a table at GoodLife and wait for my mama, who couldn't understand why I'd want to have lunch here instead of at home where we've already paid for the food.

"It's my treat, Mama."

"You need to save your money."

"Please? Meet me there?"

We'll both go to work from there. I left the house early so I could think. And pray. Or try to. I wanted to have this conversation away from home, where Mama still thinks she can send me to my room. No, this conversation needs to take place out from under her roof. We are two adults, whether she sees it that way or not.

When she walks into the café and bakery, she glances

around, eyes the baked goods in the case, which she is comparing to those at Auntie Ellyn's, then she turns up her nose. Not literally, but I know what she's thinking.

When she sees me, she comes to join me. "They call those baked goods?" She shakes her head. "They need to try Juanita's pastries."

"The food is good here, Mama, even the bakery items. You'll see."

"Why we here? What you have to say dat you can't say at home?"

"Mama, we haven't been getting along well at home lately. I thought we could do something special and relax and maybe we'd hear each other better."

"I hear just fine, thank you. And I not change my mind about him so you waste your money."

I sigh. "Can't we just relax for a few minutes?"

"Relaxing doesn't get things done. You know dat."

"Please."

"Fine. What you want to say?"

I ignore her question and make small talk until we have our food in front of us, then I look across the table. "Mama, I made a decision this week. I declared a major, or I will when I begin applying to universities."

Surprise registers on her face. This is not the conversation she expected. Though her pleasure will be short-lived.

"What major? You make a good choice, I'm sure. You a smart girl."

"Thank you. Yes, I've made a good choice. Political science."

Her surprise turns to confusion. "Why?"

"I'm interested in our governing and legal systems. After I finish my undergraduate degree, I plan to go to law school."

"Law school?" She nods, then her brow creases. "How we pay for dat?"

"I'll take out student loans. I'll pay them off over time."

"You pay a lot of interest is what you pay."

"Yes, some. But I'll work, too, so I can pay for some of the schooling without loans. I can do it, Mama. And"—I twist the napkin in my lap—"when I go to law school, I'll study immigration law."

Her eyes narrow. "So, it is all about *him*. I know you want me to come here so you can talk about him."

I lean forward. "Mama, this is about me." My tone is firm, sure, more sure than I feel with her sitting across from me. "This is about what I want. What I believe. About who I am. You taught me to value everyone, to see the good in all people. 'God made all of us and loves all of us.' That's what you've said. I am American. And I am Mexican. You and Papa gave me the gift of both. It isn't either or, it's both. And you taught me to honor both the country of my citizenship and the country of my heritage. Now I want to help the people from the country of my heritage who want to come and live in the country of my citizenship."

"You make good arguments—you make a good lawyer."

"Mama, Manuel is the same—"

She holds up her hand. "No! I not listen."

"He is as American as I am. The only difference is that"— she shakes her head, but I push on—"his parents didn't or couldn't become citizens the way you and Papa did. They came here legally; they had work visas. But when they weren't renewed, they... I don't know what their circumstances were, but Manuel was a baby, Mama, just a baby. It isn't his fault. What could he do? He didn't even know he was undocumented until he wanted to drive like all the other kids his age."

"He lie to you, Pia. Dat's all I need to know. He a liar."

"His parents lied to him; they lied to protect him. Yes, it

was a lie, but it was because they loved him and wanted the best for him."

"A lie is a lie."

"Their lie was so deep, so woven into him, that he perpetuated that lie. He owns that. He does."

Her lips are pressed together, her eyes hard.

"You taught me something else. You taught me to forgive. We are forgiven, so we must forgive others. What about forgiveness for Manuel? Won't you forgive him?"

She looks past me and says nothing.

"Mama, I want to see him. I want to spend time with him."

Still, she says nothing.

"I love him," I whisper. "Someday, I hope to marry him."

She glares at me, her eyes blazing. "No!" She bangs her hand on the table. Dishes rattle and water sloshes from our glasses. "No!"

I glance around and see people staring.

Then she gets up, grabs her purse, and walks out.

CHAPTER TWENTY-FIVE

Our job is to love others without stopping to inquire
whether or not they are worthy.
Thomas Merton

llyn

"WHAT IS WRONG WITH HER?" Pia's lovely complexion is mottled, and her eyes are red. "She won't even listen. She is so stubborn!"

"Here, honey." I hand her a couple of tissues. "Maybe I can talk to her. Not that she'll listen to me either. She never has." I shrug. "But I'm happy to try."

"I don't want to put you in the middle of it. I just had to tell someone who knows her, who literally knows how frustrating she can be."

"I do know that. But I also know she has a good heart—

well, most of the time—and I know how much she loves you. She's afraid you'll get hurt. She's trying to protect you."

"She's trying to control me. She even called the winery and told them not to let Manuel make the deliveries here."

"Oh. Actually, I made that call."

"What? Why?"

"I was trying to help. She said Manuel hurt you, and I didn't know the circumstances. It's just for a few weeks."

"I doubt that. She's determined to keep me away from him—to break us up. I better go before she comes searching for me."

"Hang in there, honey. It can only get better, right?"

"I hope so."

As Pia leaves the office, Paco comes in. I glance at my watch. "You're here early."

"Bella, he has to go."

"Who has to go? The new line cook? Why? I like him. He calls me 'Chef.'"

Paco shakes his head. "He has authority issues. Everything I ask him to do, he refuses to do. And his skills are questionable."

"Do I have grounds to fire him?"

"Not yet, but you will soon. I'm keeping an eye on him and will write him up before the end of the day, I'm sure. You better start looking for someone to take his place."

My cell phone rings and I reach for it. "Okay."

"Sorry, Bella."

I nod to Paco as I glance at the screen of my phone. Jim? What does he want? To let me out of the lease? I can only hope. Just as I'm about to answer the call, Rosa leans in the office door.

"What you tell her? I know she in here talking to you. You remember, I tell you he not good for her. You not take her side." She turns and looks down the hall toward the back room. I have to go, someone at the back door. But I telling you, she has to…" She's still talking as she walks away.

My phone beeps in my hand. A message from Jim, whose call I missed. Obviously. But just as I'm about to listen to the message, I hear raised voices, one of them speaking Spanish at breakneck speed. What in the world?

When I get to the back room, Rosa is still spewing words I don't understand, as she repeatedly jabs Manuel in the chest, him towering over her. "Uh-oh." I glance back to see if Pia's heard her mother yet but only see Paco coming to investigate what the commotion is about. "Keep Pia in the dining room!" I hiss.

I turn back and grab Rosa by the shoulders before she starts swinging at Manuel.

"I just want to see her—to tell her something. But I gave you my word. I won't see her without your permission." Manuel's tone is calm but firm.

"No! You go!"

"Please, Mrs. Sanchez."

"Rosa, can't he just talk to her?"

She whips around and points her finger at me. "This not your business!"

"You do remember that you work for me and that this is my business, literally, right?" I take Rosa's arm and begin to guide her—okay, drag her—toward the office. I look back at Manuel as we go. "You better go. This isn't the time or the place."

When we get to the office, I point to the door. "Get in there."

"I sue you for harassment."

"You do that, right after I fire you. Get in there."

She goes into the office, begrudgingly.

"Sit." I point to the chair next to the desk.

She crosses her arms over her chest and stares at me,

unmoving.

"Rosa, sit down." I close the office door and when she still hasn't moved, I take a step toward her.

"Fine. I sit."

"Thank you." I drop into my chair at the desk and sit for a minute as I catch my breath. I figure the time won't do Rosa any harm, either. When I think she's cooled a bit, I lean forward and look her in the eyes. "What is going on?"

"He just show up! He keep showing up."

"That's not what I mean and you know it."

She doesn't respond, instead she looks away from me. I work to keep my tone level, and, believe me, it is work. She is so maddening! "What is it about Manuel that has you so—"

She stands up and makes laps around the small office. "I tell her. I warn her over and over. Pia, I say, you only go out with boys who are legal, who are in school, with jobs. Only boys with papers. I tell her over and over. I tell her she get hurt, and now, what happen. Just what I say would happen. I tell her to let him go. But she not listen. If she let him go, she find someone else. He not the only fish to fry."

"Fish in the sea?"

"What?"

"Nothing." I point to the chair again. "Please sit down, you're making me dizzy."

She sits back down, arms crossed over her chest.

Is it any wonder Pia won't listen to her? She learned from the best. But as I look at Rosa, my frustration with her collapses like an overwhipped meringue. I know what's wrong with Rosa, what she's feeling. I know because... As the memories rush through my mind, so do the feelings. To admit that feeling to someone else means having to deal with it. And that's the last thing I wanted to do. It's the last thing Rosa wants to do.

"Mama"—the tenderness in my tone surprises me and it

isn't lost on Rosa—"you said something to me once that ulti-mately changed a lot of things for me."

"What dat?"

"You told me I was terrified, and you were right."

"Of course, I right." She looks away from me again.

"Look at me," I whisper. When she doesn't, I reach out and put my hand on her arm until she meets my gaze. What I read in her dark eyes confirms what I thought. "You're terrified."

She shakes her head, her denial fierce.

"You're terrified. I just don't know why. What are you afraid of?"

"She get hurt. Dat's all. I protect her."

Her response comes too fast and sounds too certain. Realization dawns. "You're...lying."

Her eyes widen and she jumps up. "How dare you..." Her voice shakes and I'm sure her little body is about to combust with anger. "You have no right to accuse me. I tell de truth. I always tell de—"

I'm on my feet and grabbing her shoulders before she knows what's happening. I look her in the eyes. "You need to go cool off. Go for a walk." I point to the door.

"I not going anywhere. There's work to do."

"Rosa, go! Take a break. Walk. Now! And don't come back until you're ready to treat me with the respect I deserve. As your boss. And as your friend—a friend, I'll remind you, that you made part of your family. I deserve your respect. I deserve the truth." I open the office door and stand there a moment. "Go." I say more gently. "Take some time."

Her shoulders drop along with her countenance, and she walks out the office door, and within a few seconds, I hear the back door open and close.

I glance at my watch. Only 3:00 p.m.? It's going to be a long evening.

CHAPTER TWENTY-SIX

Only the man who has had to face despair is really convinced
that he needs mercy. Those who do not want mercy never
seek it. It is better to find God on the threshold of despair
than to risk our lives in a complacency that has never felt the
need of forgiveness.

Thomas Merton

erissa

THE OFFICE IS QUIET. Friday afternoons often are. The others
who work in the suite of offices, including a massage therapist and a chiropractor, take Fridays off. We are a holistic
group, each serving the residents of Mendocino in a way that
utilizes our knowledge and gifts. I remind myself of that fact
today. God has gifted me for the work I do.

I open the planner, as I have so often over the last few

weeks, and look again at the empty spaces on the calendar. I have just a handful of regular clients—not nearly enough to provide adequate income to support myself, even with the hours I put in at the store. But God has gifted me for this work, and unless He provides something else, this is the work I will do.

Thank You, Lord. I will trust You.

The weight I've carried for days and days—the fatigue, the financial worry, the heartache for Twila, the darkness that has consumed me, and the longing for another, one to comfort me in the darkest moments—all remain.

"'My soul hath wrestled in it...'" I whisper the words of Saint John of the Cross.

I *have* wrestled. I will continue to wrestle. I will not give in. A shift has taken place in my soul and I will meet the darkness with gratitude. I will give thanks in *all* things. I look from the planner out the window, the shutters opened to the view. It is a crisp, clear February day, the beauty a reminder of God's goodness, even when I can't feel His presence.

As I watch a gull soar on the currents, a woman walks past the office window, head down, and talking to herself. Rosa?

I get up from my desk and quickly make my way through the waiting room and out the door. By the time I reach the sidewalk, she's turned around and is coming back my way, head still down.

"Rosa, hello."

She looks up and stops walking. "It you." Then she looks back down.

I smile. "Yes, it's me." But my smile fades. "Are you alright?"

She lifts her chin and squares her shoulders and glances at me again, then she looks away and seems to wilt. "No."

"I'm sorry. Do you have a few minutes to come in for a cup of coffee?"

She nods and we walk in silence into the building. In the waiting area, I pour myself a cup of hot water for tea and Rosa a cup of coffee from the pot I'd, out of habit, just brewed. She takes the mug from me, wraps her hands around it, and follows me into my office. "Have a seat." I gesture to one of the two chairs across from my desk, and I take the other, turning it toward her.

Rosa's silence is as unsettling, as it is unusual. I set my cup of tea on the desk and watch as she stares into her cup. "What happened?" I finally ask.

Still staring into her cup, she whispers, "God punish me. I tell a lie, and God punish me."

I consider what she's said, and while I want to validate whatever pain she's feeling, I also want to speak truth. "I'm sorry you feel that way. But you know that's not how God works. That's not who He is."

For the first time, she looks at me. Then she shakes her head. "No, I tell a lie and now I pay for it. Again."

"Perhaps the consequence feels like punishment."

"De consequences. Yes."

"Do you want to talk about it?"

"It a long time ago."

I wait for her to say more, grateful I don't have a client waiting. Grateful for the time to be present. Here. Now. *Thank You, Lord. May I be Your ears, offer Your mercy, extend Your grace, give Your love to Rosa.* As I pray, darkness, enveloping, consuming, rolls in like dense fog, blinding me. Like the bank of fog that rolled in the afternoon of Miles and Ellyn's reception. And with it, the sense of foreboding. That's when it began. That's when the darkness came for me. Just me? Or did it come for all of us?

You are here, God. I can't feel You. I can't see You. And You are here. I will believe what I can't see. What I can't sense. What I can't feel.

"I tell Pia truth is de most important thing. 'Always tell de truth,' I say. Over and over, I say it to her. I make sure she know. Nothing more important than truth. I tell her because I know. I tell a lie, and I know what de lie cost."

I lean forward. "What has it cost you?"

"My mama's life. "It cost me…" Tears well in Rosa's dark eyes. This is a woman, I am certain, who does not waste tears. Who keeps them to herself. Deep inside. And my heart aches for her.

"It cost me my mama's…life." She covers her face with her hands.

I place my hand on her arm. "Tell me."

Slowly, she drops her hands to her lap and looks straight ahead. "I was young. I fall in love and love is all dat mattered."

"Raul?"

"Yes."

She turns and looks at me and then past me to the window and beyond. But I am sure it isn't the ocean she sees.

"He tall, and handsome, and a few years older than me. He kind and smart and good. So good. He tell me he love me and he want to marry me, but he can't stay in Mexico. He have to leave. It not safe there for him. And because I with him, it not safe for me either. He warn me when we met, he told me de truth, but I didn't listen. All I could see was de good. All I could see was him. All I could see was love." She shakes her head slowly, lost in her memories. "I just like her, just like Pia now.

"When he ask me to marry him, he tell me we have to leave." She turns and looks at me. "His family have money, lots of money because of de drugs. It not safe because Raul refused to work in de business, but he not tell his family dat. He know if he refuse, he become a threat to them. So we make a plan, we get work visas, it all takes time, but step by step, we follow de plan we make. When de time finally come, I tell my mama and my papa that I going out. Just out. I tell them de lie."

She stares beyond me again, somewhere else, to another time, another place. "I take nothing with me, just a bag I packed and give to Raul de day before. I tell Mama and Papa I love them, and I see them later. But"—her eyes glisten with tears again—"I never see them again. Never. I can never go back."

"Several months later, my mama dead. De heart attack take her. I not there. I not there for her. I not there for my papa. Less than a year later, my papa go, too. It too much grief for him. And I not there."

"Oh, Rosa," I whisper. "I'm so sorry."

"And now, she do de same. Pia do de same. She love dat boy and if he get deported, she go with him. She follow him to Mexico and she never come back. No question. Dat exactly what she do. She leave me just like I"—she covers her face again—"left my mama." Her words, muffled, come out on a sob.

I get up and kneel in front of her. "Rosa, all these years, God has loved you, He has forgiven you. That is who He is." I reach up and gently pull her hands from her face. "You suffered hard and painful consequences—so much grief. I can't imagine the loss you felt. But God not only forgave you, He blessed you with a husband you loved and with a beautiful daughter. Don't believe the lie, the accusation. God is merciful and gracious—He gave His only Son as payment for our sins. Anytime we believe God is anyone other than who Scripture says He is, we believe an illusion. Let the illusion go, Rosa. Let it go."

"But I so angry. Ellyn, she say I terrified and she right. I so scared I lose Pia. I hang on too tight. I make her miserable. Soon I lose her anyway because she hate me."

"Give her to God. Trust God with Pia."

She shakes her head. "It hard. She all I have."

"I know. I understand, remember? But once you surrender, once you give Pia to God, you will rest. You will have peace."

"I believe you. But she so angry. I don't know dat she forgive me."

"Does she know why you've held on to her? Does she understand what happened and why you've been afraid?"

"She not know. I never tell her de story. I too ashamed to tell her."

"It's not too late, Rosa. Talk to Pia. Tell her."

"Now? I tell her now?"

"If you want to talk to her now, yes."

Rosa grabs my hands and holds them tight. "You come. You come with me and be there. Please? She at the café."

"I'm happy to go with you."

Rosa squeezes my hands. "You remind me of de truth. The most important truth. Thank you."

I FOLLOW Rosa into the café through the back door, the clamor from the kitchen—voices raised above the clang of cookware and the delightful aromas wafting—speak of the busyness of the afternoon as Ellyn's staff prepares for the evening.

We go through the kitchen and into the dining room where Rosa finds Pia.

"I talk to you." Rosa's tone is softer than I've heard it before. "Please."

Pia looks from Rosa to me and offers me a hesitant smile. Then she looks back at Rosa. "Now? Here?"

"Yes. We sit." Rosa turns and gestures to me. "She come, too. She listen."

Pia looks at me again, then nods.

Just as we're about to sit at one of the linen-clad tables, Ellyn bursts through the swinging doors from the kitchen, then stops short when she sees us. "What's going on?"

"Auntie Ellyn…" Pia waves Ellyn over, then says quietly. "She wants to talk."

Ellyn looks at Rosa, then at me. "Nerissa, hi. What are you…? Well, never mind." She looks back to Pia. "Okay, honey. That's fine. You talk. Take a few minutes—however long it takes." She pats Pia on the back, then turns to go.

"No, wait. Stay. Please?" Pia's plea makes it clear she doesn't trust what Rosa has to say.

Healing, Lord. Healing for mother and daughter, please.

"You stay. I need to say dis to you, too." Rosa pulls out a chair at the table. "You sit here," she tells Ellyn.

"Oh." Ellyn peeks at her watch. "Okay." She comes to the table and takes the seat Rosa has assigned her.

Rosa points to the chair next to Ellyn. "Nerissa, sit there."

"Alright." I take the seat next to Ellyn.

As Rosa takes her seat, she looks at Ellyn and points to me. "She my friend."

Ellyn leans over to me. "Lucky you," she whispers.

When we're all settled, Rosa looks across the table at me and I nod my encouragement.

"Wait." She points to me. "You come sit next to me, so I can see Pia." She looks at Pia sitting next to her. "You trade with her."

"Rosa, you do realize it's Friday afternoon and we have a full house for dinner tonight, right?"

"Okay, okay, stay where you are. I just say dis out. Now. I

just say it." She turns toward Pia. "I..." She glances at me again.

"It's okay, Rosa, tell her."

She nods, then looks back at Pia. "I sorry. I sorry I not listen and I sorry dat I try to control everything."

Ellyn leans over again, "What'd you say to her?" She whispers.

"It's what you said to her—you made her think." I whisper back.

"Shh!" Rosa glares at us. "I trying to tell her something." She turns back to Pia. "You ask me why I always say 'In America, with God, all things are possible.'"

Pia nods, and it's clear she's listening intently.

"I say dat because it true, but like you point out, it true everywhere. God de same everywhere. But I say 'America' because this is your home. This is where your papa and I want to raise you. This is where I want you to stay."

"Of course, where else would I go?"

"What happen if Manuel deported?"

Pia shakes her head. "I can't think about that, Mama. I can't."

"Well, I think about it. I think about it all de time. Because I know what it feel like to fall in love. And I know what it feel like to leave everything—*everyone*—to follow de man dat you love."

Rosa looks across the table to Ellyn. "You right. But just this time. I..."—Rosa wipes her eyes—"terrified."

Ellyn leans forward. "It's okay, Mama. It's okay."

Mama? Ellyn's tone with Rosa is tender, and for the first time I understand the love, the bond perhaps, that lies beneath the surface of their caustic exchanges.

As I listen again to Rosa's story, I see God's mercy in so many ways, including the tears in Pia's eyes and the softening in Rosa as truth sets her free. I think of Twila and Will and pray again for God's provision for them, for His love and mercy for each of them as they follow Him. And sitting next to Ellyn, I think of Miles.

Oh, Lord, how I need Your mercy, too.

"I trust you to God now. I should do it sooner, but I do it now. You call him. Call Manuel. He here earlier and want to tell you something."

"Thank you, Mama," Pia whispers as she wipes tears from her cheeks. Then she leans over and wraps her arms around Rosa. "I love you, Mama. I love you."

Tears pool in Ellyn's eyes, too.

She looks at me. "Rosa has a good friend in you."

"As she does in you."

"Well, don't tell her I said so, but we really are the lucky ones." Ellyn looks back to Rosa and Pia. "Okay, you two, enough of this. We have a restaurant to run!"

As we get up from the table and say our good-byes, I pull Ellyn aside. "I wonder…" I take a deep breath to steady myself. This is the right choice. I have my own truths to face. "May I use my rain check? Is your invitation to dinner still open?"

Ellyn stares at me a moment, then she smiles. "Absolutely. How does Monday night sound?"

"Perfect."

CHAPTER TWENTY-SEVEN

Finally I am coming to the conclusion that my highest
ambition is to be what I already am. That I will never fulfill
my obligation to surpass myself unless I first accept myself,
and if I accept myself fully in the right way, I will already
have surpassed myself.
Thomas Merton

llyn

IT'S near midnight when I finally pull into the garage. I sit in
the car a few moments as I let the day replay, at least parts of
it. Since this afternoon, I've waited for the ravages of regret I
expected to hit after setting the dinner date with Nerissa. But
the "how could I be so stupid to invite her to dinner" feeling
doesn't come. Neither does Earl's voice reminding me of my
stupidity. Of my jealousy. And that's exactly what it is, what

it *was*. It had nothing to do with Sarah, Nerissa, or Miles, did it? I created it out of the deep well of my own insecurity. But even that realization doesn't lead to the usual internal grousing. Instead, that truth—I smile—sets me free. Just as the truth did for Rosa this afternoon.

Just as I move to get out of the car, I remember the message from Jim. I never listened to it, though that's not surprising. I didn't get to a lot of things today. I pull my phone from my purse, get out of the car, and then hit the icon to listen to the voice mail as I walk into the house. When Miles doesn't greet me at the door, I assume he's gone on to bed. Who could blame him?

I drop my things in the laundry room as Jim hems and haws about an investment gone bad. *And why is he telling me this piece of news?* As I cross the living room, Miles comes out of the den and I wave, then I stop midstep. "What? You have got to be kidding me."

Miles mouths *What?*

I shake my head, pull the phone away from my ear, and press End. "I can't believe it. After all these years, after all the offers I made him, all the times I begged him—"

"What are you talking about?"

I try to assimilate the information, but it makes no sense. "Jim wants to sell the water tower."

"What about the lease?"

"He wants *me* to buy it. Good grief."

"Might be a good investment." Miles comes over and gives me a kiss. "How was your day?"

"You wouldn't believe it if I told you."

He chuckles, then puts his hand on my cheek. "Try me."

I stare into his eyes, always filled with love when he looks at me. Why haven't I believed what I've seen, what in this moment seems so obvious?

Miles loves *me*.

261

The realization nearly takes my breath. "Sure you don't mind staying up a little longer? It's late."

"There's no one I'd rather stay up with."

"That's true, isn't it?"

His expression grows serious. "It is true."

I lean into him and kiss him, slowly. Then I step back so I can see his face. "It would be a *great* investment."

Miles laughs and I keep talking. "Jim sounds desperate to sell—I'm sure I could—we could—get it for a good price. And he's already done all the work. I don't love the renovations he's done, but he certainly updated it."

Miles shrugs. "Like I said, I trust your business sense."

I stare at him a moment.

"What?"

"I'm just amazed by you. Rosa told me that the secret I was keeping—the lease—was festering inside me. She was right. I'm so sorry I didn't tell you, and now I'm so grateful you know. Thank you, again."

"For what?"

"Everything."

He smiles at me. "Tea?"

I follow him into the kitchen, where he sets the kettle to boil as I drop onto a bar stool. "What would we do with the water tower? Rent it? We don't want to be landlords, do we?"

"Not especially. But I have been thinking since we talked the other night. Maybe it's time to consider making a move."

"A move?" I look around the white kitchen, so unlike the choices I would have made for this space. For this house. "Oh."

He sits down next to me. "You were right—Sarah's imprint is on everything in this house."

"But so is yours. You worked with the architect to design this house—you put so much thought into it. And, you love it. It's your home."

He swivels on the bar stool and looks around the kitchen as I just did, then I follow his gaze to the great room. "It's a good house—I've enjoyed it, but we could put *our* mark on a place. Though that doesn't answer the question about the water tower."

"The water tower's too small for us. We need space for the kids when they come to stay." I reach out and put my hand on Miles's arm. "Selling this place would be hard on the boys. This is where they remember Sarah, where they spent their last days with her."

He nods. "But when it comes down to it, it's just a house. They'll always have their memories. Let's keep talking about it. It's a little late to make a decision about it tonight"—he looks over at the clock on the microwave—"or this morning, I should say." He gets up as the kettle whistles.

"Same with the water tower. I appreciate Jim giving me first right of refusal, although I think it was more a desperate pitch than an act of respect, but that property will sell quickly. He'll have no problem finding a buyer. But no need to decide tonight. Anyway, I don't think there's really a decision to make."

Miles fills two mugs with water, drops a tea bag in one, then looks at me.

"I'll take mine straight, thanks."

He brings the mug of hot water over and sets it in front of me.

"I meant to tell you the other night—I invited Nerissa for dinner. I thought it might give the two of you time to talk, parent to parent."

He sits next to me again and reaches over and covers my hand with his. "You're okay with that?"

"I am. Actually, when I get out of my own way, I enjoy Nerissa. Does Monday evening work for you?"

"Sure. Did she mention how Twila's doing?"

"It doesn't sound like Twila's told her much, but I did talk to Twila."

"You did? I should stay up late more often. I learn all kinds of things."

"I wasn't sure how much to share with you."

"Ah... If Twila shared something with you in confidence, I don't want to intrude."

"It's not that—I guess I just needed to work through some things first, before talking to you." I take a sip of the hot water as I recall Twila's concerns. "Evidently Nerissa is going through a difficult time. Did you know that?"

"No. I haven't seen her since the day I ran into her at the bank."

I tell Miles what Twila shared about her father and the spousal support payments. "But Twila seemed to think Nerissa's dealing with more than financial issues. She mentioned a spiritual battle, which honestly, I don't know a lot about. It sounded a little far-fetched to me, but that's why Twila's here—why she came home. She sensed Nerissa would need her."

"Will had a problem with that?"

"I'm not sure, exactly."

"I'd like to pin him down on what really happened. They're adults, I know, but if Twila felt Nerissa needed her, I'd hate to think Will would have stood in the way."

"Twila implied it was more than that—it had to do with the gift God's given her, that sense of knowing, and how she uses it. Like I said, I'm not sure."

"Well, anyway, I'm glad you invited Nerissa for dinner. The Bible is pretty clear on spiritual warfare. If that's what she's going through, she'll need support. And our prayers."

"I realize that now. I've spent more time reading this week—the Bible—and writing things down, as Nerissa had suggested. Well, not the food, I haven't written any of that down. But the other things and the reading, they're helpful."

"How so?"

"This may sound strange, but they're helping me understand myself—who I am. Does that make sense?"

"Makes perfect sense. Our identity is founded in God, who He is, and who He says we are. The enemy is bent on getting us to believe we're someone other than who God says we are. That's one of the reasons it's important to stay close to Him and lean on the truth of His Word."

When neither of us can keep our eyes open a moment longer, I rinse our mugs and leave them to dry. Miles grabs my hand and we walk through the kitchen and great room, flipping off lights as we go. As we climb the stairs, an unfamiliar feeling tags along, one I can't quite identify. When we reach the landing, it occurs to me. The feeling is ease. Comfort. And something else... I feel secure. In Miles's love for me. But more importantly, in God's love for me.

It was a long day, but a good day.

The conversation with Rosa, as frustrating as it felt in the moment, led to something valuable. It seemed God used me, and Nerissa, separately yet together, to bring some healing to Rosa and Pia's relationship.

And Nerissa's earlier discomfort when I'd invited her for dinner, or at least what I perceived as discomfort, was gone. I look forward to having her here on Monday, which a week ago would not have been the case.

When we reach the bedroom, Miles goes into the bathroom to brush his teeth. I intend to go to my closet to change into my pajamas and crawl into bed as soon as possible, but I pause for a moment and look around the room—the design Miles and Sarah decided on, the decor she chose. Yes, Sarah's imprint is here. And then, for the first time since Miles mentioned it, I recall what Miles told me about Sarah—her suggestion that he ask me out when he was ready.

I walk to the window that looks out on the cliffs and the ocean beyond. Was it just several nights ago I stood out there? Alone? I couldn't take in the love Miles offered me, the words he spoke to me. Did he speak truth? Are all the things he attributed to me that night true? Am I caring, and creative, and compassionate? What else did he say? Intelligent and wise... As I recite the list of attributes Miles sees in me, I realize they are each attributes of God.

As I step back from the window, my own image is reflected back to me, and I see, maybe for the first time, not the overweight, imperfect woman with the long, wild red curls, but I see the real me—the woman God created and is transforming into a likeness of Himself. "Thank you," I whisper.

Then I turn around and take in the bedroom, the beige linen comforter on the bed, and the white, square throw pillows. I walk over to the bed and run one hand over the straight, contemporary lines of the nightstand, and I touch the sleek lamp that sits on the nightstand. All choices Sarah made. And I consider again what Miles shared with me.

I was also one of Sarah's choices, her choice for Miles, the man she loved.

"Thank you, too," I whisper.

When Miles comes back into the bedroom, I'm still standing there, looking at each of the touches Sarah added to this room. "What do you think about redecorating?"

Miles looks around. "Fine with me."

"I think Sarah might approve."

He smiles. "I'm sure she would."

WHEN WE FINALLY CLIMB INTO bed, I roll onto my side and wrap my arm around Miles. His breathing slows, then steadies. Within moments, he's asleep. I gently roll away from him and stare into the dark, mind whirring with details of the day, including all those things I didn't get accomplished. A list begins to form for tomorrow, along with those things I won't be able to do until Monday, my day off, like place the beef order and schedule a service appointment for the freezer.

Tomorrow I'll call Jim and tell him to find a buyer for the water tower. It would be a good investment—the location overlooking the headlands with an expansive, unimpeded view of the rugged coastline, including the Point Cabrillo Lighthouse, and the ocean as far as you can see. But a rental? Neither Miles nor I have the time or inclination to deal with renters and the upkeep of a second home.

I roll over again, determined to shut off my mind. But when I close my eyes, visions of the new kitchen—all that white marble and white subway tile—invade my mind, and with it comes an idea, or at least the seed of an idea.

But it's crazy.

It makes no sense.

But the longer I consider it, the more interesting it becomes.

CHAPTER TWENTY-EIGHT

Self-confidence is a precious natural gift, a sign of health. But it is not the same thing as faith. Faith is much deeper, and it must be deep enough to subsist when we are weak, when we are sick, when our self-confidence is gone, when our self-respect is gone.
Thomas Merton

ia

IT HAD BEEN after ten when I finally left the café last night—the longest shift of my life. I'd texted Manuel as soon as my mama had given me her approval, her promise to trust me to God. I couldn't wait to talk to him, to tell him, and to hear what he wanted to tell me.

"I can call him, right? I can see him?" I held on to my mama's sleeve, afraid to let her go until she was clear, until she agreed.

She hesitated for just a second. "Yes. You call him. You tell him I give my permission."

"Thank you, Mama!" I threw my arms around her and hugged her tight, then I ran to the lockers to get my phone. When Manuel didn't answer the call, I wasn't surprised. He would be making deliveries. I left a message, telling him what had happened, and asked him to meet me after work. I would see him!

It was a busy night, but I checked my phone every chance I got. Still no message from him. No text. Nothing. I waited. I called again and again. I held my phone; I wouldn't let it go. But I must have fallen asleep.

Now, gray light filters into my room. Morning? Still groggy, I sit up as my memory clears—the calls that went to Manuel's voice mail after work last night. The texts. All unanswered. The restless night.

I reach for my phone, still next to me in bed. *Please, God, please...* But the screen is blank—no messages, no texts. I flop back down and toss the phone aside.

Where is he? Why wouldn't he call? He'd had something to tell me—that's what he told Mama, so why wouldn't he call? As I consider the possibilities, none of them make sense.

I roll over and bury my face in my pillow. I will not cry. I won't. He's fine. He has to be fine. I lift my head when I hear a tap on my door. "What?" I mumble.

My mama comes into the room and stands at the foot of my bed. "You sick?"

"No."

"It late. You sure you not sick?" She comes to the side of the bed and puts her hand on my forehead. "You warm."

"I'm fine."

"You not fine, you crying." Her forehead creases and

there's doubt in her eyes. "What happened? He not call? See, he already—"

"No, Mama. I just haven't heard from him." I sit up and my stomach clenches. I wrap my arms around my waist.

"You make yourself sick." She straightens my comforter and then picks up my pillow and fluffs it.

"Why wouldn't he call?"

"He probably just busy. He call soon, you see." But she doesn't look at me as she says it. She thinks he's done something—thinks he can't be trusted. "You rest now."

When she leaves my room, I reach for the phone again and look at the time. Almost 9:00 a.m.—late enough to call Manuel's house. I look through my contacts until I find his home number, then make the call. I wait as the phone rings on the other end, and wait. But no one answers—not his parents, his brother, no one. When voice mail comes on, I hang up. But then I call back and leave a message. Someone has to know where he is.

I finally pull myself from bed, go to the kitchen, and force down a cup of coffee and a bowl of cereal so I can function. I shower and dress, the minutes dragging by. At 11:00 I call the only number I could find online for the winery where Manuel works—he usually works on the property on Saturday afternoons. The call goes to voice mail, and frustrated, I leave another message, saying I need to speak with him and asking that they have him call me as soon as he gets there.

Then I call his home again, but there's still no answer.

I slump on the sofa, my shoulders tight, my neck aching, and my stomach nauseated. When my mama comes through the living room, she says nothing, which unsettles me even more. When the doorbell rings, my heart lurches and I jump up and run to the door. "Manuel!" I swing the door open and then my legs threaten to give out. I hold on to the door to steady myself. "What are you doing here?"

"I'm not sure. I just, like, I knew I needed to be here."

Mama comes around me and holds the door open, "You come in. You right. She need you. Something wrong."

A couple of hours ago, Mama reassured me everything would be fine, but now I know she no longer believes that.

Twila comes in, gently grasps my arm, and leads me to the sofa. "Here, sit."

I do as she tells me, then she sits next to me. We sit in silence, shoulder to shoulder, then I glance at her. "I can't, I don't want to, talk. But I need you to pray."

"I am. I have been. Since early—I woke early and I began praying. It's Manuel?"

"Something's wrong."

We sit again in silence until my phone, sitting on the sofa next to me, rings. I dive for it, look at the screen, and sob. "It's not him. It's not him!"

"Answer it." My mama comes and stands in front of me. "Answer de phone."

Twila scoots closer to me. "Answer it, Pia."

"Hello..." I listen to the voice and try to take in what I hear. "No, no, no..." I try to understand, but now I can't hear him, the sobs are too loud. "I can't understand..."

Someone takes the phone from my hand and they talk, they ask questions, but I can't... I just can't... I turn my face into the sofa as someone wails, the sound piercing my ears. The wail comes again and again and again...

"Pia!" Someone holds me and shakes me. "Pia! Listen!"

I pull away. "No, Mama, no..."

"Pia, he okay. He alive, Pia. He alive!"

I look at my mama, her eyes hard, her grip on my arms too tight. "He's...alive?" I whisper. "Alive?"

"Yes."

"Where? Where is he?"

"De helicopter take him to Santa Rosa. He at Santa Rosa Memorial."

"Why there, why so far? I need to go…" I move to get up, to go, but she holds on to me. She won't let me go.

"No. Wait. He…"

"What? Tell me. Tell me!"

"Pia…" Twila's voice is calm, soothing. "It's serious. Santa Rosa—it's a trauma center."

"No, no, no…" I cry. "What happened? What? Who called? They said an accident. What happened?"

"He in a car accident on Highway 1—head-on with another car. They take him into surgery now. You can't see him. He be in surgery a long time."

"I need to go, Mama. I need to go." She loosens her grip on my arms and wraps them around me. I lean into her and cry. "I need to go…"

She rubs my hair. "Shh…it going to be okay. He going to be okay."

I let her hold me. I cling to her.

"Shh…it going to be okay."

"He'll be alright, Pia," Twila reassures.

When my tears are finally spent, I pull away from Mama and lean back on the sofa, my head aching. I turn to Twila. "Keep praying," I plead with her. "Don't stop. Please don't stop."

"I won't stop." She reaches out and takes my hand, her touch gentle.

"Pia," my mama whispers, her tone not one I've heard before.

"What? What is it?"

"Does he…? Does Manuel have a license? A driver's license?"

"A driver's…" All the implications, all the possibilities,

everything this accident could mean assault me. And the tears begin again. "Oh, Mama..." But no, I have to be calm, I have to think, I have to help him. *Think Pia, think...*

"Yes, yes." I nod. "Yes. He just got it. AB 60—it went into effect January 15th. It's okay, Mama. It's okay." But even as I say it, I know that's just one small piece of it. Just one piece. There is so much more. So, so much more. Whether he has his license or not. A driver's license is the least of it.

It is the only document he has.

AS THE EVENING WEARS ON, I learn more. Manuel's brother, Juan, had called earlier. When I got that straight, when I remembered his voice, I called him back. Manuel had been coming home from the winery on Friday afternoon when a car crossed into his lane just south of Mendocino. As Juan described where Manuel was, all I could picture was his car swerving and crashing over the cliff, falling, falling, falling. But that's not what happened. Instead, because he was heading north, the car that hit him pushed him into the embankment. Neither car, thank God, went the other way, as so many others who've fallen to their watery grave.

But, as Juan described it, the impact of the hit, and the seat belt that likely saved Manuel's life, caused his head to whip forward, while the seat belt held his body in place. The force may have caused his brain to hit the inside of his skull. There was evidence of swelling in the brain. The details, as I listened, were overwhelming. Surgery to remove a piece of his skull to relieve pressure on his brain and to make room for swollen tissue. He also has broken ribs and sustained internal injuries.

As I listened, I wanted to plug my ears and curl into a ball. But Twila was next to me, Juan on the speaker. As he talked she took notes, she asked questions, she held my hand. And now Twila still sits next to me, the small branch of thorns tattooed on her cheek a reminder that she is here for those who suffer.

She is here for me. And for Manuel.

~

ON SUNDAY MORNING, I walk into the hospital in Santa Rosa, my hand in my mama's tight grasp. Never before have I been so grateful for her take-charge ways. She called and spoke with Juan again this morning, got an update, and then packed overnight bags for both of us as I sat and watched. That was all I could do. All I've done.

I can't *do* anything.

My mama pulls me along until we reach an elevator. As we wait for the doors to open, she turns to me. "You stand up straight. You be strong. He need you to be strong now."

"I...can't, I can't—"

"I not teach you dat. You can. With God's help, you can— He strong when you weak, remember? Manuel need you."

When we reach the ICU, Juan is in the waiting area, staring at his phone.

"Hey..."

He looks up at me, his eyes bloodshot. He stands and gives me a hug, then turns to Mama and holds out his hand. "I'm Juan, Manuel's brother. It's good to meet you, Mrs. Sanchez."

"How is he? Where is he?" I glance around the unit.

"He's the same. The swelling is down a little bit, but it could be a couple of weeks before it's down enough to replace the bone in his skull. But maybe sooner."

"Did he...wake up? Is he conscious?" I literally cannot

believe I'm standing here asking these questions about Manuel. How can this be happening?

"No, he hasn't woken up. But talk to him, Pia. Let him know you're here."

"He has to wake up. He has—"

"He wake up soon. I know. He will. You go see him."

I nod. Mama can't know what will happen, but I need her words. What would normally annoy, now gives me hope.

"C'mon, he's over there. My parents are in there now. They'll come out and you can go in. Only two visitors at a time."

"Mama?"

"You go. I wait here to meet his parents."

"Yeah, okay." I turn to go, wanting so much to see Manuel, but...

"It be okay, Pia. Go." Mama gives me a gentle push.

Juan takes my hand and leads me. As we approach the room, I see Manuel's parents through the glass—his mama bent over the bed, talking. His papa standing back, hands clasped behind his back, head bowed.

Then I see Manuel, and I stop walking, tears choking me.

Juan squeezes my hand and his papa turns and sees us.

When Manuel's mama and papa come out of the room, his mama gives me a hug, then she puts her hands on my cheeks and looks me in the eyes, *"El te ama tanto."*

Her words draw fresh tears as I hug her again. *"Gracias,"* I whisper. I know Manuel loves me, but to hear his mama tell me he loves me *"so much"* about breaks me. Manuel's papa pulls a fresh handkerchief from his pocket and hands it to me.

"He needs you, Pia. He needs to know you're here. He needs you to..." Juan clears his throat. "He needs you to pull him through."

I wipe my eyes as I nod. "Okay." I start for Manuel's room, then I remember something and turn back. "Juan, wait."

"What?"

"Manuel wanted to tell me something. He came to the café and talked to my mama on Friday, before..." I shake my head. "Before the accident. Do you know what it was? What he wanted to tell me?"

Juan shrugs. "Sorry."

What if I never know? What if...? No, I can't think that way.

I turn back and do what I never imagined having to do. As I walk into the small ICU room, a rush of cool air chills me, and the scents, the sounds—all of it makes it feel like I've walked into a different world, one I hope to never return to once we leave.

I go to Manuel's side and reach out for him but then stop. Tubes come out of his arm and run up an IV pole to bags filled with what, I don't know. A clip on his finger is attached to another machine. His head is wrapped in bandaging. Other wires are attached to his body and a machine next to the bed beeps consistently. His eyes are closed, his warm milk chocolate-colored complexion ashen.

"Oh, Manuel." I cover my mouth and stare at the man I love, the man I hardly recognize.

A sob catches in my throat, but I don't let it escape. I won't let it escape. I close my eyes for a moment to steady myself, to gather whatever strength I have. But I have none. Nothing.

God, I need You... We need You, I plead. I swipe a tear from my cheek. *Please!*

I take a deep breath, then open my eyes, determined this time to offer Manuel something, anything. I carefully reach for him again, avoiding the tubes, and find a place on his wrist where I can touch him. He is warm and his pulse beats beneath my fingers. The steady beat, the sure rhythm of his pulse, strengthens me.

"I'm here, Manuel, I'm here. You're going to get through this—you're strong and you can do this. We can do this, together. We can do this." I watch for any sign that he's heard me, that he knows I'm here, but I see nothing that gives me hope. "You have to wake up. You have to wake up soon. You have something you wanted to tell me, but I don't know what it is. You have to tell me." Still there's no sign he's heard me, or that he...ever will.

"Please God, please," I whisper. "Please save him, save Manuel..." As I say Manuel's name, as I whisper it to God, as I beg God to save him, something I've never considered before comes to mind. *Manuel*, a shortened version of *Emmanuel*, his full name, which I know means *"God with us."*

Goose bumps prickle my skin as I look around the room, searching for the presence I feel, or sense, or... "You're here," I whisper. "You're here." I wipe the tears from my cheeks. "I believe You. You're here."

I look back at Manuel. Nothing has changed.

And everything has changed.

IT'S LATE when Mama and I get to the hotel. She ate dinner in the cafeteria at the hospital—I sat and watched her. But now I'm grateful for the sandwich she bought for me. And I'm grateful she thought to bring my laptop. I sit at a small table in the area of the hotel where they serve breakfast in the mornings. I unwrap the sandwich and eat half of it while staring at the screen of my computer.

There's so much I need to know. So much to figure out. And tonight, I'm ready to face it all. Ready to learn. Ready to do whatever needs to be done. To save Manuel. And to keep him in the states—to keep him from being deported, which is now a very real possibility. Driver's license or not.

But as the flames of purpose and passion rise and replace the despondency I've felt, *Emmanuel* rises as well, and with the recollection of the moments by Manuel's bed comes a dousing of my passion to *do*.

I set my sandwich down, my stomach churning. My need to do is a need to...*control*? Just like my mama? Or at least the way she was before... Before what? Before she told me her story, before she told me the truth, before she entrusted me to God.

All things are possible...

With God.

Not with Pia. Not with me.

I'm sorry... I reach for the laptop and close it. "I'm sorry," I whisper. *I trust You. I trust You to work. I...I give him to You, God. I give Manuel to You.*" As I pray, my stomach settles. Maybe my soul even settles.

When I open the laptop again, I do so with a question. *What do You want me to do?*

CHAPTER TWENTY-NINE

How do you expect to arrive at the end of your journey if
you take the road to another man's city?
Thomas Merton

erissa

AFTER ANOTHER SLEEPLESS NIGHT, another night of wrestling,
of prayer, and of silence, I sit at the kitchen table Monday
morning disconnected from myself, as though my own spirit
hovers above and as I look down, I don't recognize the
woman below. In just a few weeks time, the woman I thought
I knew has become someone else. The woman I thought I
was seems only a mirage. An imposter of my own creation.

In the daylight hours, I resemble myself, especially when I
am with others and focused outward. But the darkness is
always there, shadowing me, tempting me toward despair,

and pulling my focus inward, to a place within I didn't know existed, an unredeemed slew of self-pity where I fear I will drown. I had spent much of the night attempting to pray for Manuel, for Pia, for Rosa. But words failed me, my prayers bouncing off the ceiling and back in my face.

The slew of self-pity is like quicksand, sucking me into its depths.

I look across the table at Twila, the exhaustion of all she's gone through with Pia the last thirty-six hours etched on her face. Yet all emotion has drained from me, and I have nothing left to offer. As I stare at her, I feel the vacancy of my expression, the emptiness. If anyone was to look closely, I suspect they'd see it, too. But no one has looked that closely in a very long time.

No one has cared.

But as that thought tries to pull me under, I know it's a lie and one I must refuse to entertain. I know what I must do, but the energy to do it eludes me.

Twila moves to pick up her mug of tea and pauses. She watches me for a moment. "You have to fight. Don't give up."

"I'm...tired. So, so tired."

She reaches across the table and takes my hands in hers, then she bows her head. Her long dark hair falls forward, draping her face. I expect her to pray out loud, but she remains silent. Her hands, cool against mine, begin to warm, the warmth traveling to my wrists, then up my arms to my shoulders. Soon, my body is infused with warmth, and the shift I felt take place in my soul a couple of days ago comes again. Stronger now. And with it the energy I lacked.

I close my eyes, the energy electric, pulsing through me, and I do what I know to do, what just moments before I couldn't do on my own—I replace the lies with truth: *Nothing can separate me from the love of God. Nothing can separate me from the love of God.* I repeat the truth over and over in my mind. Then I speak it aloud, "Nothing can separate me from the love of God."

Twila's grip on my hands tightens.

"Nothing can separate me..." I repeat it again, and again, and again, until suddenly everything stills. The mental and emotional chaos of the last few weeks recedes, and my soul quiets.

Twila's hands relax and when I open my eyes, sunlight has broken through the morning bank of fog and streams in through the kitchen windows.

"It's done," Twila whispers. "It's over."

"Yes." Joy, like the surf, rolls over me. "Yes!"

As I PULL into a parking spot near the grove of cypress trees on the headlands, I see Twila's bike leaning against a post. I sit for a moment, enjoying the refreshment several hours of deep sleep afforded me following the time with Twila this morning. When I woke and Twila was gone, I thought I might find her here.

I get out of the car and step into the crisp, clear afternoon. I turn my face to the sun and relish the warmth it offers, then I set out to find Twila. I follow the short path from the parking area into the grove of trees. As I enter the Cathedral, as it's sometimes called, I'm transported back to the day of Miles and Ellyn's wedding that took place here, under the overstory of the cypress.

Sunlight dapples the earthen floor and dances as the branches overhead sway in the breeze. I look through the clearing to the ocean, whitecaps rippling as far as the eye can see. Twila is right where I hoped I'd find her, sitting on the bench at the *end of the world*, as I've often thought of it.

This is the place she's come to meet with God since she

was old enough to ride her bike out here alone. Though unbeknownst to her, I often followed her at a distance, making sure she was safe.

Now she's the one who's watching after me, isn't she? Which is why I'm here.

I walk through the Cathedral until it opens to where the bench is set precariously close to the edge that juts out high above the surf, crashing against the jagged face of the cliff. I come around the bench and take a seat next to her.

She looks over at me. "Hey."

"I thought I'd join you for a few minutes."

We both look out at the power displayed before us, its beauty and strength unfathomable. The waves roll in, one after another, and the lie that tempted me earlier returns. Only this time, the truth arrives as well.

Someone has cared.

And someone has looked closely.

And I understand now that's why Twila came home.

She knew what was coming, long before I knew. Long before the letter arrived, Twila sensed the darkness ahead. And she came home to stand with me. To support me. To pray for me.

I turn and look at her. "You prayed for me. You fought for me. You battled on my behalf."

In her gray eyes, so filled with wisdom, I also see the pain she carries—not just her own, but the suffering of others. The gift God's given her, the knowing He's bestowed, comes with a cost.

"Thank you. God, through you. Thank you."

She turns and looks back out at the ocean, her thoughts her own.

"Twila..."

She continues to stare at the ocean.

"Will doesn't understand your gift?"

"No."

The sound of her whisper is lost to the clamor of the surf, but I read the word on her lips. And I see the tears that well in her eyes. I reach out and grasp her hand. "Honey, I don't understand it either, and I have more years of walking with God than Will has. What God has given you is unique. It's of another realm. It's supernatural."

"I have to make a choice."

"What do you mean?"

"Like, I have to choose the gift, or I have to choose Will."

"Oh, Twila…"

She reaches into the pocket of her jacket and pulls something out. She holds out her hand to me, then opens it.

"You found it!" In her palm is my ring.

"I found it when I vacuumed my room—it was in the carpet. It must have come off the night you came in and sat with me."

She hands me the ring and I slip it on my finger. I stare at it a moment and let the sense of joy wash over me, but then Twila's words come back to me.

"Why do you have to choose? Because Will doesn't understand?"

"It's what you did—the choice you made."

I look down at the ring on my finger as I let the meaning behind her words sink in. "Twila, the commitment I made is *my* path. That doesn't mean it's your path. Do you believe that's where God is leading you? Is that what He's asking of you?"

Her tears come again and as they fall, my heart breaks for her. *Oh, Lord… What are You asking of her?* I take her face in my hands and wipe her tears as I did when she was a child. "'Thou hast created us for thyself, O Lord, and our heart is restless until it finds rest in thee.'" The words, I know, are meant for her now.

"Augustine?"

"Yes. Surrender, Twila. Rest in Him. Give Will to God and rest. Let Him work. See where He leads. Let Him make that choice."

She nods, then looks back out at the sea.

I wrap my arm around her and she rests her head on my shoulder. We sit like that for several minutes, and then I know it's time to go. It's time to leave Twila alone. With God. In His hands. I will stand with her as she's stood with me. I will pray. I will trust on her behalf.

As I STAND on the front porch of Miles and Ellyn's home, a wave of uncertainty washes over me. I've not seen Miles since he haunted my dreams. I've feared what I might feel, what he might see... I take a deep breath and then ring the doorbell.

When the door opens, Miles stands in the entry, his blue eyes smiling, as they most often are. "Hey, gal, come in."

The wave ebbs and takes the uncertainty of a moment before with it. This is Miles. My friend. That's all. I step inside and he drops his arm around my shoulders, as he's done hundreds of times before.

Ellyn comes from the kitchen and crosses the great room, her smile warm and welcoming. As Miles steps away, Ellyn hesitates for just a moment, then gives me a quick hug. "I'm glad you're here."

"Me too. Something smells wonderful."

"You know you're in for a treat when Ellyn's in the kitchen." Miles pats his tummy, which protrudes just a bit more than it used to.

"Come on in, hors d'oeuvres are on the island."

Miles and I follow her to the kitchen. "Oh, Ellyn, these are beautiful."

"Thank you. *Duck pâté en croûte*, and *pissaladière*."

Ellyn's French is impeccable as are the appetizers, I'm sure.

She points to the tart. "Anchovies, black olives, and caramelized onions. You're my guinea pig—I hope to add these to the menu soon."

"I will happily be your guinea pig anytime."

"Well, a word of warning: They're full of gluten and dairy because, well, butter. And flour, too. But mainly butter. Here…" Ellyn hands me a plate. "Enjoy."

And enjoy we do. We chat, catch up, and make small talk until Ellyn ushers Miles and me to the table. "Have a seat. I'll join you in just a moment."

"Ellyn, may I help you?"

"Sit. Just sit." She turns back to the kitchen where she begins pulling things from the oven and dishing things from pans on the stove.

Miles takes the linen napkin from his place setting and unfolds it. "How's Twila doing?"

It's then I understand Ellyn's timing—she's given Miles and me a few minutes alone, and again I'm aware that what I feared I'd feel isn't what I feel at all. Instead, I'm at ease, grateful for Miles's friendship. I want nothing more from him. "She's quiet. Contemplative. She's spending a lot of time on the headlands." I take my own napkin and place it in my lap. "How's Will?"

"I think he's confused more than anything. I finally got him to open up when I talked to him over the weekend."

"Confused about Twila's gifting?"

"Yes."

"As I told Twila, I don't fully understand the gift God's given her, and I'm not sure she does either. Honestly, I'm not sure she wants the gift. She feels as though she has to make a choice between Will and God, or at least between Will and the gift."

Ellyn sets a plate in front of me. "Twila's so spiritually sensitive—it's like she's aware of a whole different dimension or something. The way God works through her is really amazing. I saw it with Sabina. And I've experienced it myself."

Miles looks from Ellyn to me. "Will sees the value in Twila's gift and seems to have an understanding of it that, honestly, surprised me. He's grown more than I've given him credit for. But his struggle, I think, is knowing where he fits into what God's doing through Twila. After talking to him, I wonder if his role isn't one of humility. Stepping back. Supporting. Encouraging. He's kind of a take-charge guy." Miles chuckles. "Stepping back may be new to his repertoire." He grows serious again. "I guess our role is to pray for them."

"Yes. I am doing a lot of that these days."

"So are we," Ellyn says.

As I make the drive home after dinner, I consider the conversation and the contentment I sensed in Ellyn. Something I haven't noticed before. She seemed at ease. With Miles. And with herself.

As I turn onto Lansing from Highway 1, rather than follow it into the village and then to the house, I turn into the park. I want a few minutes alone before I return home, where Twila will be waiting for me following her first shift at Corners of the Mouth. She's picked up some hours filling in as needed.

I pull into a parking spot, turn off the engine, and listen

to the sounds of the surf. I also tune my ear to hear the voice of the sea my father spoke of so often, but it eludes me once again. The night is clear, the moon full, its reflection dancing on the waves. As the swells bounce, I see a boat in my mind, a man's hand reaching for me...

I now know it is the hand of the One always there, ready to save me, moment by moment, and for all of eternity.

In so many ways, Miles has represented Jesus in my life. He is a man who reflects the image of God, the likeness of Christ. Not perfectly, but more so than most.

It is an image that became twisted in my subconscious. I see that now.

The longing I felt was not for the man. Not for Miles. But for the intimacy I've known with Jesus. An intimacy I'd lost sight of for a time.

"Never will I leave you; never will I forsake you." The words of the familiar verse began playing through my mind Saturday afternoon. Not the voice of the sea, but the voice of my God.

Yesterday morning, I'd opened my Bible to read the verse. I wanted to see it in print, to embed it in my mind and heart. I searched the concordance to find the reference, then flipped to the book of Hebrews, chapter 13. My breath caught as I read the full passage, now memorized, never, I hope, to be forgotten again:

"Keep your lives free from the love of money and be content with what you have, because God has said, 'Never will I leave you; never will I forsake you.'"

I hadn't remembered that the verse was about money, the very worry that nearly pulled me under over the last several weeks. Yet there it was, God's promise, attached to the exhortation to live free, to be content with what I have. However much God sees fit to give me.

Whatever happens with Daniel's request to suspend

spousal support payments, I know I will have enough, because I know I will never be alone.

I twist the thin silver band on my left ring finger, so grateful for the return of the simple reminder of my commitment to the One I love. The One who loves me for all eternity. Now and forevermore.

As the light of the moon skips across the water, I imagine that small boat, bouncing on the moonlit waves, a man reaching out to me... *"Come to me, Nerissa, come."*

I reach out and take Jesus' hand, my Savior's hand, the lover of my soul, and my heart is content, at peace, and filled with joy.

CHAPTER THIRTY

To say that I am made in the image of God is to say that love
is the reason for my existence, for God is love. Love is my
true identity. Selflessness is my true self. Love is my true
character. Love is my name.

Thomas Merton

llyn

MILES SITS AT THE ISLAND, newspaper spread out in front of
him. I hand him his cup of coffee, then go around to the
other side of the island where I can see his face. "Are you
sure?" I watch for any sign of hesitancy, though he's already
answered this question ten times, at least.

"Let's go over this one more time. The question isn't
whether or not I'm sure; the question is whether or not
you're sure. Ellyn, you used just a portion of the money your

father left you, and you used it wisely. You invested in the café, and you've built that business into something that is now supporting a dozen or more other families. You've reinvested the profits you've made, and you've done well." He chuckles. "Very well." He takes a sip of his coffee. "The money is yours to do with as you please. Period. So, are *you* sure?"

I stare at him a moment waiting for…something. Earl's voice, most likely, telling me what a stupid move I've made. But it doesn't come. "I am sure. And that seems crazy."

"Well, you've told me you felt like this idea came from God, and in my experience, those are the ideas that often do feel crazy." He shrugs as though that's a perfectly good explanation.

And maybe it is.

"Okay. Done." *Done?* I shake my head. "It's all happened so fast."

Miles smiles. "Cash talks."

"I guess. So everything's set for Monday?"

"My job is done."

"Okay." I mentally run through my list of to-dos once more as Miles picks up a section of the paper and begins reading, as if there's nothing to what I'm doing.

Then he lowers the paper and looks at me. "Enjoy it, Ellyn."

"DAT NEW DELIVERYMAN from de winery no good." Rosa stands at the office door, hands on her hips.

"What's wrong with him?"

"He not Manuel."

"You're impossible to please. You get that, right? How is Manuel? Anything new?"

"He awake, like I told you a few days ago, but he have a hard time talking. He still not tell her why he came here, what he wanted to tell her." Rosa looks down at her feet. When she looks back up at me, her eyes are laced with pain, and something else. "I shouldn't have sent him away dat day. I should have let him talk to Pia. Maybe…maybe none of this would have happened."

"You can't own that, Rosa. You thought you were doing the right thing. You thought you were protecting Pia. God knows your heart and even if you were wrong, He forgives you."

"You right, I know you right." Rosa sighs. "Manuel, he have a crooked road ahead of him."

A crooked road? "Long."

"What long?"

I shake my head. "Never mind. What happens after he's released from the hospital?"

She raises her hands. "It depend."

"On what? I don't understand."

"I don't understand it all, either. It depend on if the county program agree to pay for a rehabilitation facility. It depend on what happens legally. So many things we don't know yet."

"How's Pia holding up?"

"She understand all of it—de medical things and all de legal things. All de possibilities. She make a great attorney. She so smart. And she find an attorney, an immigration attorney to represent Manuel. She learning even more."

"She is one smart cookie. She also has a good Mama who supports her. How is she otherwise? How's her heart?"

Rosa puts her hand over her own heart. "Her heart hurts. But it not Manuel's fault. Nothing certain right now. There are no guarantees. She having to trust, to live by faith, and dat not bad, but it hard. We both having to trust. She come back to work next week—just a few hours. I tell her she need to keep busy. She spending too much time at de hospital and too much time studying. She need to be with people. She with Twila today."

"It will be good to have her back." I glance at my watch and then reach for a file on my desk. "I'm going over to the water tower to meet Nerissa and Twila. I told them I'd show them the renovations Jim did on the place. Nerissa's never seen it, and Twila wanted to see what's changed. I'm meeting them in a few minutes."

"Pia with Twila now. She probably go there, too."

"Great. Why don't you come with me?"

"I working. I can't leave."

"I know it's hard to believe, but the café will survive without you for an hour. And, news flash, we're not open today. Monday, remember? I don't even know why you're here."

"I here because Paco—"

"Save it. Do you want to go with me or not? It might be good for you to be with people, too."

"Okay, I go."

When we pull into the driveway of the water tower, Twila and Pia are already there. They sit on the steps of the side deck, obviously deep in conversation. As we get out of the car, Nerissa pulls in behind us.

"You want dat?" Rosa points to the file I left on my seat.

"Shh! No."

"What wrong with you?"

"As it turns out, nothing is wrong with me. How do you like that?"

"I like dat fine and I always know dat."

"Ellyn, this is lovely." Nerissa gives me a hug, then stands back and looks at the water tower. "Of course I've seen the other side of it from the headlands, but I hadn't seen the front of the house. It's so charming. And Rosa, you're a pleasant surprise. So good to see you." She hugs Rosa, too.

Then the girls come over and more hugs are doled out.

When we're all hello'd and hugged out, I find the key to the front door on my key ring. "Ready for the tour?" I unlock the front door and hold it open as they file inside. When I join them, Twila, the only one who knew what the house looked like when I lived there, is standing in the middle of the living room, turning in a slow circle.

She looks at me, eyes wide. "Whoa..."

"Exactly."

"It's, like, so different. Do you like it?"

"I'm getting used to it."

"It very clean and very white." Rosa walks around the downstairs, investigating every detail like she's a county building inspector.

"Literally," Pia agrees.

"Where de color?"

Nerissa is the only one who says nothing. She wanders through the living room, stands in front of the windows, and looks out at the headlands, then makes her way into the kitchen. She runs her hand over the marble top of the large island, then walks to the farm-style sink and runs her hand over the new fixtures. She finally turns to me. "Oh, Ellyn... This kitchen. It reminds me of the kitchen in Miles's house—your house—which I've always loved. It's so light and airy and spacious."

"Light it is. I'm glad you like it." I point out the mudroom off the kitchen and then show them the powder bath, which sports a new white pedestal sink.

"Take a look upstairs. Twila, why don't you show them the upper deck."

"Sure."

Rosa and Nerissa follow Twila up the stairs, but Pia lags behind.

"Hey, honey." I go and give her another hug, then look at her face, her fatigue evident. "How're you holding up?"

"Okay. Better now that I know he'll be okay. It's just been hard. We still have all the legal stuff to come and there are no guarantees. But I'm trusting God. I gave Manuel to God."

"I know. It's a lot."

"Yeah, it is. But he'll be okay. And that's what matters right now." She turns as she hears the front door open.

Perfect timing.

Pia's eyes widen as Miles walks in, Will in tow. "You're Will?"

"Pia, this is my son." Miles keeps his tone low.

"She doesn't know you're here?" Pia whispers.

"It's a surprise," Will says. "A good one, hopefully."

I hear Rosa upstairs offering her assessment of the layout, and Twila, her voice softer, telling Rosa and Nerissa something. As they leave the upstairs bedroom, Nerissa is the first to see Will. Her steps slow and she glances over her shoulder to Twila, who is still talking to Rosa.

Nerissa comes down the stairs, and as Rosa follows, she sees Will. She stops and turns to Twila. "Who dat?" She turns back around and points at Will.

Rosa, of course, knows full well who "dat" is. Twila looks to where Rosa is pointing. Her expression is one of surprise first, then blooms with joy, and then clouds. "Hi..." She comes down the stairs. "What...are you doing here?"

"I drove up this morning. I wanted to talk to you." Will goes to Twila and reaches out to hug her, then seems to think better of it.

As they've greeted one another, I've herded everyone into one corner of the living room, where we now stand. Miles stands between Nerissa and me—he holds my hand and has his arm draped over Nerissa's shoulders. Rosa stands on the other side of Nerissa, with Pia next to her.

Rosa leans around Pia and looks at me. "What we doing?"

"Shh." I point to Will and Twila just as Will pulls something from his pocket. Miles squeezes my hand.

Will clears his throat, then gets down on one knee.

Nerissa gasps, Miles chuckles, and tears sparkle in Pia's eyes.

"Twila," Will begins, "I've learned a few things over the last couple of weeks and I want to ask for your forgiveness. I didn't support you when you needed me. I'm sorry."

Tears slide down Twila's cheeks as she looks down at Will. She reaches out and touches his face, and then his hair, and then looks over at Nerissa, who is wiping her own tears.

Will glances over his shoulder at Miles, then looks back at Twila. "I've learned a lot from my dad, especially as we've talked recently. He's also set an excellent example for me of what it looks like to be a husband."

He pauses and then takes a deep breath. "I vow to love you as Christ loves His Bride—to cherish you, to honor you, to love you humbly. I vow to give you a firm foundation of support as you use the gifts God's given you, and I'll give you wings to pursue your dreams. Twila Boaz, I will partner with you in every way. And I would be honored if you'll have me, to serve God alongside you as your husband for the rest of our lives."

Miles smiles at me and then kisses me. I lean into him and whisper in his ear, "I wish Sarah were here to see this." Tears glisten in his eyes, and he kisses me again.

Rosa is now holding both Pia's and Nerissa's hands. She looks at Nerissa. "He a good man for Twila."

Nerissa laughs. "Yes, he is."

Will reaches for Twila's left hand and slips her engagement ring back on her finger, then he gets up and Twila, now a sobbing mess, wraps her arms around him and holds him so tight I fear he'll suffocate.

Miles and Nerissa, and Rosa, of course, go and offer their congratulations, and more hugs are given. But Pia hangs back, as I thought she might. As much joy as this day promised to hold, I knew this would be a painful day for Pia.

I go and put my arm around her and pull her close. I want to assure her that her time with Manuel will come, but as Rosa said, there are no guarantees for them.

Pia wipes her eyes and nods. "I'm happy for her. I really am."

"I know you are. And she'll know it, too." I turn and look at her. "Pia, your story, yours and Manuel's, it isn't finished yet. There's so much more to come, girly."

She smiles despite the pain I know she still feels.

"Do you mind helping me in the kitchen?" I figure keeping her busy can't hurt.

She follows me into the kitchen where I pull a butter cake from its hiding place in a cabinet, and pull plates, and glasses, and napkins, and utensils out of drawers and cabinets, which Pia sets out on the island. Miles joins us and takes a bottle of champagne from the newly installed Sub-Zero fridge.

As he pops the cork, I gather everyone in the kitchen, where Miles fills the glasses and I pass them around. Then he picks up his glass and holds it up. "A toast to love. Will and Twila, may you both love God with all your heart, mind, and soul, and may you reflect Him to one another every day for the rest of your lives together."

Rosa, now standing next to me, leans over. "You be in big trouble if you not invite me here today."

I laugh. "I know it, Mama. Good thing Paco called you and told you he needed you at the café this morning, right? And it's a good thing Pia got Twila here at just the right time."

"Oh, you!" Rosa swats at me.

I laugh, then I put my arm around her. "I'm only going to say this once, so listen up." She looks at me, curious. "I love you, Mama."

She nods. "I know you do."

~

AFTER CAKE IS EATEN and the champagne finished, Miles offers to take Rosa and Pia back to Rosa's car at the café, and Will and Twila walk out the back door, through the gate, and out onto the headlands. Heads together, they walk until they're no longer visible from the house.

"Ellyn, this was one of the most precious days of my life. Thank you, and Miles, for arranging the details. Will is... Well, he's special, isn't he?"

"He is, a lot like his father, I think."

"Yes, he is." Nerissa nods.

"Twila is an extraordinary young woman, but then, I don't have to tell you that."

"I'm very proud of her—she's gone through a lot and allowed it to strengthen her." Nerissa picks up a couple of the champagne flutes and takes them to the sink. She turns on the faucet, then stands for a moment gazing out the window over the sink. "It's so peaceful here."

"Oh. That reminds me. I have something in the car I need to grab. I'll be right back and then we can do up these dishes together." I walk out of the kitchen, then fumble through my purse as I search for my keys. My hand trembles as I push the key fob to unlock the car. I don't know if I'm nervous or excited, but I do know I've never felt so sure about anything in my life.

When I get back to the kitchen, Nerissa has the plates stacked and the sink filled with sudsy water. "I thought we'd wash these by hand rather than leave them in the dishwasher." She glances over her shoulder at me. "It was so wonderful of the owner to let you use this place today. Is he planning on renting it again, or—?"

"Nerissa."

She turns and looks at me.

"Oh. Sorry. I interrupted you. I was...you know...I thought... Um." I take a deep breath. "Sorry. How about if we finish the dishes in a few minutes?"

"Ellyn, are you alright?"

"Fine. I'm fine. Great. I just had... I thought... Well, I wanted to talk to you about something." Then I realize her hands are wet, dripping actually. "Oh. There are dish towels in that drawer there, next to the sink."

"Thank you." She opens the drawer and pulls out a towel, dries her hands, then folds it and lays it on the counter. All of which gives me a moment to get a grip.

"So, remember when you said to me that it's one thing to know we're created in the image of God, but it's another thing to live into that image?"

"Yes, I remember."

"Honestly, I wasn't sure what you meant when you said it, but I couldn't let it go. I've thought a lot about it, and Miles and I have talked about it. Then several days ago, Rosa mentioned something you said to her—something about how when we believe something that isn't true about God, we believe an illusion."

She nods. "Yes, I said that when we believe God is anyone other than who He says He is, we believe an illusion."

"Right. And if we believe *we* are anyone other than who God says we are, we also believe an illusion."

"Ellyn, that's wonderful insight. I haven't thought of it that way."

"So in order to truly reflect the image of God, we have to believe who He says He is and who He says we are. That came to me recently as I was writing down what I'd eaten— you know, journaling my thoughts and feelings as you suggested."

"I'm so glad that process has proven helpful."

"It has..." I stare at Nerissa a moment. Her dark curls with the thin streaks of gray frame her beautiful face, her gray eyes set off by her creamy complexion. While her features are lovely, what's truly stunning is her heart, her kindness, her compassion, the way she reflects the true image of God to others. A spiritual battle? I can see why, now, the enemy might feel threatened by Nerissa. Not unlike the way I felt threatened, maybe? It's the first time I've made that connection. Was that part of the ploy at work?

The ploy failed. *Thank You, Lord.*

I pick up the file I'd set on the counter, then I turn and look around the little house I called home for so long. "You know, I was really happy here." I look back at Nerissa. "It's the perfect home for a single woman. Just the right size. And that deck upstairs, on a clear day, you can see the other side of the world. At least, it feels that way. There's something special about this little house."

Nerissa looks around the interior of the water tower again. "It really is special, Ellyn."

"I'm glad you like it." I hand the file to her.

"What's this?"

"It's a quitclaim deed. It assigns the title of the water tower to you."

"To me? What do you mean?"

Understanding hasn't dawned on Nerissa yet. Her expression reveals nothing more than the question she's asked. "The water tower. This house. The property it sits on. We just have to sign the deed—have it notarized—and then this property belongs to you."

Nerissa opens the file, looks at the deed, then looks back at me. "I...I don't understand."

"God says He is the giver of all good gifts, and I believe He wants to give you this house."

"You can't just give me a house. This house." She walks to the large windows in the living room. "Overlooking all that. You can't just—"

"Actually, I can. I own it. At least, I did, very briefly. Now, you'll own it."

"But..." She turns from the window, eyes wide, face flushed. She looks around the living room, the kitchen, then back to me. "Why?"

I shrug. "You've committed your life to God, Nerissa. Not everyone does that. It isn't easy living as a single woman, running a business, making all the decisions yourself. I remember what that was like. I was still living that life myself less than a year ago. Add a child to the equation, even an adult child... It's a lot. Maybe He just wants to...I don't know...express His love to you. All I know for sure is that He wants you to have this gift. That seemed clear to me. As I said, He's the giver of all good gifts. And I believe He is who He says He is."

She stares at me a moment, then looks down at the ring on her hand. "And if we believe He's anyone other than who He says He is, we believe an illusion. But..."

"You know what?"

"What?"

"You look like you could use another piece of cake."

Nerissa, file in hand and seemingly a bit dazed, follows me into the kitchen.

I pull a clean plate out of the cabinet. "Oh, by the way, I stocked the kitchen with a few things, just to tide you over until you decide what to do with the place."

"Do with the place? You don't know what this means. Financially, not to have to pay rent? To know there's equity, an investment..." She shakes her head. "Do with the place? I'll...live here. I'll..." She laughs. "I'll *live* here. I can't believe it. Ellyn, I'm going to live *here.*"

"Great." Outside, Will and Twila, hand-in-hand, slowly make their way back to the house. I think of Pia again, of all the unknowns ahead of her, of the possibilities, the very things Rosa tried to protect her from.

Oh, Lord... I pray, as I have so often these last few weeks, without words. Just a simple plea. But this is a moment for joy. Here. Now. I hand Nerissa a plate with a second slice of cake and then a fork. "Here you go."

"I don't think I can eat all this."

"Enjoy it."

She takes the plate and fork, then gives me a quizzical look. "You didn't eat cake today?"

"Oh. Well. No. I have a lot I want to accomplish this week. So no cake today. I want to feel well."

"Good for you, Ellyn."

"It is good for me, isn't it? Sabina told me I'm often resistant to what's good for me. I don't know why that is, but I've decided to figure it out. I want to continue working with you. And when my therapist returns from maternity leave, I'll do some more work with her." Heat crawls up my neck to my face. "Sorry. That's probably more information than you wanted."

"No, it isn't. We're friends, Ellyn. And..." She laughs. "The large gift you've just given me aside, I'm grateful for your friendship. You inspire me."

"Friends? It appears"—I nod toward the window where, backs to us now, Will has his arm around Twila and she rests her head on his shoulder as they look out at the ocean —"we're going to be family after all." As I speak the words, the feelings of doubt, or jealousy as I finally recognized it, don't return. In fact, the only feelings I identify are those of contentment and anticipation of what's to come, for all of us. And something else? What was it Miles said to me this morning? *"Enjoy it, Ellyn."* Joy? Is that what I feel?

Nerissa is saying something about family, then she turns and surveys the newly renovated kitchen with its high-end appliances and spacious countertops. She turns back to me. "You've done so much it's ridiculous to ask for more, but…"

"What is it?"

"This kitchen, it's amazing. Do you think I could do something with it related to my business? Would you…?" She shakes her head. "Never mind. Ellyn. You've already done too much."

"Your business? What do you have in mind?"

She lifts her hands, palms up. "I'm not sure. But…I'd love to partner with you in some way. To learn from you—your business knowledge."

"Oh. Well…what about cooking classes? You know, healthy meals. You cook, right?"

"I love to cook."

"I'd thought this was a great kitchen for that purpose. You'll need a business plan, of course, and since you'll live here, I don't know that you'll need to have the property rezoned for commercial use, but we'll call the county and check on that. You may just need a permit of some sort. You'll want to consider marketing. You'll need a budget for that. By the way, you have a strong investment here. The value of this property will only—"

Nerissa's laughter cuts me off.

"What? What's so funny?"

"I don't know." She wipes her eyes and shrugs. "This is just so"—she does a slow turn, seeming to take in all the kitchen has to offer—"amazing. Unbelievable. Ellyn, truly, I don't know how I'll ever thank you."

"You don't have to thank me. Thank God. He did this."

Nerissa's expression grows thoughtful. "Imago Dei."

"What do you mean?"

"You. You're created in God's image, and you reflect His image. Beautifully, I might add."

"Oh." My face heats again and I turn away from Nerissa for a moment as I get a grip. When I turn back, she's wandered over to the range. She turns on one of the gas burners, then turns it off again. "So, what are the odds of you coming up with a dairy-free substance that tastes exactly like butter? Because that? *That* would prove profitable."

She looks at me and laughs again. "I'll get right on that."

"Good."

ACKNOWLEDGMENTS

Writing and publishing a book during 2020 proved challenging. I'd written just the first half of the manuscript when COVID-19 arrived in the United States. Quarantined at home, I listened to news briefings daily and worried about the well-being, both physical and financial, of family, friends, and so many others who were suffering worldwide. I turned that worry to prayer and trusted God was working in ways I could neither see nor understand. That trust continues today. I also opened my manuscript document daily, but my focus waned, as did my word count. It took a full two months for me to reengage with the story I'd begun writing, and then the words trickled rather than flowed.

During the long process of writing *Illusion*, the support of others was more valuable than ever.

Thank you to Julee Schwarzburg, my incredible editor, who offered flexibility and grace as I missed several of my self-imposed deadlines, which impacted her schedule. Once Julee finally received the completed manuscript, her work made it so much better. I am grateful for her partnership!

My wonderful cover designer, Diana Lawrence, found a photo I'd taken in Mendocino and posted on Instagram, and then she surprised me by using it as the backdrop for the cover of *Illusion*. I love every cover Diana has designed for me, but this one is special.

Thank you to my team, Lyneta Smith and Amy Taylor, who offered encouragement, support, and like Julee, their patience as I changed the scheduled release date for this book more than once. I also offer my thanks to Tonya Kubo, who also flexed with me as we planned to launch *Illusion*.

The group of beta readers who offered their insight on the characters and story were so helpful. Thank you!

My family—my sons, Justin and Jared, and my daughter-in-law, Stephanie—offer their love and support as I write. Thank you! I'm also thankful for the dear circle of friends who love me even when I withdraw into my fictional world for months at a time.

Thank you, especially, to my heavenly Father who knew long before 2020 that I'd write a book with a storyline that dealt with financial and spiritual battles. His timing is perfect. Always. I pray this book touches the hearts of readers in ways I'd never have expected.

COMING FALL 2021

A Mendocino Village Novel

Pia and Manuel's love story continues...

Join Ellyn and Miles and the rest of their friends in Mendocino Fall of 2021!

Interested in updates on the next Mendocino Village Novel? Subscribe to Ginny's newsletter: http://ginnyyttrup.com/contact/

Words - Christy Award Winner, Best First Novel

I collect words. I keep them in a box in my mind. There, he can't take them.

Ten-year old Kaylee Wren doesn't speak. Not since her drug-addled mother walked away, leaving her in a remote cabin nestled in the towering redwoods—in the care of a man who is as dangerous as he is evil.

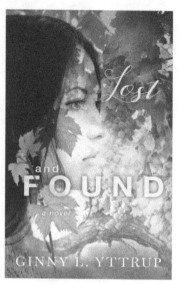

Lost and Found

Two women who've compromised for the sake of security... Will they risk it all?

Jenna Bouvier is losing everything: beauty, family and wealth. As Jenna loses her life will she find it? Andee Bell has found exactly what she wanted: fame, fortune, and respect. As And finds her life, will she lose it?

Flames

When adultery's flames explode, can fire archeologist, Jessica Weaver, preserve what matters most?

Preserving Yosemite National Park's natural and cultural resources is Jessica's job. Preserving her family's legacy is her obsession. But when betrayal's flames threaten her family and all she's fought to protect, can she preserve what matters most?

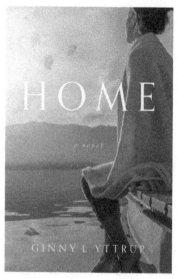

Home

When a novelist loses her way at mid-life, can her characters lead her home?

When Melanie Vander faces a looming deadline, she decides it's time for an escape to a novel-worthy locale. She's not running away. Really. She just needs to focus. But as she disappears into her writing, she encounters a man whose tenderness leaves her reeling. Dr. Elliot Hammond tempts Melanie to question everything, including her marriage. But that's ridiculous. Dr. Hammond isn't even...*real*.

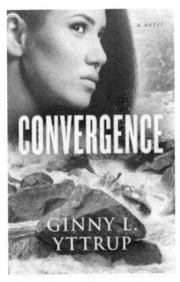

Convergence

A psychologist paralyzed by fear. A stalker bent on destruction.

Psychology professor Dr. Denilyn Rossi contends that the past is either a shadow that haunts us or a force that propels us, she tells her students. What she doesn't tell them is that her own past is a shadow she can't shake. Fear has immobilized her and is taking a costly toll. As Denilyn's past and present converge at the Kaweah River, a dangerous man bent on murder threatens her. Will he uncover the secret she's fighting to keep?

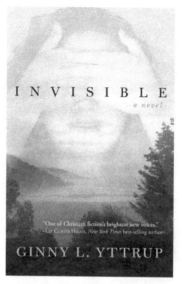

Invisible - A Mendocino Village Novel

When an overweight woman who's hidden from romance discovers a handsome doctor is in love with her, will she finally risk her heart?

Ellyn--chef, cafe owner, and lover of butter--is hiding something behind her extra weight. While she sees the good in others, she has only condemnation for herself. So when a handsome widower claims he's attracted to Ellyn, she's certain there's something wrong with him.

ABOUT THE AUTHOR

Ginny L. Yttrup is the Christy, *RT Book Reviews*, and *Foreword Reviews* award winning author of seven novels. She is a sought after writing coach and speaker. She loves spending time with her two adult sons and her daughter-in-law. She lives in Northern California.

If you'd like to receive updates on Ginny's work, glimpses behind the scenes, and frequent give-aways, subscribe to her newsletter: http://ginnyyttrup.com/contact/

CPSIA information can be obtained
at www.ICGtesting.com
Printed in the USA
LVHW041655061120
670968LV00005B/791